"A dying stranger radically alters the life of an ambitious young journalist in this remarkable debut novel by Sara Brunsvold. Winsome and wise, this thoughtful story of an unlikely friendship between two women will stick with you long after you finish the last page. Oh, if I could only be like Mrs. Kip as I grow old!"

Suzanne Woods Fisher, bestselling author
of *On a Summer Tide*

"Just as I was craving an uplifting novel, Mrs. Clara Kip entered my life. Sara Brunsvold's inspiring debut invited me into the world of the characters to bear witness to their joys and heartaches, their gains and losses, their lives and deaths. Readers who enjoy Katie Powner and Lisa Samson will want to get their hands on *The Extraordinary Deaths of Mrs. Kip*. Grab some tissues and hunker down. Once you start reading you won't want to stop."

Susie Finkbeiner, author of *The Nature of Small Birds*
and *My Mother's Chamomile*

"You don't want to miss this beautifully crafted generational story that weaves together the lives of two women in an unforgettable read. Sara Brunsvold has captured the essence of what can happen when love, grace, mercy, and God's Word are the gifts extended to those we meet on our journey through life."

Judith Miller, award-winning author
of *A Perfect Silhouette*

"In Sara Brunsvold's poignant yet inspiring novel, Mrs. Clara Kip is dying to show that living well means loving well—and dying well, if she has her way. In her st⟶

'The Lord will give you all the words you need. It's not about whether they sound pretty.' And her words are more than pretty. They're beautiful, impactful, and adeptly written and will touch the reader in heart-deep places."

Robin W. Pearson, award-winning author
of *A Long Time Comin'* and *Walking in Tall Weeds*

"Sara Brunsvold's debut has a big heart, just like Mrs. Kip. As someone who has spent countless hours in care homes and hospice situations, I loved reading a book that brought such tenderness and respect to the end-of-life experience. *The Extraordinary Deaths of Mrs. Kip* gently teaches that even in death there is much to learn about life. A thoughtful and touching read."

Katie Powner, author of *The Sowing Season*
and *A Flicker of Light*

"Sara Brunsvold's debut is a delight. She weaves stories that draw the reader in with an investment in the final outcome. Her characters are rich with individual personalities. Sara is a writer to watch."

Christina Suzann Nelson, Christy Award–winning author
of *The Way It Should Be*

THE EXTRAORDINARY DEATHS OF MRS. KIP

THE EXTRAORDINARY DEATHS OF MRS. KIP

SARA BRUNSVOLD

A Novel

Revell

a division of Baker Publishing Group
Grand Rapids, Michigan

© 2022 by Sara Brunsvold

Published by Revell
a division of Baker Publishing Group
PO Box 6287, Grand Rapids, MI 49516-6287
www.revellbooks.com

Printed in the United States of America

Library of Congress Cataloging-in-Publication Data
Names: Brunsvold, Sara, 1979– author.
Title: The extraordinary deaths of Mrs. Kip / Sara Brunsvold.
Description: Grand Rapids, MI : Revell, a division of Baker Publishing Group,
    [2022]
Identifiers: LCCN 2021045524 | ISBN 9780800741587 (casebound) | ISBN
    9780800740276 (paperback) | ISBN 9781493436354 (ebook)
Subjects: LCGFT: Christian fiction.
Classification: LCC PS3602.R865 E95 2022 | DDC 813/.6—dc23/eng/20211006
LC record available at https://lccn.loc.gov/2021045524

Scripture used in this book, whether quoted or paraphrased by the characters, is from the Christian Standard Bible®, copyright © 2017 by Holman Bible Publishers. Used by permission. Christian Standard Bible® and CSB® are federally registered trademarks of Holman Bible Publishers.

The quotations on page 272 are taken from "Anti-U.S. Tension Surges in Laos," *Kansas City Star*, May 26, 1975; and Matt Franjola, "Tragic End to Long March by Meo Tribesmen," *Kansas City Star*, August 13, 1975.

Published in association with Books & Such Literary Management, www.books andsuch.com.

Baker Publishing Group publications use paper produced from sustainable forestry practices and post-consumer waste whenever possible.

22 23 24 25 26 27 28   7 6 5 4 3 2 1

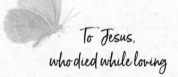

To Jesus,
who died while loving

CHAPTER 1

Monday, June 6, 2016

Clara Kip had prayed repeatedly to die in São Paulo. It truly seemed the smallest of requests. People died in Brazil every day. What was one more? Especially one who had dreamed of the country most of her life.

The Lord, however, gave her Kansas.

She watched the white line edging the Kansas City interstate pass by her window. It gently carried her toward a facility she'd hoped she would never need in a city she never thought she'd still be in, and she could only trust that the Lord was up to something. Because he usually was.

The facility's shuttle driver—a small, meaty man with a dark complexion and a nameplate above his head that read "Trey"—hummed softly as he drove. The notes floated into her imagination. She smiled, reshaping little blips of music into the dramatic, soul-tickling sounds of samba. Beats that made feet move on impulse and hearts soar with anticipation.

Her weary bones enlivened, the way they had when John taught her the dance steps.

Just once she would have loved to samba well past sundown in São Paulo, or walk along the Avenida Paulista strip, or enjoy a golden-fried *coxinha* hot from a street vendor's cart.

She looked at the Kansas sky stretched above her, streaks of clouds still tinged faint orange from the fading sunrise.

But not my will, Lord, she prayed.

Around gentle curves and over hiccup slopes, they traversed farther away from the little house that had been hers for decades, until the doctor had shown her the scan and said "aggressively metastasized." The annoying pain in her abdomen that had landed her in the hospital a week prior wasn't the UTI she had insisted it was to him and all those ER people.

After delivering the prognosis, the doctor refused to let Clara travel outside the country. Clara had called him a square.

Somewhere at a facility in the far southern outreaches of the city, her hospice team awaited her arrival.

Eventually the driver merged into an exit lane and peeked at her in the rearview mirror as they came to the stoplight. "Beautiful morning," he called back.

"Sure is, young man. God definitely got creative with that sunrise."

"That he did."

Clara considered his response. "Tell me, honey. Do you know Jesus?"

The driver's eyes twinkled. "Yes, ma'am, I do."

"Good. I can conserve my energy then."

He chuckled. "I suppose so. Although I never mind talking about him."

"Good for you, Trey. Talk about him a lot, especially when others seem uninterested. He loves that."

"Yes, ma'am." He turned onto a side street, slipping closer to their destination.

Outside the window, she caught sight of a young mother herding her kids into the SUV parked in their driveway. The littlest one skipped behind her mother, a pink backpack jiggling on her tiny shoulders. Off for another day of running headlong into new life. So much to learn and explore and discover. Clara pictured her friend Mai surrounded by her sweet little ones, specifically that one day at the airport, when their months of separation had come to a glorious end.

Only one reunion could be sweeter, in Clara's estimation. She turned back to Trey. "May I ask you something?"

"Of course."

"What do you think heaven will be like?"

He thought. "I really don't know. Bright?"

"No doubt there."

They rode in silence, then Trey asked, "What do you think heaven will be like, Mrs. Kip?"

Clara grinned. "Oh, honey. I think heaven will be the wildest ride yet."

Trey parked under the awning of the main entrance to Sacred Promise Senior Care Center. The one-story building sprawled away from the main entrance in both directions.

One side comprised assisted living apartments with their own little porches, and the other, skilled nursing residence rooms with large picture windows. A thick screen of trees wrapped around the property, giving it an appearance of seclusion from the busy shopping center beyond. Of the various facilities the kind people of the University of Kansas Medical Center had shown her in brochures, Sacred Promise seemed to offer the closest proximity to unadulterated nature. One of many reasons Clara felt drawn to it. That, and they took Medicare.

Trey hopped out of his seat and pulled her leather suitcases from the rack at the front of the shuttle. "Let me take these to the sidewalk," he said as he headed for the steps. "I'll come back to help you."

Clara grunted at his subtle suggestion that she wait. She had been walking out to get her mail just fine until a week ago. She rose and ambled after him.

When he caught sight of his passenger hobbling down the steps, he rushed over with arms extended. "Please, Mrs. Kip, let me help you."

"Honey, I'm only dying. I'm not an invalid."

Regardless, he insisted she take his arm, which she did, but only because a lady never declines chivalry.

Safely on the sidewalk, she peered down at her suitcases. Poor, sad things. They had waited with her for more than half a century to see the ends of the earth. Sacred Promise wasn't even the ends of Kansas City.

Trey lifted them by the handles and nodded to the entrance. "After you, Mrs. Kip."

Clara gazed at the sliding glass doors of Sacred Promise.

Such an odd feeling to know that once she walked in, she would not walk out. She clung to the belief the Lord had something for her here, so she shuffled forward.

The doors opened to reveal a small foyer that tried ever so hard to look homey. Burgundy wingback chairs, a grandfather clock, and floral print wallpaper made her wrinkle her nose. On either side, a hallway led to the respective wings. And in the middle of the foyer stood a young woman with fiery hair and an expression that fell somewhere between moderately welcoming and completely bored.

"Good morning, Mrs. Kip." Her voice registered minimal inflection. "Welcome to Sacred Promise."

"Thank you. How are you today?"

"Fine, thanks. I'm from administration. I believe you've been speaking with the social worker, Rosario."

"Yes." Clara started to ask the gal what her name was, but she seemed intent to get on with their business.

"Rosario is out today, so I'll be the one helping you settle in."

"Fantastic," Clara replied with a smile aimed at drawing out the friendlier side of the woman. Surely she had one.

But the gal turned on her heel and said over her shoulder, "Right this way."

Clara looked at Trey, who raised his eyebrows, clearly thinking the same thing she was.

"She seems fun," Clara whispered.

He laughed quietly.

Admin Gal led them through a door on the left side of the foyer. An etched gold plate on the wall identified it as the office.

When they arrived at the woman's desk, Trey set the bags down and stood close by as Clara lowered into the visitor's chair. "Can I be of any further assistance?" he asked her.

The gal cut in. "We can take it from here, thanks."

Trey started to respond, but Clara touched his hand. "You've been a blessing, honey. Thank you."

He smiled and dipped his head congenially. "God bless, Mrs. Kip."

"Same to you." She watched him walk away. "Such a sweet young man."

The gal gave what could be considered a smile. "Shall we begin?" Her pragmatism obviously was there to stay.

"Definitely," Clara replied. "Can't wait."

What Admin Gal lacked in pleasantries, she made up for in blazing efficiency. The paperwork blurred by.

At the end of it all, she stacked papers into a manila folder with Clara's name on it. "You'll be meeting Rosario and the rest of your care team within the next two days." She then rattled off the names of the doctor, nurses, and chaplain who rounded out the team, none of which stuck in Clara's memory.

Clara nodded nonetheless.

"Any questions?"

Even if Clara did have questions, the gal likely lacked the wherewithal for them. "I think I'm okay for now."

"In that case, let's get you to your room. I'll page an aide to help with your bags."

Five minutes later, their small parade exited the office—Admin Gal as marshal and a baby-faced aide named Jimmy bringing up the rear. *He* actually smiled, making him instantly delightful.

They trooped down the hallway toward the skilled nursing side and soon came to the activity room, the wing's central hub. Save for the buzzing nurse's station on the opposite end and a small aviary of chirping birds nearby, the room was graveyard quiet. Three other hallways radiated out from the room, one each to the north, the east, and the south. The floral wallpaper carried forward, coordinating with the cherry-finish dining table in the middle and the gaggles of emerald green–striped armchairs. Bouquets of silk flowers dotted the room, attempting to bring a semblance of nature— and life—into the place.

Had it not been for the silver tray of chocolate chip cookies waiting on the dining table, Clara would have written the place off entirely. She salivated at the sight of her favorite treat. She was tempted to break for one, but Admin Gal barreled onward to the north hallway, seeming to gather steam the closer she got.

Clara did her best to keep up, but despite her efforts, she quickly fell behind. Subsequently, so did Jimmy.

As if sensing the widening gap, Admin Gal looked over her shoulder and came to a stop. "I can get you a wheelchair if you'd like, Mrs. Kip."

"I think a race car would serve me better, honey."

Jimmy chuckled but quieted the instant Admin Gal shot him a look.

"If you believe a wheelchair would help you, I can get you one," she repeated. "We want our residents to be comfortable and safe." The words rolled out like a party line.

"I appreciate it very much," Clara replied. "If you could just hold back the pace a bit, that would do the trick."

"I'd be happy to," she said, her expression not matching her promise.

They walked the rest of the way in silence, lumbering along at Clara's slow pace. Her legs already felt the pinch.

Thankfully, only a few doors into the north hallway, Admin Gal stopped. "Here we are." She pushed open the door to room 303 and motioned for Clara to enter.

Upon first glance, the four-hundred-square-foot space seemed comfortable enough. A private bathroom adjacent to the door. A spacious chest of drawers and a small square table with two dining chairs. A comfy-looking loveseat and reasonably comfy-looking armchair, both next to the picture window. Clara skipped right over the bed—the place to avoid as long as possible—and focused her attention on the view through the window. And her heart sank.

The window gave only an acrimonious view of the front parking lot.

"The loveseat folds out into a double bed, and the armchair by the window can also recline into a . . ." Admin Gal said more words, but Clara tuned out.

That view. A fat eyeful of nothing God-created.

Clara shook her head. "Excuse me, honey."

Admin Gal's monologue came to an abrupt end. "Yes?"

"I'd like a different room, please."

"Is something wrong?"

"There are no trees."

"I'm sorry . . . *trees*?"

"Or grass. The brochure promised a serene lawn, wooded acreage, and hummingbird sightings." Clara pointed at the window. "That's not it."

The gal looked from the window to Clara. "I can assure you, Mrs. Kip, all of our rooms are identical."

"And they are lovely indeed, but surely they don't all face the parking lot, do they?"

"Well . . . no."

"Then I'd like a room that does not." To put an end to the matter, she called upon the gal's own words. "It would make me comfortable."

Admin Gal looked at Jimmy as if asking him if she'd heard correctly.

He put on a confused expression for her benefit, but as soon as she looked away, a smile inched onto his lips.

Clearly he and Clara were meant to be friends.

"Let me see what I can do," Admin Gal replied. With brisk movements, she stepped into the hallway.

When she was gone, Clara gave Jimmy a wink and said quietly, "I'm a troublemaker."

"Clearly," he whispered back.

CHAPTER 2

Aidyn Kelley zipped her gold cross pendant back and forth on its thin gold chain. While she was at the *Kansas City Star* office, she usually kept the necklace well hidden under her shirt. This day, though, was different. This day necessitated nervous motion.

She perched on the edge of her desk while her best friend, Rahmiya Hiraj, leaned forward from Aidyn's chair to read her words on the laptop. Aidyn glanced around the newsroom, alert for anyone who might look their way, then turned back to her friend.

"Tell me honestly," she said quietly. "How does it sound?"

Rahmiya waved her off, concentrating on the screen.

During the wait, Aidyn squeezed the pendant and zipped, zipped, zipped it from one shoulder to the other.

Her journalism professors had expressly warned against going around one's editor, but none of them had ever worked for Bella Woods.

She glanced around the newsroom again, nearly certain

someone was already onto her, but most of the people present were fellow insignificants, still stuck at a desk instead of out on assignment.

"You are so lucky," her J-school classmates had told her when she landed the local news job at the *Star*. Most of them had graduated to small-market papers, if any paper at all.

It certainly didn't feel lucky. A year in—after earning the highest accolades offered by the storied University of Missouri School of Journalism—all she had to show for real reporting was a couple of solo bylines on small pieces buried on page 4 of the Local section. Two months prior, she'd received an assistance credit on a page 1, but with loud protest from Shayna Reese, the senior reporter whose story was "degraded" by the cub's name in the footnote. Shayna had left her half-drunk Starbucks on Aidyn's desk every morning for a week afterward, and Woods had yet to give Aidyn another assignment of any consequence.

Aidyn glanced over at Shayna's desk separated from her own by a low wall. She could practically feel Shayna's daggers despite her absence. Though she couldn't prove it definitively, Shayna surely had all guns pointed at her, and the ear of Woods.

Please, God, let this work.

Finally, Rahmiya finished reading and spun around in Aidyn's chair. "You worded your case well, Aidie. It's professional. Savvy."

"You think?"

"Absolutely. I think you're well on your way to a feature." Her white smile offset the soft brown of her skin.

The assertion made Aidyn's heart flutter. Even though

Rahmiya wasn't a reporter, she was sharp and intuitive, and Aidyn relied on her opinion in multiple areas of life.

"Dare I say, it's very Katharine Graham of you," Rahmiya added, nodding down at the picture of the famed *Washington Post* publisher taped to Aidyn's file drawer.

The comparison to her hero inflated Aidyn even more. "Maper will say yes, right?"

"No doubt," Rahmiya said with a firm nod. "He couldn't refuse."

From the back of Aidyn's mind, however, fear encroached. Approaching the managing editor, lord of the newsroom, was serious. Particularly without invitation.

Aidyn forced a smile all the same. "Thanks, Rahmi."

"You're welcome." Rahmiya looked at the screen, then back at Aidyn. "So, you're going to send the email today, right?"

The fear drew closer. "Yes, I will. At some point." Even to Aidyn it sounded hollow.

Rahmiya frowned. "What do you mean, 'At some point'?"

"Nothing. I will. Yes, I will send it today."

"Hold up, Aidie. I've seen that look before. You're waffling. Why are you waffling?"

"I'm not, I just—"

"You texted me at freaking midnight asking me to come read this email first thing this morning because you were convinced today was the day you were going to do something about the tyranny."

"I never called it tyranny."

"You've been taking the scraps Woods throws down to you for a year. It's time you sat at the table for a meal."

"Okay, now you're speaking in metaphors."

"Because they work." She jutted her thumb at the screen. "You need to send this. Today!"

Aidyn gestured for her to calm down and shot a nervous glance around them. "I will."

"When?" Rahmiya pressed.

"Soon."

"*When?*"

"I said soon."

Rahmiya studied her. "You're not going to send it, are you?"

"Yes I will."

"No you won't. I can tell. You're going to chicken out."

"I won't."

"You totally will."

"I just want to take one more pass through, that's all."

"You're for real going to send it?"

"Yes."

Her friend squinted, clearly unconvinced. Then, in a series of fluid movements that transpired much too quickly for Aidyn to do anything about them, Rahmiya clicked Send on her behalf.

"Rahmi!" Aidyn scream-whispered and lurched toward her laptop. "I can't believe you did that!"

"It was for your own good, Aidie. I can't stand to see you waffle."

"I would have sent it when it was ready!"

"It *was* ready."

A muffled spat ensued. Aidyn fruitlessly attempted to wrestle the words back from the managing editor's inbox while Rahmiya insisted they had belonged there all along.

Their tussle became so absorbing, neither saw Woods come into the newsroom and stop a few paces away, watching. When Aidyn finally glanced up and saw her supervising editor, Woods's frown deepened around her wire-frame glasses.

Aidyn shot upright. "Morning, Woods."

"What's going on?" Woods asked. Whenever she spoke, the jowls of skin melting off either cheek wobbled slightly. In so many ways, she was like a bulldog. "Why are you here?" she said to Rahmiya.

"I was just helping her figure out some—"

"Please go back to Billing."

"Of course." Rahmiya rose with an envious regal diplomacy. She made her exit, leaving Aidyn to bear the ire of her editor alone.

Aidyn threw Woods a smile and lowered herself hesitantly into the chair. Hopefully Woods had not heard either of them say Maper's name.

Fortunately, Woods seemed too annoyed with the world at large to be annoyed specifically by a mysterious exchange between two peons. "Did you get those call notes to Reese for the July Fourth special?" Her voice sounded full of gravel, as if she had chain-smoked from the age of four.

"Working on it. I found a World War II veteran willing to be interviewed." Deep down, she hoped Woods would be impressed by the feat.

"Then I've got your next assignment." Woods plowed forward. "Kansas City Public Schools is changing its busing policy. I need two hundred words."

"On it," she replied, and Rahmi's words echoed in her ears. *A scrap, not a meal.*

Woods started to turn away, then spun back around. Something had apparently caught her eye. Something under Aidyn's chin.

Heat gathered in Aidyn's cheeks.

Woods opened her mouth, appeared to want to say something. Instead, she gave Aidyn a stern look and lumbered to her office.

Aidyn fumbled for her cross necklace and stuffed it inside her shirt.

According to a whispered consultation with Jimmy in Admin Gal's absence, the gal's name was Margaret, "not Maggie—never Maggie." The name suited her. Margaret sounded like a strong-willed name.

When Margaret returned, she ushered them down the hall to room 310 and held open the door for Clara. "Hopefully this is more what you had in mind."

Clara plodded over to the picture window to take in the new view.

At the far end of the north hall, near the exit door, the room boasted a full view of the large, lush courtyard. A thick green carpet of lawn stretched between the north and east sections of the building, then outward in a quarter circle to the wooded perimeter. Full flower beds nestled along the building, exploding with color. A hummingbird feeder hung from a pole just outside the window. In the middle of the courtyard, a pergola rose from the ground, taking a thick cover of climbing ivy with it. A decorative stone patio lounged in its shade, along with wooden benches between the pillars.

The clear June sky encapsulated the splendor, making the rich hues seem deeper, more alive.

The earth is full of your unfailing love, Lord . . . even in Kansas.

Clara turned to her companions. "Yes, this will do nicely."

"Wonderful," Margaret replied, relief discernable in her voice. "I'll update your file."

"Would you like help unpacking, Mrs. Kip?" Jimmy asked, still holding the suitcases.

"That's quite all right, love. Just set them on the bed for now."

Jimmy did as instructed. "Anything else I can help you with?"

"Not right now. Thank you, though."

He glanced furtively at Margaret, then nodded goodbye to Clara in a way that wished her good luck.

As it turned out, though, Margaret was comparatively amenable for the remainder of her time with Clara. She showed her how to work the portable call button, which she clipped to Clara's shirt, as well as how to operate the television, though Clara had zero intention of putting the latter instructions to use. Technology had never warmed to her.

Clara pretended to listen and secretly studied the young woman before her. What was her story? What did she need? And what about Jimmy? Sweet boy. He looked like he should be in college. Why wasn't he?

"Does all that make sense?" Margaret asked.

The question pulled Clara from her reverie. "Yes, certainly does," she replied, not sure what exactly had been explained.

Margaret placed the television remote on the nightstand. "Any questions for me before I head out?"

"I am having some boxes brought over from home."

"They will be here before lunch, I'm told. One of the aides will bring them to your room when they arrive."

"Fantastic."

"The nurse will be by in a little while as well to go over a few things." Margaret took a step toward the door, a hint if ever Clara saw one.

"Thank you for your time. I appreciate all you did for me."

The gal attempted another smile. "We're glad you're here."

The statement lacked empathy of any variety, but Clara did not hold it against her. She gave a friendly wave, and Margaret stepped into the hallway, leaving the door partially ajar.

Alone, Clara sighed and swept her gaze across the room. "So," she said softly, "this is where I wither."

She examined her new—and final—digs with intention. She studied the details, the curves of the loveseat and the corners of the dresser, the hue of the bookshelves and the tones of the faux-wood floor. All of it strove for coziness but fell perpetually short. The crisp lines of the sun cut across the room, drawing the eye along their perfect edges. They stretched over the loveseat, along the floor, up and over the tray table, and onto The Bed.

She refused to let her eyes linger on that thing. Not yet.

Instead, she turned her attention to the armchair tucked in the corner by the loveseat. It looked modern and highly unpromising in the comfort department. Her legs had been crying for mercy ever since the trek began to room 310, and they begged her to give the chair a go.

She scooted herself back up against the edge of the seat and began to lower onto the cushion. Despite her best effort, she landed with an unladylike plop. Most of her sits had been plops for some time, so that was no surprise. What was a surprise: the modernly uncomfortable armchair actually had substance. The right amount of support in all the right places. Almost certainly she could stand up again.

The embrace of the chair, the sun rays warming the room, and the beautiful view out her window all collaborated to draw a contented sigh from deep within her. She lifted her eyes to the blue sky and smiled. "It's no São Paulo, but I'll gladly take it."

She closed her eyes and relaxed into the chair, as if the Lord himself had provided his lap on which she could rest. Without fail, he always found a way to comfort his beloved, despite the broken dreams and the prayers yet unanswered. He always was up to something good, even if she couldn't see it. In fact, he did his best work in such times.

If only she had learned that truth earlier in life.

May 10, 1969

By the ninth anniversary of John's death, the grief hadn't gotten any easier. In many ways, it had only increased in strength, like a bully fed by weakness. Onward it plowed, through passing time and her fading memories.

On May 10, one thing dominated Clara's day. It commandeered her mind and bated her breath. The memory of the knock on her door that had thrust the younger her, so naïve and trusting, into widowhood.

"It was instant," the patrolman had told her, as if that eased anything. As if somehow that fact made every subsequent day more bearable. Her husband was still gone, still mangled with the steel around the utility pole on the side of the road. Their plans for Brazil shattered along with his bones.

She had buried him with his plane ticket.

As dusk gathered outside her damp basement apartment, she poured a glass of the Scotch she kept from John's collection, lowered the needle onto the 45 of "their song," and pushed herself back into John's leather chair. She knew none of it would help anything. In fact, it would only make things worse to wrap herself up in what once was and never could be again. But on May 10, she *wanted* to feel worse.

As much worse as possible.

The pain reminded her, with bitter irony, that she was still alive. She supposed that fact counted for something. For what, she had yet to find out. Johnny would have told her it was for God's will, but she didn't believe that. Not like he did. John and God had had a whole thing going that she never understood, nor did she want to, thank you very much.

She didn't like Scotch either, not like John did. And she hated that ugly chair, which barely fit in her tiny dwelling. And she had long stopped considering their song a pleasant experience.

But they were all the material things she had left of her husband. Those three things. All of them empty promises from a happier time when they were both too inexperienced to know what life was capable of.

She took a sip of the Scotch, rested her head against the

brown leather, and forced herself to stay in the slow-dance memories conjured by Elvis Presley's "As Long as I Have You." The recollections surrounded her as securely as John's arms once did, so young and strong—and alive. The scent of his aftershave was barely a wisp of a thought anymore, but she called across the expanse for it anyway, pleaded for it to come back to her.

It didn't. Neither did he.

The anniversary ended the way it always did. Clara sobbing herself into exhaustion, questioning the ceiling above. *Why?*

Why would a supposedly merciful God leave her alone and aching? He wasn't the kind of God she wanted for herself. Ever.

CHAPTER 3

June 6, 2016

For the twentieth time in three hours, Aidyn glanced at Maper's office door. The workday had oozed to nearly lunchtime. Still the door remained shut, and her inbox remained empty of a reply from him.

Had he seen the email?

She both hoped and feared he had. Her only interaction with the managing editor occurred when she happened to be in the vicinity and he happened to speak words that indirectly applied to her.

Instinctively she reached for her necklace for that soothing back-and-forth movement. She stopped herself, remembering Woods's expression when she had seen the cross dangling outside her shirt.

The angst mounted. Barely containable. She opened an instant message chat with Rahmiya.

I'm freeeeeeaking out, Rahmi!

Less than a minute later, Rahmiya wrote back.

Still no reply, then?

No.

He's probably busy. Give it the day at least.

I should have gone to Woods first.

Says the woman who 11 hours ago texted
me to say, and I quote, "That woman is the
Stalin of editors!"

I was drunk on adrenaline and resentment.

You were confident! STOP WAFFLING! You
did the courageous thing.

Hope you're right.

There was a long pause.

Just as Aidyn started to think her friend had gotten caught up in work, her desk phone rang. Rahmiya's name appeared on the caller ID.

"First of all," Rahmiya said as soon as Aidyn picked up the receiver, "you didn't say anything in the email that wasn't articulate and professional. Second, there was a reason why you thought to send Maper an email at all. Because you believe in your own worth. Trust in that, and for the love of all, get off the ledge! You're driving me crazy!"

Aidyn grinned. "I suppose you're right."

"Yes, I am. Now get back to work. Sushi for lunch?"

"Twelve thirty. Meet you downstairs."

Aidyn hung up, the grin lingering on her lips, her confidence a little stronger. Strong enough to open that email to Maper, reread what she had written, and attempt to see it through Rahmiya's eyes.

Dear Mr. Maper,

I'm writing to ask for a few minutes of your time. I know your schedule is hectic, and I am willing to meet whenever is convenient for you. I would like to discuss the possibility of doing a feature article for any department you see fit. In my year at the *Star*, I have shown my ability to source and gather news. The attached clip, which I wrote for the *Missourian* as a senior at Mizzou, shows my full range as an investigative journalist. This clip led to my receiving the Sifford Award, which I believe you also received during your time at Mizzou. Thank you for your consideration, and I look forward to speaking with you.

Aidyn Kelley

The email was a decent bit of writing, a demonstration in itself of her ability to strip away emotion and let the facts speak for themselves. Like a good journalist.

Before she could waffle again, she closed the email, returned to her work, and vowed to let the facts speak as loud as they would.

Just after noon, she finished her research on the school district busing policy change and started to write a draft. She looked up to see Woods on the approach.

"How's that busing piece coming, Kelley?"

She continued to type, an overt show of her focus. "I'll have it filed this afternoon."

"Good." Woods watched her work for a moment, then said, "I'm headed to a lunch meeting. When I get back, I'd like to talk to you."

Aidyn pulled her hands off her keyboard, curiosity snaking through her stomach. "Sure. What about?"

Woods glanced at Shayna's desk. "There are some assignments on the horizon I'd like to do something different with. Come by about two."

The email had worked. Maper must have talked to Woods already.

Fighting the urge to smile, Aidyn nodded. "Will do."

Though the opportunity opened up much faster and simpler than anticipated, at least it had come. She couldn't wait to tell Rahmiya and buy her a spider roll as a thank-you.

Woods lingered by Aidyn's desk, acting as if she wanted to say more. Right as she opened her mouth, the bellow of her name made both women jump.

Maper was in his office doorway. Everyone and everything in the newsroom held still. The bald, ruddy editor stalked through the aisles of low-slung cubicles, eyes trained on Woods. A white sheet of paper flapped in his meaty grip.

Reflexively, Aidyn pressed back against her chair as he approached.

He thrust the paper at Woods. "What is this?"

Unfazed, Woods took the paper. She held it at an angle that inadvertently allowed Aidyn to read it too. The first three words made her stomach plummet: *Dear Mr. Maper.*

"Did you know about this?" Maper demanded of Woods.

The woman coolly folded the paper in half. "I do now."

He glowered at her. "Keep your cub under control!" He turned sharply on his heel and marched back to his office.

Everyone seemed to hold their breath, the air too thick to take in. They stared at Aidyn and Woods.

"Mind your own business!" Woods snapped at them.

Immediately, their attention reverted back to actual work.

In the semblance of privacy, Woods cleared her throat and said in a low, tight tone, "Let's have that meeting now, Kelley."

If only she could melt into the floor. With every shred of dignity she could gather, Aidyn rose from her chair and followed her editor into her office.

In high school, Aidyn had showed aptitude in both research and persuasion, two things that made her school counselor prophesy she would be a lawyer or a journalist. "Lawyers get a higher salary, but journalists have more fun," the counselor said.

As Aidyn slunk through Woods's doorway, she wished she had opted for the money.

"Door," Woods said.

Obediently, Aidyn closed the door behind her, then snuck a glance at her editor. Woods sat on the front edge of her desk, clutching the copy of the email in her fist. She waited for Aidyn to sit, then commanded, "Explain."

No J-school course could prepare a reporter for such moments. The rule on the serial comma was practically beaten into her, along with the other fast and holy rules of the *AP Stylebook*. But no final she had taken ever asked a single question about how to overcome stupid mistakes.

She shifted in her chair, looked off to the side, tried to explain. "I want more of a challenge."

"You want a feature."

The blunt rejoinder snapped her attention back to Woods, who lifted both eyebrows, daring her to contradict.

"That's what you want," Woods repeated with a nod. "You and every other rookie."

Aidyn grasped at those persuasion skills she supposedly had. "I know I just started at the *Star*, but I believe I could be of more value to the paper. I think I've proven that I—"

"You have proven nothing, Kelley! Nothing at all except that you think you're above the rules." She flitted the email in Aidyn's face. "This is one of the dumbest things I have seen a rookie do in my twenty-three years in reporting. Not to mention one of the most arrogant, which says a lot considering the massive egos that somehow squeeze into this place." Veins popped out in the middle of her forehead.

Aidyn did her best to hold her editor's gaze; she couldn't show weakness. "With all due respect, I don't think I'm above the rules."

Woods crossed her arms. "'With all due respect,' huh?" She leaned forward, bearing down on Aidyn. "This isn't a college paper. Actual careers are at stake. In some cases, lives are at stake. Stunts like what you just pulled prove to me you *don't* understand how to give due respect where it is needed, and that is a dangerous thing. The rules and order of the newsroom exist for a reason, and if you want to continue working here, I expect you to abide by them. To *respect* them. At all times. Do you understand me?"

Aidyn nodded.

"If you have an issue, you come to me. Is that clear? And answer me *with words*."

Forcing her voice out, Aidyn replied, "Yes. It's clear."

Woods crumpled the paper into a tight ball and hurled it across the room. "Wise up. Suck it up. Do what you're told. Is *that* clear?"

Heat poured into Aidyn's cheeks and burned the backs of her eyes. Her voice shrank to a loud whisper. "Yes."

"This will never happen again."

"Understood."

"Fantastic. Now get back to work. I'm late for my meeting."

As Aidyn stood, she kept her eyes averted. The reprimand clanged at her from all angles. Her legs wobbled underneath her.

Just get to the door, she told herself.

But as she reached for the door handle, Woods stopped her. "One more thing."

Aidyn sucked in her breath and looked over her shoulder.

"I debated telling you this after that joyful encounter with Maper, but I think it's important I do tell you. You need to feel every ounce of the consequence."

Aidyn braced herself against both the bite of the words and whatever came next.

"That meeting I wanted to have with you this afternoon was about you taking on an extended sidebar for the July Fourth special." Woods paused before adding, "Page 1. Solo credit. You blew it, Kelley."

Aidyn's heart sank. No words Woods had said or could say cut as deep as those four. The higher-profile assignment, so near her grasp, had been ripped away. Her lungs begged to scream. In anger. In grief.

"Finish your work. Be happy you have it." Woods stood and turned away.

Left with no choice, Aidyn opened the door and stepped into the newsroom.

Most of her fellow peons had the decency to pretend not to have heard any of it.

One thing Clara learned quickly about being a patient at Sacred Promise was exactly how jumpy staff became when a perishing seventy-nine-year-old in a blue tracksuit went for a stroll through the building without first asking for help.

She'd made it to the activity room—had just reached toward the silver tray of chocolate chip cookies that smelled like childhood and the sweet, sweet promise of glory—when all the fussing began.

"Mrs. Kip!" she heard from behind her.

With a start, she retracted her hand and turned to find, blessed be, her new best friend, Margaret. The look on the young woman's face read three-alarm fire.

Clara smiled as cheerily as she could. "Hey there."

The gal's brow furrowed. Breeziness clearly was not her love language.

At that very moment, by the sheer grace of God, Jimmy walked into the room pushing a loaded dolly. His pace slowed dramatically when he saw the two squared-off women.

"Hello to you, young man!" Clara said. "What a joy."

He parked the dolly off to the side and approached the

women, never taking his eyes off them. "Can I help you with anything, Mrs. Kip?" He moved in close to her, a gesture symbolic of proffered strength . . . or his shared fear of her imminent collapse. Either way, it was a chivalrous act.

"I just came to get a cookie," she told him. "They seem so lonely up here."

"You're a friend to all, Mrs. Kip," he replied with a grin.

"Less work than being an enemy!"

He chuckled. "If you would allow me, I will gladly bring the cookies to you next time. You just let me know when you have a hankering, and I'll get you as many as you want. I was coming your way anyway. Look what I have over there. Your boxes arrived."

Clara followed the direction of his nod. Her two white storage boxes sat on the dolly. "What fantastic news!"

"Why don't you let Jimmy take you back to your room," Margaret said, more as a command than a question. "He'll bring the boxes down after."

"Only if he buys me a cookie first," Clara countered.

"How about two?" He picked up a napkin from the stack next to the tray and gathered two cookies into it.

"You sure know how to treat a lady."

Jimmy gently hooked her palm into the crook of his elbow. He then folded his free hand over hers, securing her palm into place, the way of a true gentleman. "Shall we?" he asked.

"We shall. Home, James."

"We have a spare wheelchair," Margaret cut in. "It's just around the corner." The poor gal would not stop fretting.

"Miss Margaret," Clara replied, "a woman glides when

she is on the arm of a man. I haven't glided in decades. Don't rob me of the blessing." She tugged Jimmy forward before Margaret had a chance to respond. "No need to worry about a thing," Clara called over her shoulder. "Strong as an ox, this young one." Then she whispered to Jimmy, "And stubborn as a mule, this old one."

He chuckled. "One of those is one hundred percent accurate."

As they progressed toward the north hallway, Jimmy moved at her pace, neither pulling ahead nor keeping her reined, like he intimately understood what it meant to be in a failing, disobedient, but still reasonably functional body.

If she'd had the ability, she would have twisted her neck so she could come face-to-face with him. "You're a good boy, Jimmy."

As if understanding perfectly, he gave her hand a small squeeze.

They entered the hall. The corridor seemed longer than before.

Her legs began to protest. She held tighter to Jimmy's arm and tried to keep her mind otherwise occupied. "I'm glad I decided to wear my motoring-about gear today. Who knew I'd have so many adventures in one morning?"

"It's been quite the morning for you, hasn't it? Sounds like a good excuse for a nap."

"Sounds like a good excuse for a cookie."

"You mean two."

"Yes, of course. I mean two."

They puttered past the doors of other residents. Many of them stood ajar, allowing a peek into the quiet rooms. What was it that made people cushion the dying with silence? The quiet was more dreadful than anything.

Quiet meant stuck.

"This place needs some dancing," she said.

"Please, Mrs. Kip, don't get any ideas."

"Too late for that, Jimmy." Though she tried to giggle, a pain stabbed through her stomach. Hiding the wince required significant energy. She pressed forward, and by the time the pain dissipated, they were at her door.

No sooner had they stepped inside than a man's loud, anguished moan caught them both. It came from the room directly across from Clara's.

She frowned. "What was—"

Another moan, longer and deeper in tone.

"Is he okay?" By instinct, and from practice, she stepped toward the noise.

Jimmy stopped her. "Let me get you settled, and I'll go check on him."

Despite her inclination to the contrary, she allowed Jimmy to do what she knew medical laws required him to do.

After getting her situated into the surprisingly comfortable armchair, Jimmy laid the cookies on the tray table next to her. "I'll be back soon with the boxes. You'll be here, right? Not off skydiving or something?"

Clara grinned. "I promise nothing, honey."

"Sounds about right." He gave her a wink, then stepped into the hallway, pulling the door completely shut behind him.

In the space that followed, Clara strained to listen for anything from across the hall, but with the door closed, she could hear only muffles, an acoustical fact Jimmy likely knew well and acted on accordingly.

Regardless, her heart still resonated with the man's pain. Keeping her eyes toward her door, she prayed, *Be close to him, God. And if I can be your love and mercy, show me a way.*

A second later, her gaze landed on the cookies.

CHAPTER 4

The essence of survival in a newsroom is appearance. It is everything. It is reality even if it tells a lie.

If a reporter appears confident, she is regarded as such. If a reporter appears uninformed, she is regarded as a liability.

If a reporter leaves her editor's office after a tongue-lashing with anything other than an uplifted chin, she will be considered weak, too emotional for an emotionless job.

Unworthy.

Aidyn denied the gelatin feeling in her legs, clenched her fists to hide the tremble in her hands. She returned to her desk with carefully righted posture and an air of purpose. Though she sensed the glances her direction and the whispers behind hands, she pretended she didn't.

She convinced herself the office walls were thicker than they were.

When she sat at her desk, she immediately opened a blank document and began to type. It didn't matter what came out—all gibberish. What mattered was the appearance of importance. The appearance of being unfazed.

A minute later, Woods wordlessly strode by on her way to her delayed lunch meeting. Aidyn pretended not to notice.

Type, type, type. She typed to give herself space to calm down, for her heart to stop thumping as hard as it did, for her muscles to relax.

Just breathe, she told herself.

Her IM dinged.

Rahmiya
Ready?

Aidyn winced. Lunch.

Not only did she not want to appear like she was running out to lick her fresh wounds, but she honestly couldn't stand the thought of food at the moment.

Sorry, Rahmi. Better pass today.

??

Aidyn tapped the keys in thought. How much should she say? Especially over IM, and especially so soon.

At last, she replied,

The answer was no.

Even Rahmiya would know the real story held much more complexity than that.

Aidie, I'm so sorry. Talk later?

Call you tonight.

Rahmiya sent back a heart emoji. The signal of sisterhood gave Aidyn enough solace to continue with her fake work.

But staying put in the newsroom proved to be a bigger challenge than she'd anticipated. Twice in the space of the hour, someone walked by her desk slower than necessary. Though she refused to look up, they undoubtedly sneered at her.

When she went to the printer to retrieve the copy of the busing policy story she'd printed out for her final checks, snickering drifted from a nearby desk. Against her better judgment, she glanced toward the sound. Two reporters, both cohorts of Shayna's, quickly looked a different direction. Their attempts to hide their sly grins were pathetic, likely by intention.

She needed to leave.

In movements as purposeful as possible, she returned to her desk, grabbed her messenger bag from her file drawer—the one with the picture of Katharine Graham sitting in her office—and made a show of being busy with something on her phone as she walked out of the newsroom.

The midday June heat enveloped her as she descended the front steps of the brick *Star* building. She turned right, toward the Grand Street corridor, and started walking south without a destination in mind. Maybe around the block. Maybe a couple of blocks.

The burn behind her eyes intensified. Her throat tightened. Quickly she retrieved her sunglasses from her bag and slid them on. She kept her head down, breaking all Midwest social decorum by ignoring people she passed. There were enough voices in her mind; she didn't need the polite hellos from strangers.

The voices sounded like Woods. Like Maper. Like Shayna. Like the snickers. Like her own.

They spoke of her stupidity.

They preached on her foolishness.

So loud and convincing, they shut out all other thoughts. She couldn't break away from them for a second, not even to attempt to hear the answer when her heart cried, *What now, Lord? What do I do now?*

Clara scuffled across the hallway and knocked on the partially open door of room 309. "Anybody home?"

The door moved slightly with her small force, but the man did not answer. He did not stir.

She glanced down the hallway to ensure no one spied her. In her years alongside her friend Mai, she had learned that where there is pain, there is a calling. A duty. And a great and wonderful commission.

She brought the cookies with her.

"Hello?" She gently pushed the door open all the way and stepped inside.

The silence that hung in the room had the same heaviness that had once sunk into her own bones in her basement apartment. It was the shape and weight of profound loneliness.

Lord, shower your mercy here.

Her new neighbor lay still in his bed. He was a waif of a man, with sunken cheeks and a blank stare stuck on the bookshelves across the room. A crown of kinky gray curls horseshoed the back and sides of his head, and darker patches of skin speckled the bald place on top. Even from the doorway, the rasp was clear in his respiration. His thin arms splayed at his sides on top of what looked like a homemade quilt, weathered like its owner. A gold wedding band encircled the ring finger on his left hand.

Clues of unspoken stories. Stories she might earn the right to hear.

"Hello, neighbor," she tried again, louder, as she took a few steps forward.

The space between her words and the man's reaction stretched for days. When he did receive her, it was with a rather acute scowl. "Who are you?" he demanded with a gravelly voice.

"Fine way to greet a lady, my dear."

"I'm not your dear. I don't even know you."

"My name is Clara Kip." She smiled and trundled halfway to the bed. "I just moved in across the hall. Thought I'd come by for a visit."

"What for?"

"To be human, of course. You know, before I don't have a chance to anymore." Giggling, she gave him a little wink.

The scowl stayed put.

"Would you like a cookie? I swiped a couple from up front." She peeled back the edge of the napkin to show him the loot.

"No," he barked.

"Do you not like cookies?"

"I don't like strangers coming into my room."

"Now, honey, I'm not a stranger. You know my name. That makes me an acquaintance."

"I don't want to be acquaintances. I want you to leave." The gravel in his voice grew sharper at the edges.

"That's fine." In perfect composure, she took another step forward to let him know she was not easily offended or deterred. "If you want me to leave, I will. But I would so enjoy the chance to get to know you. Will you at least tell me your name?"

He stared at her for a moment, as if evaluating her sanity. Not the first time she had received such a reaction.

"If I tell you my name," he said, "you'll leave?"

"If that's what you'd like, yes." Purposely she left out how *long* her promised departure would take.

The man watched her another moment, then licked his top lip, cracked and flaked with white from dehydration. "Charles Slesher."

"How lovely. Nice to meet you, Charles Slesher. I've always liked the name Charles. I told my husband if we ever had a son, I'd like to name him Charles. Such a dignified name. With a dignified name, you must have had a dignified career too. Let me guess . . . Doctor? Lawyer? Real estate agent? If you say insurance agent, I might not give you a cookie at all." She chuckled. "You're not, are you?"

His scowl tightened. "You're not going away, are you?"

"Nope. Might as well answer the question."

He shook his head and looked away. "Just get out of my room."

To the inexperienced or fearful, his reaction may have been reason to drop the pursuit. But to Clara it meant something quite different. A pained body with a broken spirit tends to recoil when the hand of grace first finds its wounds.

"Look, Charles Slesher. The way I see it, you can either kick me out and go back to the great big empty to-do of being alone, or you can enjoy the company of a rather funny and compassionate woman who is willing to share cookies that she risked life and limb to retrieve. A rather generous offer, if I do say so myself. You stand to gain a relative fortune here."

She waited for the words to stir within him and craned her neck as far as it would allow (which wasn't far) to try to discern his expression.

Work, Lord.

Charles turned toward the picture window on the other side of his bed. For a long moment, he was silent. Then, so quietly she had to strain to hear him, he said, "I was an engineer."

"An engineer! Oh, that sounds interesting. You must have all kinds of stories about projects you worked on. Any projects I would recognize?"

Slowly he turned back to her. "Maybe."

That was an opening if ever there was one. She shuffled over to his bed. When he did not object, she unwrapped the treats in her hand. "A cookie for a story?"

He looked between her and the cookie, clearly still unsure.

"I'll tell you as many stories as you can stand about my life, Charles." She laughed, and for the first time, the tip of his mouth ticked upward.

He held out a gnarled hand, palm up. She tucked a cookie snugly into it.

For the next twenty minutes, she sat in the armchair next to his bed and listened to his stories of work, of his wife, of the other things that brought him joy. She helped him forget he was widowed and dying.

The tender worship of companionship.

A hard art to learn.

October 5, 1969

"The babies saved me."

That's what she would tell people of her job at the busy nursery inside the University of Kansas Medical Center.

"It took me nine years to find my way to them, and nine minutes for them to show me the way out of the hole."

Though people chuckled at the sweet notion, thinking it was nothing more than that, she meant it at a level they couldn't appreciate. Without her newfound career, she feared she would have stayed in that old armchair drinking that old Scotch and longing for that old dream for the rest of her prematurely old life.

The suggestion to be a nurse's assistant came from Martha Rendall, a neighbor who was always talking about two things: her church and her nursing job. Clara put up with the church talk because Martha was a doll, and she was eventually intrigued enough by Martha's stories of working in the hospital that she decided to follow her friend's suggestion.

Her first day at KU Med alongside Martha came nine years, three months, and two days after John's accident, and she had found nowhere softer and more flourishing to land than among new, untainted life. Crying, sleeping—it didn't matter how the babies chose to spend their time during her shift. She held them all the same. The crying assured her they were learning to adjust to the outside world. The sleeping convinced her peace could still be found in the world.

She arrived at the nursery with Martha one October morning to the immediate summons of a night nurse. The woman held a swaddled, screeching little thing wearing a fuzzy pink knitted cap.

"Clara, please work your magic." She barely waited for Clara to put down her purse before holding out the bundle.

A baby girl named Estelle. "Been at it for a while?" she asked as she gathered the darling to her chest.

"Almost all of them were at it for the past twenty minutes. She's the holdout."

"Now, Miss Estelle," Clara said in a soothing voice, "we talked about your manners yesterday, did we not? Shhhush, madam."

The baby hesitated in her crying.

"That's right, darling." With a firm, comforting grip, Clara began to twist at the waist, swaying side to side, just the way Estelle liked. On a three-count beat, she whispered, "Shh-hush."

The space between cries grew longer.

Martha watched her friend in action, a smile spreading on her lips. "They should give you a raise."

"More like a Nobel Peace Prize," the nurse said and bustled off to where the oncoming nurses gathered for the shift report.

"Every baby has a formula," Clara said. "Estelle's was a bit harder than most to figure out, but I finally caught up to what you were telling me, didn't I, Miss Estelle?" She snuggled her cheek against the baby's cap, offering the extra warmth and assurance of protection.

"You are a godsend, friend." Martha patted her shoulder, then left to join the shift report.

"She speaks way too highly of me," Clara whispered to the baby. "If only she knew, right?"

As if in response, the baby heaved a sigh.

"Attagirl, Miss Estelle." She continued to sway, encouraging Estelle to drop off into sleep. As she did, Clara glanced over at the bassinet at the far end of the nursery. Baby Elijah.

Though she wasn't supposed to have favorites or get attached, it was impossible not to with Elijah. Besides having the most chub of all the babies, he possessed the calmest eyes, as serene as fresh-fallen snow, like he'd come into the world with a full-grown soul. He was due to leave the next day, and she already felt his absence in the depths of her heart.

After she settled the sleeping Estelle back in her bassinet, Clara abandoned her list of check-in tasks to pay Elijah a quick visit.

A fateful decision.

Her steps lightened the closer she got to him, the little man snug in a swaddle, tips of his black hair sticking out from under his blue cap. His thick body rose in a gentle slope from the bassinet pad, and his head had rolled to the side, facing away from her.

Clara came around the side of his bassinet. His pacifier had fallen out. She reached for it, then stopped cold. Foam trailed from his blue-tinted lips.

A feeling like fire spread over her.

"Martha! Martha!" She reached for him but forced her arms to stop. Her training had taught her not to pick him up.

Within seconds, nurses surrounded the bassinet, jostling her to the side. Things went blurry. The blur of white tunics. The blur of shouts. The blur of movement.

Somehow in the haze, she ended up at the rocking chair in the corner, the chair she often used to soothe the babies, assure them they were safe, watched, and loved. Because she had believed they were all of those things. She had believed depravity could not pass through the nursery door.

Not until Martha lifted Clara's chin minutes later and told her the news with only a look did it become clear the nursery never was a sanctuary.

Clara melted into sobs.

With hands as gentle as Clara's, Martha laid her friend's head against her own chest and held her. "Jesus is holding him now," she whispered. "We can take comfort in that."

Clara nearly spit. More church talk. "Jesus could have held him right where he was. Why rip him from his mama's arms?"

"I wish I could answer that, friend."

Clara let out an anguished cry. "He didn't do anything wrong! Why take him?"

"It's devastating." Martha stroked her back. "It never gets easier."

"I can't do this, Martha. I can't watch babies die too. I can't!"

Martha pulled away to look at her. "You can. You can love and care for these little ones while you have the chance, regardless of what happens. That is your choice. We live among perishing bodies, and we don't get to call the shots."

51

Clara shook her head, tried to move away.

Martha held her firmly. "Listen to me. I am convinced precious Elijah knew perhaps better than all the babies how loved and cherished he was by you. I have no doubt he did."

The sincerity and truth in Martha's expression were too intense. Clara bowed her head, a new wave of tears pouring out. All she could think about was Elijah's mama hearing the news, how it would plow through her, rip her open, and leave her ravaged. Why would God let anyone feel such pain? That wasn't merciful. That was selfish. The God Martha and John loved so much had shown himself to be nothing but a bully.

Martha wrapped her again in a hug and clung to her. "Keep the fight in your veins, honey. Never let it fade."

But how could she?

Death had won once. Then twice.

She was certain she was done taking the hits.

CHAPTER 5

Tuesday, June 7, 2016

The tree limbs outside of Clara's window bobbed with the invisible streams of wind. Swish, swoosh. A comforting rhythm, a melody in itself, like a soundless lullaby. The leaves shimmied in their raucous play. In the background, the sky had started to spread out its full-day blue, buttoned with white wisps.

Clara watched from the armchair, her Bible open in her lap. A prayer stirred in her heart and spun softly off her lips into the expanse outside her window.

"Lord, your world and your people are treasures to me. Thank you, God, for these gifts. Thank you for the staff here at Sacred Promise. Thank you for this place to shelter in your care. Show me how I can serve you today among these people. Amen."

The Lord never failed to answer a request for work to do.

She closed the Bible and set it on the nightstand next to two framed pictures. Few personal effects had made the move from her house. The Bible was by far the most important, followed closely by the pictures. Each captured the handsome face of her sweet John during a momentous occasion: their wedding reception and his visit to what would have been their São Paulo apartment.

She blew a kiss to her husband, her forever love. Then, with much grunting effort, she pushed herself up to a standing position. Once securely on her feet, she shuffled over to the two storage boxes Jimmy had placed on the small dining table on the other side of the room. Her goals for the day were twofold: enjoy time in the courtyard (so help her, God) and go through those boxes containing her last remaining possessions.

And maybe eat a cookie.

Jimmy had lined up the boxes in a perfect row on the table, arranging them according to the labels she had scrawled on the outside. Though they had been tucked away in her bedroom closet for many years, she remembered exactly what they contained—the stories she had not wrapped herself in for so long.

She started at the beginning, with the box labeled 1.

The journals were arranged in a row along the bottom, spines facing up. A single newspaper clipping lay on top, folded and browned with age. Gently she removed the fragile paper and opened it.

Her breath caught when she saw her younger self alongside Mai Khab. She had not seen her friend's beautiful face for decades. Without her reading a single word, the events, faces, and hopes of that tumultuous—and rewarding—post–Vietnam War era began to rouse.

A knock at her door brought her back to the present.

"Good morning, Mrs. Kip." The voice belonged to a middle-aged woman with a gleaming smile, a smooth, round face, and wavy, dark hair pulled back into a ponytail. "I'm Rosario Dia. We've been speaking on the phone."

"Rosario! Am I glad to see you! Come in."

The woman stepped into the room. "It's so nice to finally meet you."

"Same to you, honey. I missed you yesterday."

"Yes, I hope you'll forgive me that I wasn't here." Her slight Spanish accent charmed Clara. "Though I try to make it a point to be here when my patients arrive, yesterday I needed to be with my mama. She isn't doing so well, and she lives alone."

"Your mama is very lucky to have you."

"Thanks for understanding. I know you were in good hands with Margaret, though." Her smile drew in slightly, and she eyed Clara. "Everything go okay yesterday?"

Clara paused at the loaded question. "Tell me what you heard."

"I heard everything, Mrs. Kip."

Clara shrugged. "What can I say? She started it."

Rosario chuckled. "You're going to keep us on our toes, aren't you?"

"There's a rowdy one in every bunch," Clara replied with a giggle. "But in all fairness, Margaret was quite kind to move me to this room. The view is perfect. I'm still working on settling in, though." She nodded toward the open storage box and the newspaper clipping in her hand. "I'm trying to figure out what to do with it all. I have so little left, but it's still too much."

Rosario peered closer at the article. "Is that you?"

"It is. And my old friend Mai Khab. She came to us from Laos back in '75." She handed the clipping to Rosario, who studied the picture. Clara had always loved that picture, life and renewal beaming in her precious friend's eyes. The photojournalist had captured Mai's spirit so perfectly.

Rosario took in the words of the accompanying article. Soon enough, her lips parted. She had clearly come to *that* paragraph. Her jaw practically dropped to her clavicle.

"Mrs. Kip," she said in disbelief. "You did that?"

"You make it sound like I cured cancer." She blinked at the irony of her joke. "If only I had."

But the humor was lost on the stunned Rosario. "That is amazing," she said.

"The Lord did the work. There were many of us involved. I was blessed to be part of it."

Rosario peered into the box. "Are those your journals?"

"Yes."

"Are they from the seventies too?"

"They are."

Rosario suddenly seemed eager. "What do you think you'll do with all this?"

"Beats me, honey. I don't think anyone is all that interested in owning an old woman's ramblings."

Rosario grinned. "Actually, I know someone who would love to see this."

Clara frowned. "You do?"

"Definitely. She's an old dormmate from college. Mind if I reach out?"

"Be my guest. But I won't be offended if the answer is no."

"I seriously doubt it will be."

"You sound awfully sure."

Rosario nodded. "A thousand percent sure. She lives for an undiscovered story."

Aidyn dropped her messenger bag into her file drawer and kicked it shut, the same way she had done every weekday morning for nearly thirteen months. In all those times before, the kick was a declaration of dominance over the day ahead, a swift, perfunctory statement of confidence.

This time, however, the kick possessed barely enough potency to close the drawer.

At 8:30, she was already exhausted from fitful sleep and from pretending not to care about the sideways glances from every person she'd passed on her way into the building. Apparently, what happened in the newsroom did not stay in the newsroom.

Woods was already in her office, per her usual early-morning habits. With any luck, she would stay holed up for a long while—one less set of critical eyes darting Aidyn's way.

As soon as she could, she busied herself with checking email and tackling the menial assignments on her list. The busyness provided her a veil of importance and therein a degree of solace.

Until Shayna arrived.

The unmistakable caw-like laugh alerted Aidyn to her entrance. Against her better judgment, Aidyn turned her head just enough to see the newsroom door out of the corner of her eye.

The pear-figured, big-haired Shayna huddled with three other reporters. She was all smiles, irreverent and loud. At one point, she directed the reporters' attention to Aidyn, who quickly turned away. Their laughter carried.

With cheeks on fire, Aidyn forced herself to concentrate on her screen and held fast to her flimsy veil even as Shayna approached. Well before she was emotionally prepared, she heard the thud of Shayna's overstated Vuitton knockoff as it hit the desk.

"Sounds like one epic email," Shayna said. "Well done."

Aidyn held her tongue and continued to type.

"I hear Maper wants to ship you out to a bureau."

Her fingers halted midstroke.

"That's what I'd do if I were him, anyway. You'd be covering senior citizen luncheons and county fairs the rest of your life."

Aidyn dared to meet her gaze. "I'm not going anywhere."

Shayna put her fists on her desk and leaned toward Aidyn. Her bright-red suit jacket, already tight around her girth, pulled dangerously hard at the shoulder seams. "Don't be too sure. Maper never thought you deserved your job anyway, and who can blame him now?"

Aidyn fought to hold in the rejoinder that shot to her lips like cannon fire. She returned to her work and prayed for strength.

Fortunately, Shayna allowed a reprieve as she settled in. She sat, took out her laptop, and began clacking away at the keys. After several minutes, however, she started up again.

"Send me my notes for the special yet?"

"Yesterday."

"They better be good."

"They're better than good."

"I hope so. I have to make up for your sidebar."

Aidyn whipped her head toward Shayna. "How did you know about the—" She stopped. It was a silly question.

Shayna confirmed it. "Woods would never add to my feature without talking to me first." She closed her laptop and grabbed a pen and pad. "Speaking of which, it's nine o'clock, which means I have a meeting with Woods. Because that's what reporters do—talk to their editors. Someday you'll learn that." She shoved back her chair, then promenaded toward their boss's office with her shoulders thrown back in a queen-bee posture.

Aidyn covertly watched her. Disgust and envy ate away at her bones.

———

"Are you decent?" Rosario poked her head into Clara's room.

Clara looked up from the journal in her lap. "Fancy seeing you twice in one morning. Come in! Have a seat over here with me."

Rosario headed for the loveseat next to Clara's armchair.

"You didn't bring any cookies?" Clara asked, disappointed.

"Mrs. Kip, it's only ten a.m."

"No time is the wrong time for cookies, honey."

Rosario chuckled as she sat. "Duly noted. I hope what I *do* have is something you think is even better than cookies."

"Try me."

"Remember how I was going to talk to my old college friend?"

Clara shut the journal and raised her eyebrows in anticipation. "I do."

"I got in touch with her."

"So soon?"

"I know, I was a little surprised too. But she wasn't that hard to track down. I told her about you and your story, and she said she would love everything you have!"

"Everything?"

"Yes, everything!" Rosario reached over and squeezed Clara's hand. "What do you think?"

"I'll be," Clara breathed. "I'm not sure what to make of that."

A light filled Rosario's eyes. "Mrs. Kip, this is going to be such a blessing to so many people. Bigger than either one of us realizes."

Clara's curiosity was piqued. These stories had been around for decades. Why would they be resurrected now?

Lord, what are you up to?

My office.

The IM was simple and straight to the point, and that was the scariest part. Slowly Aidyn rose from her chair and headed for Woods's office.

She knocked before she entered. "You wanted to see me?"

"Sit." Woods continued to write on a notepad with unimpeded ferocity. The tip of her pen scraped loudly on the paper.

Aidyn lowered into the same chair she'd occupied the day before and waited, hands gripping the armrests.

Finally, Woods dropped the pen, heaved a sigh, and looked at her with intensity. "We need to talk about your future here at the *Star*."

Aidyn's breath caught.

"I rejected hundreds—*hundreds*—of applicants for your job. The market is so tight right now I would have no problem filling any hole you left. None. Which is why I find it infuriating that you view your job with such disregard."

"I don't—"

Woods thrust up her hand, silencing her. "Don't try, Kelley. You proved yesterday you don't appreciate what you have. You consider your work to be far beneath your talent. You made that very clear. To everyone."

Aidyn looked down at her right hand, the thumb of which had started to pick at the side of the armrest.

"Ambition is a two-edged sword. Use it wisely, you become a trailblazer. Use it foolishly, you become a chump. Your one job as a rookie is to prove you're not a chump. How do you think you're doing at that, Kelley?"

Aidyn ventured a glance at her editor. "Not good."

"Not good," Woods repeated for emphasis.

Sweat moistened Aidyn's palms. Her fingers itched to touch her cross necklace.

Woods leaned back in her chair and crossed her arms. "Maper has more or less written you off. Quite frankly, I agree with him. Which means you have to do something to prove to me you offer more to the *Star* than bravado."

Aidyn held her breath.

"I have an assignment for you. You will take it with absolutely no complaints, and you will complete it at full

Sifford Award capacity. And I mean *full* capacity. Is that clear?"

"Yes. Completely."

Woods reached toward her computer monitor and pulled off a sticky note. "You'll start by talking with her."

Aidyn took the bright yellow square of paper. "'Sacred Promise Senior Care Center,'" she read with a frown. "Can I ask what exactly this assignment is?"

"It's an obituary."

She blinked. "An . . . obituary?"

"Yes."

"But . . . aren't obits written by the family?"

"Not in this case, it's not."

"But—"

"Kelley, I specifically said no complaints. What about that was not clear?"

"Nothing," Aidyn replied reluctantly.

"Good." Woods sat forward and picked up her pen again. "Then I expect some award-winning work. You have what you need. Go." She shooed Aidyn to the door with a swipe of her hand and resumed writing.

Without a word, Aidyn returned to her desk, humiliating assignment in hand. How could writing an obit possibly be the way to prove herself worthy of a feature? The two had nothing to do with each other.

She dreaded Shayna's reaction to the news.

But more than anything, she dreaded having to talk to a dying person.

CHAPTER 6

"You're kidding," Rahmiya said through a mouthful of spicy tuna roll.

"I *really* wish I were." Aidyn could only poke at her own food with her chopsticks. The meeting with Woods had cut her appetite dramatically. Even being with Rahmiya at their favorite sushi spot couldn't correct it. "An obit, Rahmi! An obit is lower than a scrap. It's barely a morsel. It's not even legit writing."

"Families submit those," Rahmiya said.

"I know."

"They shell out big to have them run too."

"Exactly! It's just paid advertising."

Rahmiya shook her head in sympathy. "Now that I think about it, I can't remember ever reading an obit, to be honest."

"That's because no one reads them except the family." Aidyn jabbed at her roll, then dropped the chopsticks with a sigh. "Shayna's going to have a field day with this."

Remorse colored Rahmiya's expression. "I feel responsible for this mess."

"What? Why would you feel responsible?"

"Because I literally sent that email. I didn't respect—"

Aidyn waved off the apology. "It's not your fault. It was my idea to send the email in the first place, and I would have sent it regardless, so this is totally on me. You were just trying to be supportive."

"Still, I feel bad. I wish there was something I could do."

"You are doing something, Rahmi. You're listening to me whine."

"I'd be whining too, sister." She picked up another roll with her chopsticks. "So, what happens now? Is the family sending you something to help you write the obit?"

"No, it's completely from scratch. I actually have to go meet this woman today at three."

"You mean she's still *alive*?" Rahmiya asked, nearly spitting out the bite.

"Yes, in hospice care at a skilled nursing facility. Somewhere in Olathe."

"That sounds delightful."

"I know. Hospitals are bad enough. I seriously have no idea how I'm going to stomach being in a place like that."

"But she's cognizant?"

"From what I understand."

"And why can't her family write the obit themselves?"

"The lady I spoke to at the facility said the woman doesn't have any family. Though she did kindly assure me that this woman is—and I quote—'a total hoot.'"

"If she were a crank, would they really tell you?"

Aidyn chuckled. "Probably not. Whatever this woman is like, I hope to get the info I need quickly and get this over with."

"Good plan." Rahmiya took a sip of her water. "How long does the obit have to be?"

"Woods didn't give me a word count, but I assume maybe a hundred words or so."

"That's not so bad. One hundred words is a fairly short road to redemption."

Aidyn grinned. "I suppose so."

"And that's the point of this, right? To redeem yourself by proving you can be humble?"

Aidyn shrugged. "Woods does think I need to learn my place. It's humiliating however you want to categorize it." Surrendering to her lack of appetite, she pushed her plate away and put her cloth napkin on the table.

Rahmiya took one last bite and chewed with a thoughtful look. "This may seem like an odd question, but do you at all wonder if there's more to this?"

Aidyn frowned. "What makes you ask that?"

"I'm not exactly sure. I guess . . . if I didn't know Woods, I'd think there was a bigger reason why an editor would give such an unorthodox assignment to a rookie reporter."

Aidyn huffed. "That's assuming the editor actually wants the reporter to have a career." She waved the server over to request a to-go box. "Trust me, Rahmi, Woods doesn't like me well enough to put in that much effort. Especially with Shayna around."

Charles looked worse. The tone of his skin crept closer to waxen. The rasp in his breathing had worsened. His eyes were closed, and his mouth hung ajar.

It was hard to put her finger on what was stealing his breath bit by bit, but the feel of death gaining ground within him was unmistakable. It was winning more than he was fighting.

She stepped closer to his bed and spoke softly. "Hi, friend."

His eyelids flickered at the sound of her voice, then shut.

"It's Clara," she said. "I'm back, like it or not."

Almost imperceptibly, his bottom lip quivered, as if he struggled to drum up his own voice.

"Don't worry, I didn't come empty-handed. Look here. Cookies fresh from the oven." She unwrapped the cookies in her hand and held them out as if he could see them. Though it was obvious he couldn't eat them—he had only held the cookie in his hand the day before—the gesture surely meant something to him. "Don't they smell divine? You're lucky I have restraint, honey. I have to be honest, these almost didn't make it down the hallway today."

The more she talked, the harder he worked to turn his head her direction. Slowly he faced her. He struggled to keep his eyes open long enough to see her. "Who . . . you?" he asked in a near whisper.

"Clara. Your neighbor. The one who brings you cookies." She set the treats on the tray table and rolled it to his bed. "I suppose I should bring you some milk to go with these cookies. Or at least some water. You strike me as a bendy-straw fella. I could find you one of those too."

"Clara?" he asked.

"That's right, honey. Clara. We had a very nice chat yesterday afternoon. So nice I decided to come back every afternoon. You told me a lot about your sweet Emma, and I told you more stories about my Johnny than you could possibly ever want to know."

His eyebrows shoved together momentarily. "I . . . don't . . ." He coughed faintly several times, flinching with each one.

"It's okay if you don't remember, Charles. I'm not offended."

Recovered from the fit, he managed to look up at her. "Was I . . . nice?"

"You were a doll."

He scrunched his brow and huffed, obviously having his doubts.

"Don't you fret, Charles. I did sort of spring myself upon you. And meeting new people isn't always easy, is it?"

"No," he breathed. "Espe . . . cially now."

With a giggle, she conceded the point. "It's definitely more challenging." She watched him for a moment. Her heart panged with empathy as he flinched against a hidden pain. He licked his lips in a futile attempt to give them relief.

"Do you mind if I sit here next to you in this armchair, Charles? This old bag of bones doesn't hold up as well as it used to."

He nodded his consent.

"You're such a gentleman." She gingerly sat, thankful Charles's room was arranged slightly different from her own so the armchair was on the door side of the bed, and close enough to him that she could take up his hand if she wanted. She adjusted until she found a comfortable position, then gave Charles her full attention. "You look tired, honey. How about you rest, and I'll tell you some more of my stories?"

He nodded, his head drifting back to center.

"I promise I won't eat your cookie."

One side of his mouth tipped up in a subtle smile.

Before she began, she said a quiet prayer for him. *Lord, I don't know if Charles knows you, but if he doesn't, please, Father, draw him into your presence. Give me the words to speak to him. He is precious to me.*

She cleared her throat and settled her folded hands in her lap. "Speaking of meeting new people, guess what I've got going on this afternoon? I'm meeting someone new! A young gal, from what I'm told. A friend of a friend of a friend, or something like that. I'm supposed to share stories with her too. I can't imagine I'll enjoy that any."

She giggled at her own joke and pretended he laughed with her. He appeared to nod off, his eyelids too heavy to keep open all the way, his jaw too much of a burden to keep shut at all times.

"To tell you the truth, Charles, sometimes I get a little nervous when I'm about to meet someone new. I worry about their intentions toward me or whether I can be a true friend to them. I worried about that with you, by the way. You were a bit of a tough cookie, mister. Pardon the expression. But we got through okay, didn't we?"

She paused as if to allow him to respond. Though he gave no indication he heard, she believed he had, and that he appreciated her desire for conversation with him.

"You know what I've learned over the years, Charles? People can be the worst, but they also can be quite the adventure if you're willing to open yourself up and have the courage to stick with them. Some of the biggest blessings I've received have come because I chose to have such courage. It's a hard choice to make, don't get me wrong. But almost always the Lord has taught me more when I took the hard path with someone instead of the self-protective one."

A pinch of pain in her stomach made her pause. Rubbing it, she continued, "Of course, some people know better than others how hard they are to stick with. To be fair, I'm positive people I once knew would say that about me. Actually, I'm sure they would."

The pain sharpened. She sucked in her breath and waited until it passed. "You may find this hard to believe, Charles, but I did not always have my act together. I definitely was on the ignorant side about things more often than I care to admit. But the Lord has a way of breaking our pride not one moment too late."

April 14, 1971

Clara stood abruptly, nearly knocking over her coffee mug.

"Friend, wait," Martha pleaded. "Please don't misunderstand me."

Customers at the neighboring tables glanced their way. Clara could not care less. She was tired of hiding—of denying—her true feelings.

"Have you ever lost someone, Martha? Ever?"

"I don't mean to pry," Martha said in a soft voice, low

enough to encourage Clara to follow suit. "But I think this would be good for you. It's been eleven years since John died. Counseling can help you find the healing you never—"

"Answer my question!"

Even the counter staff stopped to look at them.

"Have you ever lost someone?" Clara insisted. "Not patients. Not acquaintances. But someone whose heart is part of your own?"

Martha's face reddened. "No."

"Then how could you possibly know what it's like? How could you possibly understand what I'm going through?" She snatched her purse off the back of her chair. "I don't need to talk about my feelings to some stranger who gets paid to spout off opinions about my life. And I certainly don't want to be the one paying him to do it!"

"Honey, please," Martha tried again.

"Don't 'honey, please' me! This is my life, my decision, and I've made it. Don't ever lecture me on how to grieve properly."

She stormed out of the café, certain her friend was nothing but a nosy, naïve know-it-all.

Absolutely certain.

Except for a little whisper of doubt telling her otherwise.

June 7, 2016

Aidyn's stomach began to knot the moment she left the *Star* office. The twenty-five-minute drive to Sacred Promise afforded her plenty of time to imagine what she might see. The mental images were derived from what she knew of hospitals, which was derived mainly from movies and television.

Sacred Promise was probably a stoic, carved-stone building, industrial in structure and personality. Inside would be a matching set of stoic people scurrying here and there, prodded by calls over the intercom. Tile floors, plain windows, and the unshakable aroma of bleach and antiseptic. All practical to the point of impersonal.

When she arrived, though, the real-life facility challenged every one of those assumptions.

She took in the place as she pulled into a parking spot. The facade comprised carved wood beams and a light-brown plaster, giving the building a warm, earthy complexion. A rich lawn and a generous screen of mature trees along the edges of the campus gave the place an unexpected serenity. As she stepped out of her car, the melodic chatter of birds wafted over the distant hum of traffic. A gentle breeze swept across her face, taking the edge off the midafternoon heat.

Pleasant. Lovely. But none of it did much to settle her nerves.

Only an hour or so. That was all that would be required, God willing. She strapped on her messenger bag, clung tightly to the strap, and ready or not, headed for the entrance.

Inside the foyer, a heavyset woman with a bright smile waited for her. "Aidyn Kelley?" The voice sounded like the one from the phone.

Aidyn nodded. "You must be Rosario Dia."

"Pleasure to meet you." The woman extended her hand. Her nails were neatly manicured, her grip commanding.

Hopefully Aidyn's was neither too weak nor too sweaty.

"Thank you so much for coming on such short notice."

"Of course."

"I have to be honest, I was a little surprised when you agreed to this. I understand this is an unusual way of going about things."

"A little," Aidyn agreed. Rosario didn't know the half of it.

"All the more appreciated then. I do think once you meet Mrs. Kip, though, you'll understand this was well worth the effort."

Aidyn smiled politely, hiding her skepticism.

"I'll have you sign in here." Rosario pointed to a white guest book on a small desk outside the office door. "We ask all visitors to sign in and out, and we prefer media members to come between nine a.m. and five p.m. on weekdays. But if you need additional time, let me know."

Aidyn half listened as she picked up the pen next to the book and signed under the few other names on the day's record.

"Would you like bottled water or a cookie? We have some down in the activity room," Rosario said.

"Thank you, I'm fine for now." Aidyn set down the pen and righted. "Will I be speaking with Mrs. Kip in a conference room?"

"She gave permission for you to come to her room, and I'll take you back to meet her. Before I do, though, I'm just curious. Have you had much experience with the end stages of life?"

The question felt like a test, and one Aidyn would fail. "Not really, no."

The woman nodded knowingly, as if she had read that in

Aidyn the second she walked in. "Most people don't when they come here. If you ever have any questions, please feel free to ask me or any of the staff members. This stage can be uncomfortable and confusing to witness, but it has so much unappreciated dignity to it as well. We strive to emphasize those parts. After you spend some time with Mrs. Kip, I'm sure you'll understand what I mean."

Unsure how else to respond, especially through her increasing doubt, Aidyn nodded.

"Any questions for me?"

Aidyn shook her head. "Not that I can think of. Maybe later."

"In that case, let's go meet Mrs. Kip." Rosario waved her forward.

As they started across the foyer, Aidyn sucked in her breath and cleaved to her bag strap as if it were the only thing keeping her to the ground. She walked side by side with Rosario down the hallway.

"I told you Mrs. Kip is a seventy-nine-year-old widow, no children, correct?" Rosario asked.

"Yes," Aidyn said. "And that she is still fully aware and interactive."

"Interactive?" The woman laughed. "Well, that's one way to put it. Perhaps I should have used a different word. Mrs. Kip is . . . more like . . . adventurous."

Aidyn nearly stopped walking. That word sounded way worse. "What exactly does 'adventurous' entail?"

Rosario looked at her sideways and grinned. "Just wait. It'll be obvious."

CHAPTER 7

Had Clara known they were coming down the hallway, she would have scooted out of Charles's room sooner. She would have made it back to her chair in time both to avoid that look from Rosario, who had made her thoughts on Clara's freewheeling clear, and to be ready to receive Aidyn Kelley with something much warmer than a startle of surprise.

As it was, she had been oblivious to their approach, absorbed in the work of cracking the shell of the dying curmudgeon next door. She had gotten him to laugh, and it was by far her crowning moment.

"Later, tater," she called to him as she backed out of his room. Quietly she shut the door, praying for the Spirit to nurture the seeds she had sown in their hour-long visit.

When she turned around, the two women stood there, staring at her.

"Oh," she gasped.

Rosario pursed her lips.

The girl raised her eyebrows in uncertainty.

"Hello," Clara chirped.

Shaking her head, Rosario replied calmly, "Mrs. Kip, please let us help you when you want to move about. We'd hate for you to fall."

"I'm perfectly fine, honey. See? I made it out alive." She ambled toward them. "And just in time to meet my new friend here. You must be Miss Kelley."

"I am. Pleasure to meet you, Mrs. Kip." Her voice was pleasant, friendly, but tainted with apprehension.

Clara came closer, getting her old eyes within range to observe the girl's features better. A beautiful face with sky-blue eyes framed by blond locks that swept past her shoulders. Taller than Rosario by a solid inch. On sight, professional and put together. But the way the girl clung to her bag strap with color-drained knuckles revealed her inexperience in such situations.

When Clara's gaze lingered on hers a beat too long, the girl looked away, then nervously at Rosario.

Sweet child.

The courage the girl attempted to wear was inauthentic, following a pattern not meant for her. In so many ways, Aidyn reminded Clara of her younger self.

"Miss Kelley is the reporter we've been waiting for from the *Star*," Rosario said—needlessly, in Clara's opinion.

"I hope I can be interesting enough for you to write a few sentences," Clara offered.

"Oh, I'm sure she'll end up with more than that, Mrs. Kip," Rosario said.

But the girl looked dubious. She attempted to cover it with

a smile, which wasn't much of a smile at all. She looked like her lips were caught in a contraction.

Aidyn Kelley would require a different kind of work than Charles.

Clara grinned. *Yes, Lord. Show me the way.*

She hobbled to her door and motioned for the girl to follow. "Come on in, Miss Kelley. Let me gab in your ear awhile."

Aidyn and Rosario trailed behind the demure, white-haired woman into room 310. The burgundy tracksuit hung from the woman's body, large flaps of fabric collecting around her arms and legs and sagging down her abdomen. She walked with an uneven gait, her left leg more cumbersome than her right. What must it take for a body to be like that? Aidyn cringed at the thought.

Only an hour. Then she could escape.

"Make yourself at home," Mrs. Kip said over her shoulder as she traversed around her bed.

The room was similar to Aidyn's freshman dorm room, though more lavishly furnished and larger. The only indication of the room's medicinal purpose was that hospital bed in the middle. The comforter appeared undisturbed. Oddly, the room smelled like flowers.

Mrs. Kip labored toward the armchair in the corner by the picture window. "You like my view, Miss Kelley?"

Aidyn looked through the glass to the landscaped lawn with a pergola in the distance. A hummingbird feeder hung from a pole a few yards from the window. "It's very nice."

Mrs. Kip flopped noisily into the chair and clipped her

call button onto her jacket. "Hummingbirds come by every now and again, but I'm still waiting on those deer I was promised. I'm beginning to think they hooked me with false advertising."

"They'll show up eventually," Rosario said. "You keep watching. Preferably from your chair, with your call button on. Unless, of course—"

"Unless I ask for assistance," Mrs. Kip finished. "Yes, yes. You've mentioned it a few times."

"Apparently it bears repeating." Rosario grinned. "And since you're in good hands now, I'll take my leave and let you two visit. Call me if you need anything." She paused and leaned closer to Aidyn. "Do me a favor?" she said quietly.

Heaven only knew what a lead-in like that might bring. Directions on how to corral the old woman? What to keep her away from?

"What's the favor?" Aidyn asked.

"Savor it," Rosario replied, giving her a wink. Then she left, leaving the door open behind her.

Slowly Aidyn turned to Mrs. Kip, who looked up and smiled. "Hope you don't mind, but I just need to catch my breath for a minute. That neighbor of mine wore me out."

"Not at all. Do what you need to do."

"But at least come sit with me." Mrs. Kip motioned toward the loveseat under the window. Her hand was bent with arthritis and so thin every bone protruded with the slightest movement. A puff of breath could have lifted her off her feet and snapped her in two.

The prospect of going near something so fragile was terrifying, but Aidyn had a job to do. A reporter always gets the story. She walked over to the loveseat and sat on the side farthest from the old woman. She slid her messenger bag onto the cushion next to her. This close to Mrs. Kip, the finer details of her appearance came into focus. The hollow cheeks, drooping earlobes, and lips so pale and thin they practically didn't exist at all. She wore oval glasses atop her stub nose, and her wispy hair left parts of her scalp exposed.

Mrs. Kip was like a shriveled, paler version of her grandmother, though exponentially more gregarious.

Partly for something else to focus on, Aidyn dug out her notebook and pen. On one page, she had written a list of questions based on example obituaries she had found on the *Star*'s website. The sooner she started with questions, the sooner she could leave.

"Aidyn?" The woman rolled the name on her tongue. "Aidyn. Never heard that name for a girl before."

"My dad picked it."

Mrs. Kip harrumphed. "Yep. Sounds like a man's doing."

Actually, Aidyn liked her name, and she started to tell Mrs. Kip so, but the woman spoke first.

"My father had the same bent. He gave me the middle name Lu. As in Lou Gehrig, but spelled L-u because clearly that makes it more feminine."

Though unaware of it, the old woman had partially answered Aidyn's question about her full name. Quickly she jotted it down.

"Gehrig was the cat's pajamas back in the day," the woman continued. "Is he still famous among you kids now?"

Aidyn shrugged. "Didn't he have some kind of disease?"

"Among other accomplishments, yes. You should look him up sometime."

Aidyn agreed politely, having no intention to research another person because of their death. She looked at her list of questions to determine the best one to kick things off.

Once again, Mrs. Kip spoke first. "How long have you been with the *Star*?"

"About a year."

"Have you written anything like this before?"

Carefully selecting her words, Aidyn answered, "It's not really my department's forte."

Something flashed across Mrs. Kip's face—like a flinch—so fleeting it went as fast as it had come. Mrs. Kip carried on as if nothing at all had happened.

"Is that so?" the old woman replied. "This is something new for you then. That's good. Always good to try something new. Keeps things interesting."

Aidyn nodded. No point in disagreeing with an elderly woman.

"So, tell me about yourself, honey."

"Mrs. Kip, I'm supposed to be asking you that."

"Still catching my breath." The woman gestured to her chest.

Maybe catching her breath had something to do with the elusive flinch. In case it did, Aidyn indulged her with high-level facts only. Brevity usually discouraged a lot of further inquiry.

"I graduated with honors from Mizzou. I've wanted to be a reporter since high school, and I want to own a paper someday."

Mrs. Kip nodded. "You sound very career-oriented."

"In this industry, you have to be."

The woman regarded her, eyes narrowing slightly. The weight of her gaze made Aidyn look down at her page. She tapped it with her pen until she could think of something to say.

"Did you work, Mrs. Kip?"

"I did. Various odds and ends. Spent most of my years at KU Med."

"Were you a nurse?"

"A surgeon. Head of the neurological department for ten years."

Aidyn felt her eyes widen. "Really?"

"No. But I'm glad to know I can still tell a convincing story." The old woman covered her mouth as she giggled like a precocious schoolgirl. Her eyes twinkled with delight.

Aidyn smiled like she didn't mind. "Funny."

"I thought it was," Mrs. Kip said with a shrug.

"So, you were not in the medical field?"

"Sort of. I did work at the hospital for many years—that part was true. It wasn't what I set out to do, but that's where the Lord placed me. Which reminds me, I have a couple of pictures I want to show you before this Swiss-cheese brain of mine forgets." With noticeable stiffness, the woman turned to the nightstand between the bed and chair. She picked up two framed five-by-seven pictures one at a time, then handed the first to Aidyn. "That's my husband, John, and me."

The young couple in the black-and-white photo smiled at something or someone to the left of the camera. What appeared to be a dance floor stretched out behind them.

In the shadows along the outer edges of the floor, barely perceptible, were linen-covered tables occupied by people. The dark-haired John Kip wore a white dress shirt opened at the chest. His sleeves were rolled to the middle of his thick forearms. His joyful laugh, caught perfectly for all time, matched that of his bride, whose tousled hair and flushed cheeks gave a vivid picture of the energetic dancing they had just completed.

"That was our wedding reception," Mrs. Kip said. "We did the samba for everyone. Took us months of practice, but these two left feet of mine finally got the rhythm."

"You look very happy."

"We were. The happiest time of my life. And here's my favorite picture of him." She handed the second frame to Aidyn.

Also in grayscale, Mr. Kip stood on a balcony with a city sprawling out in the background. The buildings were boxy with flat roofs. Telephone and electric wires crisscrossed over top. He stared directly into the camera, arms crossed, as if daring anything to scare him.

"Where is he in this picture?" Aidyn asked.

"São Paulo. Brazil."

"Was he on vacation?"

"He was there for business. He had plans to return, but that ended up being his only trip."

"Why is that?"

Mrs. Kip paused. "He died, honey. Not long after he got back."

The answer hooked into Aidyn. "I'm so sorry."

"I was sorry too. For a long time."

Aidyn looked at the two pictures again, comparing the groom of the reception to the man of the balcony. The difference in his appearance was minimal. "He must have been so young."

"He was, Miss Kelley. And so was I."

"How old were you?"

"Twenty-three."

The answer was a gut check. Only one year older than Aidyn.

In the brief silence that followed, she struggled with what to say next, caught between wanting to give respect for the hard topic so soon after they met and wanting to ask a dozen more questions that rushed forward as a result of the tiny glimpse into Mrs. Kip's life.

But suddenly Mrs. Kip slapped the tops of her thighs. "What do you say we spring out of here, Miss Kelley?"

Aidyn frowned. "I'm sorry?"

"It's a beautiful day. Let's go outside." The woman unclipped her call button.

Immediately, Aidyn tensed. Glancing toward the door at where Rosario once stood, she asked, "Are we allowed to?"

"They certainly didn't go to the trouble of building that pergola out there only to have no one enjoy it. Come on, honey. It's calling my name." She scooted herself up to the edge of her chair and started to rock as if attempting to build momentum so she could stand.

"Are you sure?"

"I think better out in the sun. The heat brings it out of me." With one big swing forward and a grunt, Mrs. Kip shoved off the seat. She made it halfway up before losing steam and flopping back down. "Well, that was graceful," she muttered, then giggled.

"Maybe we could just stay here," Aidyn suggested. Images battered her mind of the old woman face-planting on the sidewalk or trying to make a break over the fence. It was hard to say which would be worse.

"Nonsense. Hold out your arms for me." When Aidyn didn't immediately understand, Mrs. Kip gesticulated repeatedly until Aidyn finally put aside the framed pictures and, with reluctance, went over and stuck out her forearms, palms up. Mrs. Kip grabbed hold of each in the middle. As an extra measure of stability, Aidyn gently gripped Mrs. Kip's arms in return—her unnaturally thin arms.

When Aidyn felt the woman begin to lift off the chair, she pulled Mrs. Kip up, bringing her safely to her feet.

"Haha! Thank God for leverage!" Mrs. Kip said.

But Aidyn couldn't smile. Apprehension mounted.

No way this would end well.

The old woman shuffled around her with noticeably unsteady legs.

Remembering the phantom flinch, Aidyn offered, "I can get you a wheelchair."

The old woman huffed. "I don't like that kind of attitude, Miss Kelley."

Aidyn bit her bottom lip, unsure what to do.

Mrs. Kip made the turn around the bed and tottered toward the door, clearly with no intention of staying put or being persuaded to. She called over her shoulder, "If God is for us, who can stand against us? Be on the side of angels, honey!"

She couldn't let the woman leave the room without an escort. That really would upset the staff. Aidyn groaned quietly. She stuffed her notebook and pen into her bag and strapped it on. If ever anyone needed an angel army, it was Aidyn Kelley at precisely that moment.

CHAPTER 8

Some things get better with age, and the caress of sunlight rated high for Clara, as it naturally would for someone who couldn't get warm even in a full tracksuit in the middle of a June day in the Midwest.

When they stepped through the exit door, Clara paused and closed her eyes, basking in the first glorious touch of sunlight. As much as the lingering pain in her lower abdomen would allow, she pulled the open air into her lungs. The sweet, simple joy of breathing fresh, sun-soaked air.

Better than cookies.

She opened her eyes and surveyed their surroundings. The lawn was dressed in vivid greens and yellows, reds and violets—the full brilliance of summer blooms. Towering daylilies reached up toward their Maker. Purplish-pink and soft-red flowers adorned the trumpet honeysuckle growing up the trellis along the building.

Clara let out a contented sigh. "This is more like it. Don't you think, Miss Kelley?"

"Yes, it's beautiful," the girl answered, but restlessness showed in her expression.

Clara had hoped the change of scenery would help soften the transition for the girl, offering a bit more of the "normal" everyday environment Aidyn was used to. The poor child had been hit smack in the face with death at every angle and through every sense. Clara partly regretted the story of John that early after meeting her. The girl didn't need one more reason to be unsettled by death. She needed a reason to embrace it. Or at least unclench around it.

Help me find a way, Lord. I can't tell her the good stuff about life if she's too uptight to receive it.

"Let's jaunt over to the pergola, Miss Kelley." She motioned to the pine-beam structure down the paved pathway, about thirty yards from the door. Climbing ivy covered the half-moon shape, affording a long, wide spot of shade underneath. Coordinating benches waited to be of service within the shadow. A perfect spot to do their visiting.

Clara stepped with confidence toward the shady, peaceful goal with the girl beside her.

Within a few feet, though, she felt the pinpricks in her legs. That grating harbinger of the exhaustion to come, and sooner than was conducive to Clara's intended schedule. Her tummy fussed at her with more frequency. She concentrated on moving one foot in front of the other, working through the protests.

The girl kept her pace slow to sync with Clara's. "You must like the outdoors, Mrs. Kip."

"You bet I do. God's world is better than man's."

"No doubt."

Clara peeked over at her. "You believe in God?"

After a brief pause, Aidyn replied, "I do."

"You seem unsure about that, honey."

"Force of habit, I guess. I'm not used to talking openly about it. Newsrooms aren't exactly harbors of faith."

"Well"—Clara willed her feet to keep moving—"I don't know much about newsrooms, but I do know the Lord has his warriors in surprising places."

Aidyn turned to look at her, as if wanting to say something.

Just then, a stabbing pain in Clara's stomach stopped her in her tracks—exactly the thing she wanted to avoid in front of the girl.

"Mrs. Kip? You okay?"

Clara waved her off. "No need to worry. It was only a little how-do from the innards." She chuckled to show how okay it all was, but Aidyn didn't look convinced. "Really, I'm fine." Clara took a breath, commanding the pinch to release, and motioned up ahead. "Look, we're almost to the benches." She resumed her slow pace.

Aidyn proceeded with her, noticeably tenser. Clara wished she could rewind that moment and cover up the involuntary wince, like she had when they were in her room.

Finally at the pergola, Clara chose the bench that was both the closest, for her own sake, and completely in the shade, for the girl's sake. She flopped into the seat with a heavy exhale. "Made it. No problem."

Somewhat timidly, Aidyn sat next to her, setting her messenger bag by her feet on the decorative concrete patio. She turned her attention to the lawn and seemed to drink it all in.

Beleza, Clara wanted to say. Beauty. One of the few Portuguese words she remembered. *Tanta beleza.* So much beauty. But that story would have to wait. When getting people to relax, Clara had found over the years that the topic that settled people's nerves most efficiently was themselves. She would start there.

"Do you have siblings, Miss Kelley?"

Aidyn barely glanced her way. "Yes. Two." That was all she offered, then she reached into her bag for her notebook. She was like Charles, but less surly.

"Are they older or younger?" Clara prodded.

"Older." She opened her notebook and readied her pen, clearly prepared to get on with the business she came for. "What about you?"

"Do I have siblings?"

Aidyn nodded.

"No. I was an only child."

"What about cousins? Other relatives?"

The basic bio questions somewhat confused Clara. The girl had yet to ask anything remotely hinting at the Mai story. Regardless, she replied, "I have no living relatives . . . that I can remember, anyway." She chuckled, hoping to get Aidyn to do the same.

Instead, the girl scratched down a couple of notes—a curious thing, though Clara didn't presume to understand the ways of a reporter—and continued with her seemingly irrelevant questions. "Did you go to college?"

"No. I went to the altar."

"What year were you married?"

"September 22, 1959. It was a gorgeous Saturday. Weather

could not have been more perfect." Crisp memories swept into her mind—the sunbeams through the sanctuary, the velvety cake in her mouth, the tingle when Johnny asked her to dance. She smiled, the vibrant memories ready, willing to dance out into the open. Oh, how she wanted to tell the story!

Aidyn, however, clearly had no interest in them. "When were you born?" she asked.

Disappointed, Clara answered, "April 6, 1937. After the Depression but before the war. I guess you could say I like to be in the middle of things."

"Where did you grow up?" The girl didn't even look up from her paper.

"I was born and raised in Granada, Colorado."

"What brought you to Kansas City?"

"I moved here for John, which is kind of an interesting story."

"What year was that?" Aidyn asked, as if she didn't hear any word except "John."

Clara sighed to herself. "That would have been 1958."

"Did you ever live anywhere else?"

Clara couldn't help herself. Too much fact strangles the heart of the storyteller. She had to fight back, and the tale practically spun itself—so easily she could not be held responsible for anything that happened as a result.

"We had to move to California for a year or so when I was in grammar school. Dad got temporarily banned from Granada and its surrounding counties in 1944 for helping some people escape from the Japanese internment camp outside of town." Clara hid her grin and waited.

At first, Aidyn jotted down the information. Then her pen

slowed. Soon it stopped altogether. She looked up at Clara. "Is that true?"

"Do you believe it is?"

"No."

Clara giggled, not bothering to cover her mouth.

With that trying-to-be-polite smile, Aidyn crossed out a couple of lines of copy in her notebook.

"Don't fault me too much, honey. I have so little entertainment these days." She laughed and patted the girl's arm. "Besides, I'm afraid you may think my real life is exceedingly unimpressive. I'm a childless widow about to check out. Not exactly the stuff of headlines."

"Regardless," Aidyn replied evenly, "your real life is what I'm here for."

"You could make it up and no one will know the difference."

"The truth is always better."

Clara considered the words. The girl probably didn't understand the wisdom she spoke. "That it is, honey. That it is."

Deep tiredness began to creep into her extremities, an unwelcome reminder of how low her time of wakefulness ran. If she was going to say anything of value, she needed to say it soon. She needed inspiration, a way to break into the monotony of the business the girl insisted they stick to.

Above them, leafy tentacles of ivy draped off the beams like long, lean fingers reaching down, asking for an embrace. Her gaze landed on a solitary yellow leaf in the middle of one finger, a stark outsider in a verdant world. Clara squinted to try to get a better view.

"What is it?" Aidyn asked, tilting up her head as well.

"That leaf there. The yellow one. See it?"

"I do."

"Get it for me, would you?"

The girl's brow scrunched.

"Unless you want me to," Clara offered with a grin.

"That's okay. I'll get it." Aidyn stood and evaluated the best way to reach the leaf.

At first she tried to lift onto her tiptoes. When that didn't work, Clara suggested she stand on the bench. Aidyn glanced at the door of the building, as if fearing someone might burst through it, screaming a reprimand.

"Go on, Miss Kelley. No one will care."

With the nimbleness of youth and the hesitation of an ardent rule follower, Aidyn climbed atop the bench, snagged the leaf, and brought it down for her.

"Thank you." Clara cradled the leaf in her palm. "Look at that. It has freckles."

Resuming her place on the bench, the girl observed the soft brown specks with palpable disinterest. "That's nice."

"It's more than nice, honey. *Look.* Closely."

She did, but she clearly didn't see. The girl's inexperience and obvious presumptions would not allow her to.

"I have some truth for you, Miss Kelley, if that's what you really want to hear."

"I do," Aidyn said.

"A leaf is a silent proverb. Did you ever consider that? When it buds on the tree, people rejoice. Throughout its prime, they love it for the shade it provides. But only when it reaches the end of its time on the tree does its brilliance come through. Sometimes yellow, sometimes orange, sometimes deep red. Dazzling in its artistry, like a drop of sunset you can see at all hours of the day." Clara smiled. "A leaf has the most extraordinary death. There is so much beauty to it."

She admired it one last time, then gently tossed it into the air. Together they watched it float softly to the patio.

"I think that's something to pay attention to, don't you, Miss Kelley?"

For another thirty minutes, Aidyn attempted to pump more information out of Mrs. Kip. For twenty-one and a half of those minutes, the woman mostly evaded the questions and rambled on about, among other things, flowers, sunrises, and cookies. Three times the woman nodded off for several moments, awakened only when Aidyn loudly cleared her throat.

When Mrs. Kip nodded off a fourth time, Aidyn looked at her watch. Almost 3:45 p.m., and all she'd managed to capture was three-fourths of a page of notes. Reading through it, she realized, by no small mercy, she had answers to many of her questions. Perhaps she could fill in the rest with research and never—ever—have to come back to Sacred Promise.

She turned to the dozing old woman and touched her arm. "Mrs. Kip?"

The woman startled awake. "Yes. Heard every word."

"Actually, you were the one talking, Mrs. Kip."

"I was? What was I saying?"

"You were telling me about your friend's cookie recipe."

Mrs. Kip furrowed her brow, clearly trying to remember. Finally, she shrugged. "I told you my life was exceedingly unimpressive. I bore even myself."

When Mrs. Kip giggled, Aidyn smiled, but she calculated how long it would take to extricate herself from the facility. "You're tired, Mrs. Kip. We should go inside."

"I'm fine, honey."

"But I do need to get back to work."

The woman's countenance sagged. "Of course. It's a workday. I forget these things. It's been so long."

"I have enjoyed our visit," she offered.

Mrs. Kip smiled as if knowing the truth. "Me too, Miss Kelley." She patted Aidyn's arm. "Let's get inside before they send out a search party." That giggle again.

Despite everything, the easy, bright laugh of Mrs. Kip felt like a warm hug.

She gathered her things and stood. "Would you like me to help you up?"

"Let me give it a whirl first." Through a series of groans and puffs, Mrs. Kip managed to push herself up to a standing position. But her legs were noticeably more unsteady than before.

Not wanting to offend Mrs. Kip more than she may have already, Aidyn refrained from asking her if she needed an arm for support—and from looking worried.

Their sojourn back to the building took longer. Aidyn repeatedly snuck glances at Mrs. Kip. What would she do if the woman collapsed? For both of their sakes, hopefully the building had security cameras feeding into a nurse's station somewhere.

When they finally reached the building, Aidyn breathed a sigh of relief and stepped ahead of Mrs. Kip to open the door.

A young man in light green scrubs greeted them.

"Jimmy!" Mrs. Kip lit up. "What's shakin', bacon?"

"I was looking for you. You weren't in your room." The guy looked barely out of high school. He glided over to the old woman and hooked one of her hands into the bend of his elbow, without protest from her.

"I busted out. Miss Kelley here helped me. Isn't she great?"

Jimmy nodded a hello to Aidyn. "That was very nice of her. And you two are headed back to the room now?"

"I suppose it's that time."

"Let me escort you then."

The kid had an effortless way with Mrs. Kip, an ease in how he chatted with her and guided her down the hall, into her room, and over to her chair. For a kid, he seemed to have an abundant understanding of the old.

Aidyn waited near the dining table in Mrs. Kip's room. Two storage boxes caught her eye, and she noticed the simple numerical labels. She looked away in time to see Jimmy hold Mrs. Kip's hands as she started to lower herself into the chair.

The woman's legs suddenly gave way. She fell straight down, landing cockeyed on the cushion. Jimmy expertly caught her before she toppled forward onto the floor face-first.

He held her for a moment, assuring her he had her. Then he gently scooted her back into the chair. "That was a surprise, wasn't it?" he said.

Mrs. Kip pushed her glasses back into place on her nose. "Guess I need to work out more."

"Or start drinking milk with all those cookies," he offered as he clipped her call button back on her jacket.

Mrs. Kip took his hands in hers. "You're a good boy, James."

SARA BRUNSVOLD

She appeared more vivacious—and vulnerable—with him. Aidyn felt strangely jealous.

"If you're settled, Mrs. Kip, I better finish my rounds. I'll let you and Miss Kelley get back to your visit, and I'll see you later."

"Bye-bye, darling." She waved to him as he rounded the bed.

Approaching Aidyn, he motioned for a conference.

Subtly, she stepped to meet him, and he leaned in to whisper, "You might want to wrap things up. She needs to crash."

"Will do," she whispered back, glad for the affirmation to end the visit.

As Jimmy stepped into the hallway, Aidyn thought about how to make her own exit. Mrs. Kip seemed to have deflated in a matter of seconds. Her eyelids drooped.

Still, she beckoned Aidyn over. "Come sit, Miss Kelley. Just a quick minute."

Clutching the shoulder strap of her bag, Aidyn returned to the loveseat. No sooner did she sit than a wince crossed Mrs. Kip's face. The woman did not try to hide it and in fact hunched against the source, taking several beats to collect herself. Despite her instinct, Aidyn didn't ask if she was okay but only waited with her for it to pass.

Once it did, Mrs. Kip rested against the back of the chair and met Aidyn's gaze. Her expression revealed that all kidding had been put aside.

"You asked me for the truth about my life. Here's something I want you to know about me up front."

Aidyn's ears perked up, ready to receive the words.

"I've lived some years. I've done some things and saw

95

even more. I've been to the highest highs and through the lowest lows. I've had dreams broken and dreams given, love lost and love won. I'd go through it all again if that's what the Lord willed. But if I'm being honest—if I had a vote in the matter—there is one thing and one thing only I would change." She paused to pull in an obviously pained breath.

Aidyn waited, then gently coaxed her. "What would you change, Mrs. Kip?"

"I would change the way I die."

"You mean, as in live longer?"

"Heavens no, honey. I'm past done with this place." She winced again, shorter this time, and rubbed the side of her lower abdomen. "I mean I wish I could die a better way. Not here in this place, wilting my way into glory. I'd die of something . . . with pizzazz."

Aidyn frowned. "Pizzazz?"

"Yes. That's a good word, right? Pizzazz! As in, something memorable. Instead of people saying, 'Bless her heart,' they'd say, 'Wow, she really lived.' Does that make sense?"

"I think so."

"Does it? Fantastic. Because I'm too tired to explain it any better."

Aidyn grinned. "Then I really should go and let you rest." The interviewee gave no protest, so Aidyn stood. "It was a pleasure meeting you, Mrs. Kip."

"Same to you, Miss Kelley. I look forward to our chat tomorrow. Same time?"

Aidyn fought to keep the smile on her face. She didn't have the courage to tell Mrs. Kip she had all she'd come for.

She nodded anyway.

Aidyn did two things when she walked out the main doors of Sacred Promise. First, she texted Rahmiya and let her know she'd survived.

Rahmiya replied,

FaceTime me later. Tell me details.

Second, she drove twenty minutes out of her way to Homer's Coffee House, her favorite in all of Kansas City, and ordered the most indulgent beverage on the menu.

By her estimation, she had earned every calorie.

CHAPTER 9

For the remainder of the evening, Clara thought about young Aidyn. She contemplated the girl from every angle, especially those pieces left untouched in her brief (and mostly conscious) time with Aidyn. As she drifted in and out of sleep in her armchair, she wondered about the girl's home life. Had her childhood been happy? Did she live alone now or surrounded by love? As Clara picked at her dinner, she wondered what food comforted Aidyn the most. As she stared out at the pergola in prayer, she asked the Lord to reveal what spoke most to the girl's soul.

Help me truly see her, Lord.

Clara realized she had fallen asleep again only when a hand on her arm roused her. Michelle, her night nurse, was there, bent down to her eye level.

"Looks like you were having a nice rest," the nurse said.

"For the tenth time today. I've turned into a sloth."

"That's quite all right, Mrs. Kip. You sleep as much as you need to. It's good for you."

The truth underneath that statement—the truth Michelle kindly left unspoken—was that sleep would soon comprise most of Clara's day. Sleep to avoid extraneous wear on her wasting body. Sleep to avoid the pain. An idle slip through time until she landed at heaven's doorstep.

Tiredness was a bridle she couldn't escape.

"Let me check your vitals real quick," Michelle said. "Then we'll get you ready for bed."

"Bed?" Clara glanced outside. Dusk kissed the earth. "It got late quick. What time is it?"

"About 8:30."

"My word," Clara breathed.

After checking her vitals and making notes in the tablet she carried, Michelle asked if she needed help getting to the bathroom. When Clara declined, Michelle graciously accepted the bid for independence and went to retrieve Clara's nightclothes.

With a quiet struggle, Clara got to her feet, grateful the nurse did not see, or at least that she didn't say anything if she had. Her legs felt tighter than earlier, and her back did not want to straighten like she wanted it to. Regardless, she moved across the room. Slowly.

The nurse waited next to the bathroom door with a patient smile.

"These bones just don't want to move tonight, honey. I think I'm getting old."

"Happens to the best of us, Mrs. Kip." The nurse took her into the bathroom and closed the door. "Would you like to try to use the restroom?"

"I'll give it a try." The tumors in her bladder constantly gave her brain mixed signals, leaving her unable to discern when the sensation was a need for relief. It was anyone's best guess.

She ambled to the toilet, held on to the safety bar on the wall, and allowed Michelle to help her lower her track pants.

"Let's just go ahead and change your undergarment too," the nurse said.

Clara remained standing as Michelle pulled at the seams running down either side of the disposable underpants. They ripped apart easily, and the filled cotton slumped away from Clara's body.

Though the nurse tried to quickly roll the pants to hide the contents, Clara could see the brownish yellow. She hadn't even felt it come out. Or smelled it.

Her cheeks warmed.

As she lowered onto the toilet with the nurse's help, Clara closed her eyes and prayed to renounce her pride. Somehow it never got easier. After all that time, surrender to death remained a long, slow, shocking process. Little by little, the Lord showed her when and where to let go and step into trust. Always, always, he taught her.

The nurse handed Clara wipes to clean her delicate areas, and once the new underpants were on, she had Clara step into her cotton pajama pants while she was still sitting. The pants were a happy, bright yellow with small white bunnies eating carrots. The waistband sagged around her middle.

"These are my favorite pj's," she told the nurse. "They make me feel like a kid again."

"They're super cute. I wouldn't mind having my own bunny pj's."

"JCPenney, honey. Use the coupon."

Michelle chuckled. "I'll keep that in mind."

With practiced expertise, she helped Clara strip off her track jacket and shirt, then she guided Clara's arms through the sleeves of the matching bright-yellow shirt.

Michelle stood back and admired Clara. "You look ready for a slumber party."

"Wouldn't that be a hoot."

By comparison, the rest of the night prep was cake. A light brush of the hair, a swipe of the face and extremities, the removal and care of her dentures. Clara caught a glimpse of herself in the mirror over the sink. Without her teeth, her hollow cheeks practically disappeared in on themselves. She looked more colorless than she remembered. It was a fraction of the face she once had, the one that had snuggled against John's and smiled into the camera with Mai.

Back in her room, Clara pulled down the bedcovers and eased her way underneath them.

"Anything else I can get for you before I go, Mrs. Kip?" Michelle asked.

She thought for a moment. "How about a nightcap? A Shirley Temple would hit the spot."

Michelle grinned. "I'm afraid the bar is closed for the night."

"Then just the night-light, if you would."

"Of course. I'll be back later to check in, but call me if you need me. Good night, Mrs. Kip."

"Good night, darling. Thank you."

On her way out, Michelle ensured the small light in the bathroom was switched on. Then she stepped out into the hall and pulled the door mostly closed behind her.

Silence instantly draped the room.

Clara pulled in a breath and let it out slowly.

Loneliness. Silence. Dying.

Three flaming arrows impossible for anyone to deflect without help.

Clara closed her eyes.

Lord, help me feel your presence here. This breath I have is fading, but it still comes from you, still for your purposes. Despite what my body does or refuses to do, embolden this spirit of mine to stand on in this battle. Empower these weak arms to hold fast to the shield of faith. Like a mighty warrior for your glory, God.

Once again, Aidyn's face came to her mind. The beautiful young girl. Timid yet trying to hide it. Sky-blue eyes revealing a heaven-held soul.

The image tugged on her heart.

Lead me, Lord.

August 5, 1971

The counselor wore brown tweed, smelled of pipe, and didn't take notes in their sessions. The latter disturbed Clara more than anything else. His thick sideburns were second on her list.

"Tell me about a time when you did something you were proud of." He leaned back in his leather chair, rested his elbows on either arm, and brought his hands together.

"You mean in my entire life?" she asked. His placid way was supremely annoying.

"However you want to answer. Something recent or something from years ago. Whatever comes to mind."

How in the world was that supposed to help her get over her loss of John? She sighed. "I don't know. I suppose I'm proud of finding a home for the stray cat I came across the other day. Normally I keep them, but I've gotten in trouble with my landlord one too many times. This time I found a friend to take her home."

"You do this often, taking in stray cats?"

"Yes. Occasionally a different kind of creature, but I'm partial to cats."

"Why do you think that is?"

"Why do I like cats?"

"Why do you feel the need to take them in?"

Clara blinked. "They're helpless animals. They're defenseless to the elements, and you know as well as I do what humans can do to them."

"Are you scared of what humans may do to them more than you're scared of what the elements would do to them?"

"Hadn't thought about it, but probably. Humans are nasty to each other, but they can be downright cruel to animals. I volunteer at the shelter sometimes, and the cases I see absolutely break my heart."

The man nodded empathetically. "Would you say you are a fixer?"

"A what? What does that mean?"

"A fixer is someone who sees a problem and feels compelled to solve it. They cannot rest until it's solved. They commit to finding a solution in order to bring peace."

Clara shrugged. "I suppose so. Martha would probably agree with that, although she labels it a bit differently."

"How does she label it?"

"She calls it my bossy-pants mode."

The man grinned. "Martha sounds like a good friend."

"She is."

The counselor adjusted in his chair, a look of concentration on his face. "Tell me, Clara, how does it make you feel that you can't fix John's death?"

Cold sliced through her. The cold of accuracy.

The man was gentle in his follow-up. "I believe the anger you've been feeling stems from your inability to fix this situation you find yourself in. You've lost someone very important to you, and you don't have the tools in your tool belt to fix it, let alone change these emotions running wild inside you."

She drew her arms across her body and looked away.

"If this sounds like an accurate description of how you feel, Clara, know it's normal for someone who has gone through all you have gone through."

Tears pooled in her eyes.

"I am going to help you get the tools you need," he said. "They won't fix anything so much as recalibrate your understanding. You'll learn a lot about grief and how to carry it gently but firmly. How does that sound?"

Clara wiped her eyes and sniffed. "No offense, Doc, but I have my doubts about all this."

"That's normal too."

She shifted in her seat. "We're not talking about some kind of drug or that yoga stuff, right?"

"Not at all."

"Then what?"

He leaned forward, resting his elbows atop his thighs. "Have you ever tried journaling?"

Wednesday, June 8, 2016

Aidyn powered on her laptop and opened her notebook. The goal for the morning was simple and straightforward: Write an obit, gain good graces with Woods.

Doable and nearly done. And it helped that Shayna was on assignment.

Following the language and structure of the examples she had pulled from the *Star*'s website, Aidyn typed with relative ease, leaving placeholders for information she would need to fill in later.

> *Clara Kip, 79, of Kansas City, KS, passed away on . . . Services will be held at . . .*
>
> *Clara Lu (. . .) Kip was born on April 6, 1937, in Granada, Colo. She was the only child of . . . She married John Kip on Sept. 22, 1959. They were married for . . . years. They made their home in Kansas City, KS, where she worked as a . . . at the University of Kansas Medical Center.*
>
> *She was preceded in death by her parents and her husband.*
>
> *Clara was a woman of strong Christian faith who enjoyed the outdoors and baking. She was active and social*

until her final days, and she loved to laugh. Anyone she met was an instant friend.

Tributes / in lieu of flowers . . .

More than one hundred words in rough draft. The missing pieces would add about half that, at least. She reread the words and smiled to herself.

Not bad.

After printing off a hard copy, she took a highlighter to mark the holes. Underneath the text, she made a bulleted list of sources she could potentially use to find the missing information. KU Med's HR department might be willing to do an employment verification. A newspaper or library near Granada might be able to help identify Clara's parents. As far as the length of marriage, she could figure that out based on what Mrs. Kip shared.

Aidyn smiled wider. Everything seemed to come together.

The marriage length would be easiest to figure out, so she started there. She took Mrs. Kip's birth year and added twenty-three, her age when her husband died. With little effort, she did the math and got the answer: 1960.

She stopped. Could that be right?

They had married in 1959.

Realization sank in.

Mrs. Kip had been a married woman for one year and a widow for fifty-six. Aidyn's chest hitched. The words Mrs. Kip had said almost as a side note replayed in her mind: *"I was sorry too. For a long time."* Those words had not sounded all that meaningful when Mrs. Kip said them. The truth was, they were packed with meaning.

Mrs. Kip's husband had been young, newly married, barely started out in his career.

What had happened to him?

At that moment, Woods came out of her office and strode over to Aidyn's desk. "What did you get yesterday?"

"Almost everything I needed for an obit. I'm working on a draft now."

Woods's brows pulled together in a confused frown. "She told you everything?"

"There are a few pieces I still need, but easy enough to track down."

The frown deepened. "Let me see your copy."

Aidyn handed her editor the highlighted working draft.

After reading it, Woods looked irritated. "Kelley, how long were you with Clara Kip?"

"About an hour."

"You were with her for an hour and this is all you got?"

"Was I supposed to get something else?"

"Yes, Kelley. Her *story*."

"But that is—"

"This is not her story. This is her vital statistics put in slightly narrative form, and not all that well, I might add." Woods wadded the paper. "Go back there, sit with her, and *listen*, Kelley. Listen better than how you listen to me."

Aidyn clenched her jaw.

"A good writer knows how to find the story. She can hear it where no one else does. That's the essence of what we do." Woods tossed the ball of paper onto Aidyn's desk. "Don't give me another draft until your copy reflects that."

CHAPTER 10

Aidyn refused to look at the obit for a couple of hours. The sting was too fresh, the anger too raw. Though she tried to occupy herself with the other tasks on her to-do list and by texting Rahmiya to make lunch plans so she'd at least have something to look forward to—and stop herself from dwelling on another 3:00 visit to Sacred Promise—Aidyn kept drifting back to Woods's instructions.

Get her story, she grumbled to herself. *How can I when she won't tell me? What kind of story could it possibly be if even the teller is bored with it?*

She banged out an email with strokes harder than they needed to be. Her laments clashed and clanged in her mind, the noise and activity of which served only to make her more irritated.

Get her story. Mrs. Kip herself doesn't even care about her story!

Suddenly she stopped. Was that true? Had Mrs. Kip not shown any interest in any part of her story?

Aidyn carefully rewound the conversation in her mind.

Had the woman at any point been desirous to share details? Had she voluntarily offered up information? Seemed to want to offer more?

In one clear instance, she had. Her husband.

Aidyn flipped to the page of scrawl in her notebook and read everything she had written down about John Kip.

Brought Clara to KC. Married September 1959. Danced the samba at their reception. Dark-haired, dark-eyed, sun-kissed complexion. Wanted to work in São Paulo, Brazil. Died young.

He couldn't have been much older than his wife when he died.

Question after question marched forward.

Why São Paulo? What was his work? Was he from Kansas City? How did he and his wife meet? Was he an only child too? Did he love to dance?

And of course, the biggest burning question: How did he die?

If John Kip was a story his wife wanted to tell, then maybe Aidyn should show an interest in hearing it.

She wrote down her questions for their meeting and tried to leave it at that, but that one question wouldn't leave her alone.

How did John Kip die?

It was the question that promised the biggest payoff. Perhaps knowing the answer would illuminate Mrs. Kip in new ways. If he'd been sick, the story would have one feel. If he'd been murdered, another. If he'd died of a heart attack or something sudden, still another. How he'd died was an important piece of Mrs. Kip's life.

Unfortunately, death certificates were not public record, and she didn't yet know anyone in the clerk's office who could grease the wheels for her.

Then an idea presented itself. If John Kip had died in Kansas City, the odds were great that the *Star* had run his obit, which might offer clues.

Quickly Aidyn jotted down his name, death year, and last known residence on a sticky note. Before she left her desk, she sent a quick IM to Rahmiya.

Will meet you out front at 11:30. Have to go
to the archives for a minute.

Then Aidyn made her way upstairs, to the tucked-away storehouse of archived material. The archivist, a silver-haired woman named Phyllis who wore thick-framed glasses and smelled faintly of must, looked over the sticky note. "How soon do you need this?"

"As soon as you can."

"I'll see what I can do."

Aidyn thanked Phyllis and headed out.

Please find an answer, she prayed as she descended the stairs into the main lobby. The potential of what Phyllis might uncover consumed her so much, she ran straight into Shayna.

"Sorry, didn't see you."

"Then pay attention." Shayna stalked away.

Normally a run-in like that would affect Aidyn more, but Rahmiya was already waiting outside, and there was too much to tell her about the morning.

Four bites were all Clara could manage. The rest of her lunch sat lonely and unwanted on the plate. Food had quickly become more of a burden than a comfort. Even the appeal of cookies began to wane.

She rolled the tray table away from her armchair and turned to the window. The sun toasted the earth toward the ninety-degree mark, but it didn't seem to bother the tenderest of creation. Flowers opened wider to embrace the full rays from above. Orange-bellied robins sailed through the blue sky as they went about their eager business. At the feeder hanging from its pole in the sliver of shade offered by the building's shadow, a hummingbird discovered a treat of nectar.

The tiny, enchanting creature positioned itself over the plastic-flower spout. It suckled there, not once stilling its imperceptible wings. Clara watched with wonder as the ingenuity of man met the delicate needs of nature. She imagined the nectar spreading throughout the hummer's petite body, refreshing it cell by cell.

The bird took its time to enjoy its reward.

She chuckled. "You have more of an appetite than I do, darling."

A moment later, another, larger hummingbird moved in. It edged closer and closer. When the bold little guy didn't move aside, the larger one encroached and virtually shoved it out of the way. Defeated, the little bird flew off while the newcomer took its fill.

Clara tsked. "Bully."

A knock on her door preceded a voice. "Mrs. Kip?" Rosario appeared in the doorway.

"How wonderful. I was hoping I'd see you today."

"Really? Why is that?" Rosario came over and sat on the loveseat.

"I just enjoy your smile, honey. It makes me happy."

Rosario ducked her head for a second. "Mrs. Kip, you're making me blush. And I'm happy to give you company whenever I can." She glanced over at Clara's uneaten lunch.

Clara should have covered it with a napkin.

Thankfully, Rosario didn't comment on it. "Speaking of company, how did your visit with Aidyn Kelley go yesterday?"

"Oh, she's a lovely girl. She put up with me well, and she even took me out to the pergola."

"Yes, I heard you two had a little adventure."

"It was more for her than me," Clara said, though it was clear by her expression Rosario had doubts. "I was hoping it would loosen her up a bit. She was a little tight on the conversation."

"Maybe she's not used to someone as vivacious as you."

"She's had a sheltered life then."

The younger woman laughed. "She'll warm up to you, Mrs. Kip. You have that way about you."

"I hope so. But I know it's not easy for a young person to walk into a place like this. I appreciate her doing it."

"I know you do, Mrs. Kip. What did you two talk about?"

"This and that. We didn't go deep on anything. She had a whole list of questions that she ticked off, one right after another. To be honest, it kind of felt like I was applying for a job."

"Did you share any of your stuff with her?" Rosario motioned to the storage boxes on the table.

"Not a lick. She didn't even ask me about it, which surprised me. Like I said, she seemed so focused on her questions."

Rosario nodded. "Yes, about that. I received an interesting phone call from my friend Bella Woods this morning." She crossed her legs at the knees and wrapped her hands around the top one. "I think I told you she's Aidyn's supervising editor. I didn't realize this, but it turns out there's a bit of subterfuge happening on Bella's end."

Clara leaned forward. "Now that's exciting. What's the ruse?"

"Apparently, Aidyn thinks she's here to write your obituary."

Clara turned the words over in her mind, verifying that she heard correctly. Then she laughed heartily. "Oh, that explains so much! I thought she was just a terrible interviewer." She giggled, making Rosario laugh too. "But why in the world would her boss tell her to write my obituary? I already have one."

"You do. I have it in your file. But Aidyn doesn't know that, and we are not to tell her. Bella needs her to think she is to write an obituary that perfectly and eloquently captures your life."

Clara raised an eyebrow. "There has to be a story behind that."

"Oh, yes. Apparently, Aidyn got herself into some trouble with the big boss over at the paper. He forbade her to work on anything but small tasks. Bella was very disappointed about it because Aidyn is a talented writer with amazing potential, but that youthful ego . . . you know."

"I know. Got me into trouble too."

"It gets all of us," Rosario said. "When Bella heard about your story, she knew she wanted Aidyn to take it. She said a story like yours requires a certain soul—a tenderness—to write it, and Aidyn has that in spades."

Clara nodded. "I could see that about her."

"The thing is, because of the hot water Aidyn landed herself in, Bella couldn't give her the story. At least not outright. So she came up with a little workaround. She convinced her boss that Aidyn's 'discipline' should be to write an obituary for you. Bigger papers don't typically assign staff to do that anymore, so it's considered a truly lowly assignment. Based on that fact, the boss agreed, and Bella had the green light to send Aidyn out here to talk to you. Of course, Bella's hope is that the more Aidyn learns about your life—"

"The more she'll discover the history," Clara concluded.

"You got it."

Clara sat back and pondered it all in amazement. "So, this friend of yours is trying to give Aidyn her big break?"

"So it would seem."

Clara smiled. "I love the way she thinks."

Rosario winked. "She's always been clever."

"She also must care about Aidyn, going to all this trouble."

"Clearly she does."

"Is she a believer too?"

Rosario nodded. "She is."

"Praise God for his hidden warriors."

"Amen."

Clara smiled, feeling the lightness in her heart—that sensation of the Lord's hand at work, orchestrating his people to be part of a generous answer to prayer.

A thought came to her. "You're saying Aidyn doesn't know about any of that?" She pointed at the boxes.

"Correct. And that's where Bella could use your help, Mrs. Kip. Let Aidyn find the story on her own. She needs to listen closely enough to ask questions that open up an opportunity for you to share about that part of your life."

"In other words, don't volunteer it?"

"Correct. She needs to lead you into it. Do you think you can get her to do that?"

Clara clapped with delight. "Hot dog! This will be fun!"

When Aidyn returned to her desk after lunch, an email from the archivist was waiting for her. Two PDF files were attached. The message read,

> Attached is an obit for a John Kip from Friday, May 13, 1960, along with a small piece run the Sunday after. The latter uses a similar name (likely his). Hope this helps. The name Kip turned up other results too, though not for a John. Let me know if you want those curated as well.

Eager to read the attachments, Aidyn did not pay much heed to the last part. She opened the obit, which turned out to be a scanned image of a microfiche—and much shorter than she anticipated.

> Services for John Mateus Kip of Kansas City, Kan., will be held at Parallel Parkway Baptist Church on Monday, May 16. Visitation begins at 10:00 a.m. with funeral services beginning

at 11:00 a.m. Mr. Kip passed away tragically on May 10, 1960. Born on January 22, 1936, he was the son of Paul and Ana Kip of Saint Joseph, Mo. He is survived by his parents and his wife of eight months, Clara (Rooker).

Aidyn's heart panged at the phrase "wife of eight months." School years lasted longer.

Pushing the emotional reaction aside, she took out her notebook and jotted down the details she could glean. Mrs. Kip's maiden name. Her husband's parents and their hometown. The fact they may have been Baptist. His age at death: twenty-four. The tragic nature of his death.

But the obituary brought up more questions than it answered.

His parents had lived in Saint Joseph, but did he grow up there? Was he born there? What did he do for a living? Did he not go to college either? Most curious to her: John's middle name. It clashed with its distinctly Anglo-Saxon bookends.

She wrote in her notebook, "What origin is Mateus?"

Eager to know more, she opened the second attachment, an equally cursory piece from the local police beat. The information, however, proved heartbreakingly enlightening.

Kansas City Police assisted the Missouri State Highway Patrol in a single-car fatality accident along 210 Highway in North Kansas City. The accident happened around 2:30 a.m. Tuesday, May 10. A four-door sedan traveling westbound left the road and collided with a utility pole. The driver and only occupant, later identified as J. M. Kip of Kansas City, Kan., was pronounced dead at the scene.

A car accident. That was how he'd died. Tragic and alone.

Aidyn had thought that finding more about his death would satiate her questions. Instead, one more equally burning question was birthed.

What could he possibly have been doing in a secluded part of the metro at 2:30 a.m.?

Clara reached into the storage box and took out the next two journals. Each journal in the boxes contained nearly a year's worth of her young adulthood musings and daily happenings. Her slow, steady progress through the stages of grief. Her realization that God was more than she had given him credit for. Her first time at church with Martha. The joy of her baptism day—June 10, 1973—"Hallelujah" written in all caps at the top of the page.

Reading them brought back all the memories, good and bad, and more than a few things she had long forgotten, which was exactly what she'd hoped would happen.

If young Aidyn were going to eventually, hopefully, obtain these journals, Clara first wanted to make sure she remembered accurately what they said. Age has a way of diminishing details. The more she remembered about her life, the better she could spot those opportunities in their conversations to share something that would prompt Aidyn to ask the right questions.

She sat back down in the dining chair—a highly unsatisfactory piece of furniture compared to the snuggly armchair—and opened one of the newly retrieved journals. The first entry was dated August 3, 1974.

"Oh my," she breathed when she saw the date. She didn't have to read the entry to recall what it said.

It was the day she'd found out crisis had come. Funds were gone. The mission trip to Brazil had been cancelled—again.

She lifted her gaze toward the nightstand, at the framed picture of John on the balcony, the place she'd tried so hard to get to. Though she couldn't physically see the image from across the room, her memory easily formed the lines, shapes, and shadows from countless hours of studying it. She closed her eyes and imagined she stood on the apartment balcony at last, with John, within heartbeat distance of him. São Paulo stretched out before them, the burgeoning wealth of the city center in full view but both of their souls bent toward the destitute favelas rimming its edges.

Every ounce of the ache rushed back to her.

She opened her eyes and began to read what her heart-broken younger self recorded.

It feels like losing him all over again. Lord, I want so badly to go where John was unable to return. I want to see what he saw, all of it. God, I know I'm still new at this and I have a lot of rebellion to make up for, but please hear my prayer. I am willing to go in his place. Please send me. Please, God, won't you send me?

"Oh, sweet child," Clara whispered and stroked the words with her timeworn fingers.

The same raw confusion and disappointment she had felt as a young Christian stirred within her, but it was tempered with the knowledge of what happened next. What she knew now, her younger self still had to grow up into.

Something great lay ahead. Something beyond her wildest dreams.

Because pain, too, has a purpose.

Her years with Mai Khab taught her that such bitter sorrow can be an excellent way maker.

May 8, 1975

Clara's shift was about to begin, and she ran late, as usual. Babies awaited her, fresh to the world and unsure they were on board with it. Desire grew in Clara to hold them and reassure their sweet little minds. As she made her way down the hospital's maze of hallways, ideas about what songs to sing over which baby rolled through her mind. She had so many praise songs she was learning from Martha and her church—now Clara's church—and all of them tended to be her favorites.

As she passed by the orthopedic ward's open double doors, something caught her eye.

She stopped.

A woman about Clara's age stood against the wall, arms squeezed tightly to her stomach, gaze fixed on a spot on the floor. Her petite frame was crowned with long, straight dark hair, and her brown complexion stood out against the white of the walls. Even from the distance, Clara could tell the woman's cheeks ran with tears. Others passed right by, throwing odd looks the woman's way. They deserted her in the sadness she carried.

Clara's heart twisted. A grieving woman, abandoned. She of all people could not pass by. Without thinking, she walked through the doors.

The woman looked up as Clara approached. Her eyes widened, and she immediately wiped her cheeks.

"Do you need help?" Clara asked gently.

"I'm okay," the woman replied so softly her voice was nearly drowned out before it reached Clara's ears. She had a distinct accent.

Instinctively, Clara touched the woman's arm. It trembled under her fingers. "My name is Clara. What's yours?"

The woman looked away. "I'm okay," she repeated.

"That may be, but I still want to help." Clara rubbed her arm, encouraging the woman to look at her.

After a moment, the woman did.

"What's your name, friend?" Clara asked a second time.

With hesitation, the woman replied, "Mai Khab."

"Hello, Mai. That's a beautiful name. Are you with a patient?"

After another pause, the woman nodded. "My husband, we came for friend."

The accent was thick and Asian, but Clara did not have the gift of languages enough to identify its roots. "Is your friend in one of these rooms?"

The woman pointed a couple of doors down on the opposite side of the hallway.

"Is your husband in there with your friend?"

The woman warily pointed farther down the hall, toward

the waiting area. "On phone." All waiting areas had at least one pay phone.

Clara considered what to do next. The scared woman probably thought she was crazy, and she obviously wanted to shrink away from Clara's touch.

"Mai," she said, "I don't know what is going on, but I can tell you're upset. If I can do anything for you, please tell me. If nothing else, I'll gladly pray for you."

The woman perked up at the last words. "You Christian?"

Surprised at the reaction, Clara confirmed she was.

The woman grabbed her arms and burst into eager words directed at the ceiling in a language Clara did not understand. Just as quickly, she switched back to English and looked at Clara in earnest. "I ask God for help. I ask him, and you came."

A warm sensation spread through Clara—a feeling she would come to recognize later as the breeze of God's hand moving things and people into place.

"Help with what, Mai?"

Through limited English, the woman explained what had brought them to KU Med. Her husband, Mahasajun, and their friend were both officers in the Laotian army, which, according to the news, was a crucial partner to the US military in Vietnam. The two countries had an agreement for Laotian officers to receive specialized training from American forces. Mahasajun and their friend were among a handful of Laotians selected to attend several rounds of training at an officers' academy at Fort Leavenworth, Kansas, just an hour outside the city. This was the men's third trip and the first time Mai had come along. Their friend had broken his leg in several places during a training exercise and had been transferred to KU Med for surgery.

"We come tell him bad news," Mai said. "Pathet Lao, they take over."

Clara nodded. The news reports had been heart-wrenching. The Communists had seized control of several Southeast Asian countries, exactly what the Vietnam War had tried to prevent. "I read that in the paper," she said, then the deeper meaning dawned on her. "You can't go back, can you?"

Mai shook her head. "Not safe for army." Her bottom lip quivered as she added, "Or their families."

A shadow descended in Mai's eyes. Clara recognized it instantly. The fear of a mother separated from and helpless to save her babies.

Her own pulse quickened. "Your children are still in Laos?"

Mai's face scrunched. Tears erupted.

Clara gathered her into a hug. The woman fell against her shoulder. Dampness seeped through Clara's shirt and onto her skin. The pain of one human spilling onto another, hearts and lives beginning to intertwine in ways neither of them could imagine.

Clara closed her eyes. Even though she was still new to all the faith stuff, the only action that made sense in that moment was to plead for help.

Lord, show us what to do next.

CHAPTER 11

June 8, 2016

Aidyn walked toward the front doors of Sacred Promise with her bag slung over her shoulder, still trying to sort out what to ask and how to ask it. Not only for the sake of writing something Woods wanted to see, whatever that was, but also for the sake of satisfying her curiosity about John Kip's death. Hopefully the latter goal fed perfectly into the former.

Absentmindedly, she took out her gold cross and trailed it back and forth on its chain as she walked. She continued to mull over the husband angle.

How would a young woman live the rest of her life as a widow and not go crazy? Would Aidyn be able to do that? What did losing her husband so young do to Mrs. Kip's life? What about the way he'd died? And the timing of his death, so early in their marriage? Why did she never remarry?

The main doors slid open, and Aidyn stopped once she was inside. The place held a certain vibe, foreign and provoking. Her stomach tightened. She released the cross and instead clung to the strap of the bag.

Following the instructions Rosario had given her the day before, she first went to the small table outside the office to sign the guest book, then headed down the hall. As she passed through the activity room, she spied a silver tray of cookies on the dining table.

An idea hit her.

She grabbed a napkin and wrapped three cookies. One for herself and two for Mrs. Kip. Perhaps a delectable treat would encourage the woman to stay on topic. She tucked the cookies into the outside pocket of her bag and headed down the north hallway. Purposefully, she kept her eyes straight ahead and breathed through her mouth.

From halfway down the hall, she saw Mrs. Kip's door ajar. She quieted her footsteps—more out of fear than respect— and craned her neck to peer into the room.

It was empty.

"Great," she muttered. She could practically picture the old woman scuffling about the building to places unnoticed, as if in a slow-motion game of hide-and-seek.

She rotated on her heel and looked down the hallway— for what, who knew? Maybe for Mrs. Kip herself. Maybe a staff member to help her seek. She had to figure out what to do.

Then, Mrs. Kip's voice. Soft and rhythmic in its cadence.

She turned toward the sound. It came from the room across the hall. It floated through the sliver of space between the door and the jamb.

Aidyn approached silently and peeked into the room.

Mrs. Kip sat in the armchair next to the bed. She held a black-covered book with gilded edges.

"Would you like me to read the next one, Charles?" she asked in the same soft, rhythmic voice.

Aidyn moved her gaze to the man in the bed and immediately sucked in her breath.

His alarmingly skeletal face was the color of milk. He slept in slack-jawed oblivion to his company. Mrs. Kip was much more pleasant to observe by comparison.

The demure woman adjusted the glasses on her nose and found her place on the page once more.

"This one is titled 'A Night Prayer.' It says, 'Answer me when I call, God, who vindicates me. You freed me from affliction; be gracious to me and hear my prayer.' Oh, I like that, Charles. I like it quite a bit. That's from Psalm 4. Would you like me to keep reading?"

Mrs. Kip carried on so normally as if unbothered by the death before her, let alone within her.

How? How is that even possible?

Suddenly the sense that someone was nearby crawled across Aidyn's skin. She looked to her left and startled at the sight of Jimmy. "Oh, wow. I didn't hear you." She kept her voice hushed and stepped toward him.

"Sorry I took you by surprise," he said in an equally quiet voice. "You were clearly enthralled with whatever is happening in there."

"Yes, well, kind of. I promise I wasn't snooping. I came to talk with Mrs. Kip, but she wasn't in her room. I found her in there, reading to the man."

Jimmy laughed. "Go figure, she's up again without asking. Let me guess, she's reading the Bible to him."

The kid's accuracy was impressive. "She is, in fact."

Jimmy sighed contemplatively and looked in the direction of the man's door. "She does that. I've caught her in there several times."

"Must be hard to be here on your own," Aidyn said. "I bet she's lonely."

Jimmy regarded her, then replied gently, "No, Miss Kelley. *He* is lonely. And she can't bear the thought of it. Frankly, I can't blame her. I've seen loneliness kill faster than cancer. She's giving him a gift that medicine can't provide."

The words were too dense to understand in the moment. Aidyn tucked them into the back of her mind.

"I need to check on him," Jimmy said, pointing to the door.

"Of course." Aidyn moved to the side to let him pass. "I'll wait out here for Mrs. Kip."

For some reason, her words drew a chortle from the kid. "You might as well come in too, Miss Kelley."

"Isn't there a law against that?"

"Not in Mrs. Kip's world."

Aidyn shook her head. Surely they would both be in a world of trouble if she were caught in another patient's room. Trouble she couldn't afford.

Seeing her reluctance, Jimmy sighed. "Look, Miss Kelley, I'd inform Mrs. Kip you're here and have her come out, but I can already tell you she won't have any of that. She'll insist on introducing you to Mr. Slesher, so you might as well come in with me."

"But it violates HIPAA," she insisted.

"You're fine if he's okay with it."

"How do we know he's okay with it, though? He looked like he was . . . asleep." It was the most polite way to describe it.

"Because Mrs. Kip won't let him be *not* okay with it," Jimmy said. "She has that effect on people."

In desperation, Aidyn threw up one last defense. "I don't want to disrupt what she's got going on in there."

Her reply was easily deflected by the grin seeping onto Jimmy's face. "Don't worry about that either. Mrs. Kip wants all her friends to know each other."

Clara felt sorry for the girl. The poor thing tried to hide her horror at seeing Charles that way, but her stiff body language betrayed her. The first time a person sees the fingers of death strangling a breathing body irreversibly amends the psyche.

Better she sees it now.

Aidyn lingered halfway to the bed, as if the distance offered some assurance of safety, a buffer between herself and the decay.

Clara let her be. Eventually the girl would come closer. In the meantime, Clara turned toward Jimmy, who was on the other side of the bed busily tucking pillows under Charles's entire right side. The prop tilted the man's right half upward about ten degrees, and his head rotated an inch or so toward her, affording a fuller view of his face. His lids hung heavy over his eyes. He hadn't spoken in a while.

"There you are, Mr. Slesher," Jimmy said. "Hopefully that feels more comfortable."

The old man's lids moved ever so slightly.

"I'm going to pull the sheet back over you," Jimmy explained, "but I'll leave it untucked, the way you like it." He took hold of the sheet gathered at the man's waist. It caught air as Jimmy pulled it up high and over Charles's thin torso, which was hidden by a standard-issue hospital gown. The air created bubbles under the fabric that gradually dissipated as the sheet gracefully settled against him.

Graceful like a leaf.

"I'll leave you now to talk with your lady friends," Jimmy continued. "Nurse Nora will be by in a bit to give you a thorough check, okay?" He waited a beat for the man to reply.

Charles's eyelids sank lower.

"See you later, Mr. Slesher." As Jimmy came around the side of the bed, Clara held out her hand for him to take.

"Jimmy, sweetheart, I'm so glad Charles has you to help keep him spritely."

He grinned. "Same to you, Mrs. Kip. I'll check in with you before my shift is up."

"You better. I'll be bored otherwise."

He chuckled. "Can't let that happen. See you later." Releasing her hand, he turned to Aidyn. "Enjoy your visit, Miss Kelley."

The girl breezily nodded her thanks, but as soon as he was gone, anxiousness pooled in her expression. The poor thing didn't know what to do with herself.

Clara spotted the gold cross dangling from her neck, a message from the Lord reminding her to whom the child belonged and to whom she should teach her to turn.

Lord, be my words.

"Come on over, Miss Kelley." She pointed to a dining chair. "Pull up a seat."

A flash of panic streaked across the girl's face. "I was thinking . . . we could go back to your room. Let him sleep."

Clara waved off the suggestion. "He sleeps regardless, honey. Grab a chair."

Aidyn tucked her bottom lip under her teeth and glanced quickly at the door. As if realizing she really didn't have much of a choice (because she didn't), she took hold of a dining chair and placed it by the bed so that she sat perpendicular to Clara. Her movements were rigid and restrained.

The work with Aidyn would be difficult, but the fruit that could come from it would be sweet. The effort would be worth the energy spent.

"I'm so glad you're here," Clara said. "I told Charles you were coming. He's been looking forward to it as much as I have."

The girl smiled warily.

"Would you like me to introduce you two?"

Aidyn glanced at the bed, a distinct note of misgiving in her expression. "Sure."

"In that case, Miss Aidyn Kelley, I'd like to introduce you to Mr. Charles Slesher. He was an engineer for Black and Veatch. Charles, this is Miss Kelley, the one I told you about. She's a reporter for the *Star*."

Besides taking a shallow, raspy breath, Charles remained still.

"Tell him about your work. I'm sure he'd be glad to hear about it. He's a great listener."

The girl looked between them, clearly unsold on the idea.

"I could tell him my own version," Clara said, "but I know how much you value the truth."

Aidyn's mouth turned up slightly at one end, a reluctant acquiescence to Clara's point. She took a moment to prepare her thoughts, or perhaps gird herself. Likely both.

"I've worked at the *Star* for about a year." She stumbled for her next words, clearly unsure how to talk to a dying man who couldn't talk back. Her gaze drifted to other points in the room as she spoke. "I mostly assist the senior Local News reporter with fact gathering and initial contacts. Periodically I write smaller pieces. Depending on what my editor allows me."

The short exposition offered several clues into Aidyn's life. Of particular note, the touch of acidity when she mentioned her editor. Apparently, Aidyn was not aware of who Bella Woods really was.

Aidyn folded her hands into a tight ball in her lap and looked at Clara. "I don't know what else to say. That's about it."

"That was wonderful, Miss Kelley. Thank you for sharing. You just remember, Mr. Slesher may not be able to respond in the normal way that you and I can, but I promise you he heard every word, and he appreciated each one." Clara smiled with as much warmth as she could, hoping the girl felt a little more at ease. "You have a very pleasant voice to listen to, you know that? There's a sweetness to it you can't fake. It's pleasant enough to listen to all day."

Aidyn seemed to turn over the compliment. "Thank you, I guess."

"So pleasant, in fact, it gives me an idea." She reached for the closed Bible in her lap and held it out to Aidyn. "You could help me read to Mr. Slesher."

The girl looked at the outstretched Bible, obviously unsold on that idea as well.

Clara pushed the Bible closer. "Never shy away from sharing the treasure with someone else, Miss Kelley. Please take it. It's getting heavy."

Slowly the girl took the Bible from Clara's hand and brought it to her own lap. "What should I read?"

"We were working through the Psalms, but feel free to read whatever you'd like." She added with a smirk, "Maybe not Numbers, though. He gets enough sleep."

To Clara's delight, Aidyn gave the smallest of grins. It was tiny, but progress. She opened the Bible and flipped through the pages absently, as if trying to determine where to start.

"What have you been reading lately in your studies?" Clara asked.

"I . . ." Aidyn glanced up sheepishly. "I haven't been reading as much as I should."

"Well, I'm not one to judge a lapse in personal devotions. Life has a way of stealing our attention for seasons. The good news is, though we sometimes find ourselves out of the Word, the Word always remains in us. I bet you know the twenty-third Psalm by heart, yes?"

"I do."

"You can start there, then." She gestured to Charles. "Speak it over him, honey."

Aidyn glanced furtively at Charles.

"Go on."

The girl closed the Bible and gripped it with both hands. She paused a moment as if debating if Clara's lead was truly worth following. Then, softly, she called forth the old, familiar words. "The LORD is my shepherd; I have what I need."

The sound of the girl's voice wrapping around the Scripture pleased Clara greatly. Two believers gathered together before the throne of the Lord for the sake of one lost sheep. No more powerful thing on the earth exists.

Clara silently prayed along with the words Aidyn spoke. *Surround Charles with your love, Lord. Your mercy especially. Bring him into your fold.*

"He lets me lie down in green pastures; he leads me beside quiet waters."

Bring him stillness and peace. May he know the sound of your voice, God. As long as there is breath, there is time. God, in your mercy, draw him to you and help him lay down his own will. Save him today, God.

The beat went on like that, Aidyn beautifully praising and Clara fervently praying. They boldly spoke into heaven from the humble patient room. Word after blessed word, until Clara felt a stir. Strong. Mighty.

And Charles suddenly opened his eyes wide.

Both women startled.

"Charles?" Clara leaned toward him, heart beating wildly. Breathless, she waited. Aidyn was still as stone beside her.

A soft clucking sound emanated from Charles's mouth, as if he was trying to get his tongue to function. He progressed to a mumble, his words indecipherable. He stared straight in front of him at something—or Someone.

"What is it, Charles? What do you see?"

His brow scrunched, and then, bit by bit, it raised high, pushing his forehead into deep wrinkles, as though whatever he saw, whatever he clamored for, filled him with overwhelming emotion.

"Yes, Charles," Clara said. "That's him. He's waiting."

She peeked at Aidyn. The girl's face had blanched, and she gripped the Bible with white knuckles.

"It's okay, honey," Clara whispered. "The Word is powerful."

Aidyn didn't move. Her eyes remained fixed on Charles.

Clara reached for his hand and gathered it in both of hers. With Aidyn watching and hopefully listening, she continued on to Psalm 25, watering what the girl had sown.

"'LORD, I appeal to you. My God, I trust in you.' Let that be your answer, Charles."

Please, Father God, help him heed the Shepherd's voice. Open the eyes of his heart, Lord, that we may be together in paradise.

She lifted Charles's hand to her cheek and comforted it with what little warmth she could offer. "Dear Charles," she whispered, "please answer."

His eyelids flickered. He made a soft noise that sounded like the letter *n.* Then his eyes fell shut.

In that position, he remained, thin, raspy breathing coming at long intervals.

Whatever happened, only the Lord knew. Clara lowered his hand to the bed and turned to Aidyn. The girl's brow was furrowed, and her mouth was drawn tightly in consternation.

"Quite a ride, huh?" Clara asked.

Aidyn didn't respond. She moved only her eyes, looking at Clara briefly, then back at Charles, as if waiting for the next weird thing to happen.

Clara leaned toward her and whispered, "Ours is a God of new life, Miss Kelley."

Of the many things Clara desired to say to the girl, none ranked more important than that.

It was the core, the epicenter, the root of everything yet to be spoken.

CHAPTER 12

Aidyn sat stunned.

She believed in the power of Scripture, of course. Or at least she thought she did. If she didn't, her faith had, at best, been a white lie. Still, what she saw the atrophying man in the bed do struck her as freakish and unsettling rather than a testament of spiritual wonder as the old woman apparently saw it.

Mrs. Kip saw the world in colors Aidyn could not discern.

More than ever, Aidyn itched to leave Mr. Slesher's room. But Mrs. Kip seemed to be in no mood to even consider it.

The old woman motioned for the Bible in Aidyn's lap. Aidyn handed it over and watched her open it and resume reading aloud.

Mrs. Kip's clear and utter love for the words dripped from her voice, as if the words sprang directly from the deepest chambers of her heart. Little pieces of herself offered up to someone who could give nothing in return.

Aidyn felt torn between settling into the lull of Mrs. Kip's voice and insisting they leave.

Fortunately, a few minutes into the oration, the nurse walked in. Aidyn grasped at the glimmer of hope that their stay would soon end. Surely the nurse would observe the HIPAA violation before her and send them shuffling across the hall.

The nurse, however, only smiled. "Jimmy told me you were entertaining some ladies, Mr. Slesher." She stopped at the wall pump near the bathroom door to spritz sanitizer on her hands. "Mind if I cut in for a minute?"

"We don't mind one bit, Nora," Mrs. Kip said. "We were just having a walk through the Psalms."

"Sounds lovely." Nora skirted the bed to the opposite side. "Psalms is one of my favorite books. It's beautiful, isn't it, Mr. Slesher?" She bent over slightly to get a better view of the man's face, studying it as if searching for clues.

The whole thing felt increasingly uncomfortable.

Aidyn leaned over to Mrs. Kip, clinging to one last thread of hope. "Should we give him some privacy for this?"

Hearing the question, the nurse spoke first. "You don't have to leave. I'm just taking a quick peek and will come back later for an exam."

Aidyn bit the inside of her lip.

Before every move, the nurse explained to the man what she was about to do.

"I'm going to take a look at your legs, Mr. Slesher. You might feel a breeze when I move the sheet."

Nora peeled back the lower edges of the white sheet and let it double over his shins, exposing his feet and ankles.

Aidyn nearly retched.

The thin skin over his emaciated ankles had a sickening anemic hue. Every ridge of bone seemed to poke through. A bluish tint colored his toenail beds.

She tore her eyes away.

"I'm going to slip my hand up to your knee, Mr. Slesher," Nora said. "I won't squeeze. It's only a touch."

Aidyn imagined the weight of Nora's hand crushing his fragile joints, the stick legs snapping off at horrific angles. She clasped her hands in her lap and shook away the thought. Feeling eyes on her, she glanced at Mrs. Kip.

The woman looked at her the way a grandmother would take in a hurting child. A look that said Aidyn was safe and completely understood. She reached over and cupped Aidyn's arm.

The empathetic gesture compounded Aidyn's uneasiness about the situation. Who was she to accept grace from a woman whose body would soon be in a similar breakdown? She sat there with Mrs. Kip's hand compassionately resting on her arm, eyes averted from the bed, and prayed for the opportunity to finally leave.

"You're doing great, Mr. Slesher," Nora told him. "We're almost done."

Aidyn dared to look at Nora's activity and found the nurse bending over to look at the bottom of his feet. Immediately after seeing them, Nora threw a glance at Mrs. Kip.

Something passed between them. A hidden message. A continuation of an ongoing, intimate conversation. Mrs. Kip sat back against the chair, drew her hands to her lap, and bowed with eyes closed, the posture of prayer.

Mrs. Kip's vigil for Mr. Slesher obviously ran much deeper than could be observed.

Who is this woman?

Nora replaced the sheet, thanked Mr. Slesher for his patience, and came around the bed. "You're due for an exam too," she said, looking at Mrs. Kip. "I'll be by after your company leaves. Please be careful about your energy level. You've been up a lot today."

Mrs. Kip dismissed the suggestion with a wave of her hand. "I'm fit and fine, honey."

"Still. Perhaps you and Miss Kelley can finish up your visit in your own room."

Aidyn perked up.

"Is that a suggestion or a command?" Mrs. Kip asked.

"Both."

The woman sighed. "Message received, warden."

A bemused smile came to Nora's lips. "You'll appreciate me someday."

"We'll see."

As Nora stepped into the hall, Mrs. Kip gestured at Aidyn to get up. "Come on, honey. Let's bolt before she calls in the dogs." With much effort, and stubbornly without help, the old woman fumbled into a standing position.

Aidyn, meanwhile, rose as if on springs and took the chair back to the table, eager to get through the door. When she looked back to find Mrs. Kip, though, she saw her lingering beside the bed.

The old woman stared down at the frail man. Both of her hands wrapped around his left one. She clung to him like she didn't want to let go. Like she held a jewel that was in danger of being lost. She leaned down as far as her unsteady body allowed and whispered, "Sweet dreams, precious one."

In that instant, it was abundantly clear that Mrs. Kip would come back to his room as soon as she possibly could. She would break all the rules if she had to, upset all the nurses, come what may.

Aidyn's curiosity doubled. *Who is this woman, and where did she get such fierce love?*

Clara settled into her own armchair with a heavy exhale. A dull throb beat in her belly. All her bones ached from the inside. She positively hated to admit Nora was right about the energy level thing. Had it not been for Aidyn's company, she would have allowed herself a little snooze right then, in her armchair overlooking the serene lawn, warmed by the sunlight. Dying was an exhausting business, both doing it oneself and watching someone else do it.

But when she looked at the girl lowering onto the love-seat—on the side closest to her this time—her heart reminded her of the work yet to do. This child God had given her out of the world needed tending too, just as much as Charles did.

Clara commanded her body to full attention and prayed for the Lord to lead the way.

Aidyn pulled her messenger bag onto the cushion beside her and searched inside. She was still stiff and measured, and Clara recalled how scared the poor thing had looked when Nora peered under the sheet. The girl couldn't even watch.

"Not easy to see someone in that condition, is it, honey?" she asked.

Aidyn opened her notebook on her lap and shrugged with obviously forced nonchalance. "It's all part of it, I suppose."

Sweet child.

"That it is," Clara agreed. "But it sure doesn't make it easy. No matter how many times I've been with a loved one on this side of life, it never gets easier." Though she hadn't seen what Nora did on the bottom of Charles's feet, experience told her the blooms of purple had gotten darker. The cells slowly asphyxiated from lack of circulation. "If you ask me, Miss Kelley, it's all kind of gross."

Aidyn raised her eyebrows in surprise at the assertion.

"Don't you agree?" Clara asked. "I know I could do without it."

"Yes, it's just . . . I didn't expect the bluntness."

Clara chuckled. "There's more where that came from."

The girl smiled uneasily. "I have no doubt." She looked down at her notebook page lined with questions she had clearly come prepared to ask. Questions that drove at what she thought was essential.

Clara could tell one question in particular swirled in her brain.

"If you're in a blunt mood," Aidyn began, "I have a blunt question."

"Those are my favorite kind."

Despite the permission, the girl hesitated, as if unsure she should speak the words. "Did you watch your husband die too?"

The question pinged at Clara's heart, both because it

drummed up the painful memories and because it wasn't asked in a reporter kind of way. It came wrapped in tenderness, with notes of empathy. The product of ears learning to listen for the heart as well as the facts.

"It's a complicated answer," Clara began. "Technically he died in a car accident, but really he was dying long before that."

"How do you mean?"

Clara gathered her hands together, pulling herself in against the rush of emotion. "He battled the bottle, honey. For as long as I knew him."

The note of empathy Clara had heard in the girl's voice showed up in her eyes as well.

"Johnny was a good man. Generous, loving, hardworking. He believed in Jesus long before I did, but he never learned to deal with his demons. He took their power for granted. And if I'm being honest, so did I. I watched him slosh to his death and didn't try to stop him. That was a guilt only many years of counseling could help me let go of."

The girl was quiet. Her gaze fell to the page again, as if in her eagerness to know, she had not considered what it would be like to have the knowledge.

Clara understood perfectly well what that was like too.

"I had a friend named Martha Rendall who was so important to me during those years after John died. God bless her richly, she put up with a lot of lip from me."

The girl grinned, clearly appreciative for the levity, and started to write notes.

"She helped me see an important truth, Miss Kelley, and it was the one I shared with you back in Charles's room. Our

God is the God of new life. Carve that in a stone somewhere, because it is the gospel truth. It was exactly what happened with me. And wow, what a new life it was! I was a giant mess, and he rescued me from it all. Because of him, my view of this fleeting life completely changed. He gave me a new vision. Would you like to hear it?"

Aidyn glanced up from her note taking. "I would."

"Good. Then write this down: The grave is not my final home. I want to live as if I believe that. By God's grace, I will live because I believed that."

Slowly the girl's pen came to a halt. She lifted her eyes and stared at Clara, as if the words ran through her mind over and over, bringing light to places long in the dark.

Clara gestured at her stilled pen. "Write that down, honey. It's gold."

Roused back to her task, Aidyn grinned and continued writing.

The dull pain in Clara's stomach began to sharpen—a warning. But the girl was finally on the right path, and Clara couldn't let a little discomfort get in the way. She pressed through and hid the wince.

"May I ask another blunt question?" the girl requested.

"Fire away."

Aidyn lifted her pen and met Clara's gaze. "What are you dying of?"

The question did not surprise her. "Besides old age?"

"Yes. Besides that."

"Cancer, Miss Kelley. Got it all over. Quite the weasel, this disease. Didn't know it had even set up shop until about a couple of weeks ago."

The girl's eyes widened. "That must have been a shock."

"You can say that again."

"I'm so sorry."

Clara shrugged. "It definitely created some havoc in my life, that's for sure. But honestly, I'm thankful I don't have to put up with chemo and all that. I've watched too many people suffer through treatments. I knew it wasn't for me."

Aidyn nodded, considering. "Would you like me to include something about cancer in your obit?"

Clara screwed up her face. "Yuck, no."

"Thought I'd ask. Some people do."

"They do, but I told you yesterday I don't want people being all weepy about it. My death is a victory long awaited, and I want people to think of it that way."

"Right," Aidyn said. "A death with pizzazz."

"Exactly. A death with—"

The comment caught Clara. It stirred her into thought.

An idea mustered in her mind. One that encouraged seeing death for the lie it was. One that would break the restraints on the girl's courage and teach her that from the very institution of fallible bodies, death had been destined for a complete rewrite.

With each piece that fell into place, a tingle coursed through her, covering the growing sharpness in her gut.

She looked at Aidyn, who had apparently been watching her in the moment of silence with increasing curiosity. "Miss Kelley," she said in a tone that revealed her excitement, "I have one request for my obit."

The girl looked dubious. "What's that?"

Clara leaned forward, her elbows on the armrests. "I would like you to write me a death with pizzazz."

Aidyn's brow scrunched. "I'm sorry?"

"At the end of my obit, I want you to write a new death for me. Something that wakes people up, gets them riled. Something riveting. Something memorable. Something . . . extraordinary!"

The frown deepened. "You mean . . . make something up?"

Clara shook her head. "I mean inspire!"

Confusion morphed into apprehension in Aidyn's expression. "Mrs. Kip, I appreciate what you're saying, but I can't turn in an obit with an obvious lie in it. My editor would never approve."

"Where is your imagination, Miss Kelley? This is my obit, isn't it?"

"Well . . . yes."

"Then tell your editor I can have what I want. I'm paying for it."

Aidyn opened her mouth but seemed to stall on what to say. She looked down at her notebook, at all the questions left to be asked, all the information left to be found. Clara wanted her to discover it all, and so much more. Everything she didn't know she lacked.

The pain stabbed at Clara's stomach. Her minutes were limited before her body's protests were too loud to ignore.

Which prompted her to make the offer that would change the course of their time together. And set Aidyn up for the discovery of a lifetime.

"Look, Miss Kelley, you want answers, and I want an extraordinary death. We can help each other. For every extraordinary death you suggest for me to consider, I'll answer three questions you have about my life. Any three of those questions you have there in your notebook, or ones you think up on the way. Blunt or mild or boring. No question is off-limits. And I promise I will always be truthful." Subtly she pulled her hands to the middle of her belly and pressed in on the pesky ache. "What do you say? Three stories for a suggestion. Sounds like quite an offer, if I do say so myself."

Aidyn looked up at her and bit her bottom lip.

CHAPTER 13

"Whatever it takes," her J-school adviser would say—usually when Aidyn showed a hint of reluctance to stretch beyond the norm to find that one tidbit that would throw open the story. "Whatever it takes, Kelley, get in there. You can't be intimidated to be what you aren't normally to get what you can't otherwise."

She was no stranger to trading favors or exploiting a chink in the armor, but how in the world did she find herself in a place where what she needed to do for a small, insignificant, throwaway assignment was to rewrite an actual person's death?

This day keeps getting weirder.

Unable to think of any counter to Mrs. Kip's offer, she sighed heavily.

The woman responded with a giggle. "I'll take that as a yes." Her eyes shone like a child presented with a pony.

Deep within her, Aidyn liked that she was partly the reason

that look came to Mrs. Kip's face, but more than anything, she dreaded what it meant for her now. The deal would be either a giant distraction or, at best, extremely annoying.

"Does that mean I need to come up with a suggestion right now?" she asked.

"Now's a great time, honey. Have at it."

Reluctantly, Aidyn willed her brain to sputter out an idea. Her mouth twisted as she thought. Finally, she blurted, "Saving a child from a fire."

A blank silence followed.

"Not good?" she asked.

Mrs. Kip shrugged. "A tad unoriginal, but it'll do for your first try. You'll get better."

The compliment did little to encourage her.

"All right, then," the woman said. "My turn. What's your first question? Ask me anything."

The list of questions stretched long on her notebook page. With the newly installed suggestion-to-question ratio, she had to be far more selective and strategic in her inquiries. She scanned the list, looking for any questions with a higher probability of producing more than a one-sentence answer from Mrs. Kip. Questions that went beyond what her parents' names were, her hobbies, her profession.

What Aidyn needed were questions that would prompt Mrs. Kip to tell stories. Revealing stories.

At last, she asked, "If you had more time, what would you do?"

Mrs. Kip grinned, as if the question pleased her more than it did Aidyn. "If I had more time, I'd go to São Paulo." She turned to the picture of her husband with the city behind him. "We were supposed to move there in August 1960, which ended up being three months after John died. He had joined the foreign services with the hope he would be stationed in Brazil."

"Why is that?"

"He was born in São Paulo."

His middle name, the foreign-sounding one that clashed with the Midwestern bookends—it must have been Portuguese. She looked closer at the picture of John on the nightstand. Dark hair, dark eyes, a complexion two shades deeper than his wife's. It was all clearer.

"He was raised by his aunt and uncle in America, but he was born in Brazil," Mrs. Kip continued. "His father was an American businessman on a weeklong trip. His mother was, shall we say, a naïve waitress. A baby was out of the question for her. But her sister, who had married an American and lived here in the Midwest, agreed to take him. He lived with his adoptive parents from the time he was two months old." Mrs. Kip looked again at the picture of her husband, admiration thick in her expression. "He was one of the lucky ones. He escaped the favelas before he ever really lived there."

Aidyn wrote fast to keep up. "I'm sorry, what are the fa— what did you call them?"

"Favelas," Mrs. Kip repeated, slower. "Slums, basically."

Aidyn wrote the definition as well as the pronunciation in her notes: fuh-veh-luh.

"São Paulo had so many orphans, Miss Kelley. It would break your heart. Those sweet babies left to their own devices. John and I wanted to stay on in the city after his service and set up a home for them. But that plan wasn't meant to be."

"Because John died," Aidyn said.

"Because the Lord had other ideas," Mrs. Kip corrected. "I didn't see it that way when John died, but I wasn't a woman of faith then. Now I see it clear as day. Even in pain, God's up to something."

Aidyn nodded, wrote down some notes, and pretended to understand completely the desire to abandon one's dreams for God's will. But really, the very idea sounded excruciating. It would hurt beyond measure to give up her own dream of being like Katharine Graham.

"What did you do after your husband died?" she asked, prepared to capture even more of the woman's verbosity.

But Mrs. Kip grinned in that ornery way. "I think you're forgetting something."

"I am? What?"

"That was your fourth question."

Aidyn felt her mouth fall open.

Mrs. Kip started to laugh, but pain flashed across her face. It caught her voice and pinched her brow.

Aidyn paused and watched her carefully.

"It's nothing," the woman said once she was back to relatively normal, though clearly it wasn't nothing. "Go ahead, honey. Amaze me with your creativity."

Putting aside her worry, Aidyn thought about what might please Mrs. Kip. "How about . . . attempting to swim the English Channel?"

Mrs. Kip nodded, even began to smile, but another wince grabbed her. Her face contorted harder and longer.

"Mrs. Kip?"

The woman eventually unclenched and forced a smile.

"I'm fine." But she still clutched her stomach. "Go ahead with your questions."

Aidyn's mind bounced between mounting fear and respect for Mrs. Kip's wishes. Hesitantly, she repeated the question she last asked. "What did you do after your husband died?"

The old woman took a breath that sounded tainted with discomfort. "I did a lot of hard things. But hard things usually end in the biggest blessings." Mrs. Kip nodded at Aidyn's notebook. "Write that. That's gold too."

Aidyn did, but she kept one eye closely on the woman, who used the break in speech to lean forward into an upright C, as if the compressed posture would help.

An urge to move closer gathered within Aidyn. She ignored it and continued to write as Mrs. Kip resumed speaking.

"I stayed in the basement apartment of some friends for a long while. It was the size of a sardine can, but I grew to love it." Her eyes closed, and she pulled in another labored breath. Her voice began to break and weaken. "My first job was . . . as a checker in a local grocery store . . . Then Martha got me in the nurse's assistant program at KU Med for the nursery . . . That's where I—" Her whole face wrenched. She groaned and hunched further.

"Mrs. Kip?" Aidyn thrust her notebook and pen to the side and moved to the edge of the loveseat.

The woman cried out.

Aidyn reached forward and touched her knee. "Mrs. Kip? Should I—"

In an instant, the woman went limp. The weight of her head spilled her body forward, pulling her headfirst off the chair.

Aidyn dove, landing on her knees and scooping her arms forward in time to catch Mrs. Kip under the shoulders. The woman's head wedged against her chest.

Aidyn's heart raced. *What do I do? What do I do?*

She stayed on her knees, propping up the old woman and trying to think through the panic.

God, help me!

Suddenly she saw the cord to the clip-on call button—the one Mrs. Kip was supposed to wear at all times in her room. The woman apparently had left it hanging over the arm of the chair when she went to visit Mr. Slesher. Aidyn lifted one knee to support Mrs. Kip's head and quickly reached for the button. She pressed it three times, as if the repetition would somehow indicate to the nurse's station the urgency of the request. Then she placed her hand back on the woman's body. She could feel her bones through her clothes.

"It's okay, Mrs. Kip," she whispered in a shaky voice. "The nurse will be here soon. Hang in there."

The assurance was as much for herself.

They will be here soon. Hang in there.

Though Mrs. Kip weighed maybe one hundred pounds, the pressure of her upper body bore down into Aidyn. Something sour drifted up to Aidyn's nose. The unmistakable stench of urine.

"It's going to be okay," she repeated to keep the retch at bay. "The nurse is almost here."

She looked at the door. But the threshold remained empty.

Her knees ached against the hard floor. *Please*, she begged.

Then, as if on a gentle breeze, a single word floated into her mind.

Extraordinary.

It stirred in her heart, beat back the fear in her mind, parted the clouds of confusion enough for her to understand.

Tell her an extraordinary death. Something that helps her wake up.

Aidyn pulled in a trembling breath and, without feeling compelled to explain to Mrs. Kip what she was doing, began to speak suggestions.

"How about . . . trekking through the Himalayas to . . . raise money for Tibetan children?"

She prayed the awkward, stumbling words meant something.

"Or . . . fighting off elephant poachers in Africa? Or . . . rescuing young girls from the red-light districts?"

She waited, hoped, for Mrs. Kip to respond. But the silence that lingered was heavier than before.

She closed her eyes. *Please, God.*

Finally, footsteps at the door.

Aidyn turned and saw Nora's eyes go wide.

"Oh, Miss Kelley!" The nurse rushed over and expertly lifted the old woman back into the chair, freeing Aidyn to stand.

"I'm so glad you were here," Nora said, though Aidyn wasn't nearly as grateful. "What happened?"

"I don't know. She was having pain and then just passed out."

"I need to get her in bed. Do you mind helping me?"

Aidyn gritted her teeth but agreed. "What can I do?"

"If you could stand at the foot of the bed, then you can help with her legs."

Aidyn moved to the assigned spot and watched Nora hook her elbows into Mrs. Kip's armpits, resting the woman's head on her shoulder. With trained deftness, Nora lifted the unresponsive woman from the chair, pivoted on one foot, and brought the woman's backside to the mattress.

Mrs. Kip appeared even smaller draped helplessly against her nurse.

Nora laid the woman's torso on the bed first, then motioned for Aidyn to lift her legs.

Aidyn squatted and gripped Mrs. Kip's ankles. Her stomach lurched at the fact that her fingertips easily overlapped. It was amazing Mrs. Kip could walk at all.

As Nora adjusted the woman's position on the bed, Mrs. Kip began to rouse. First with a small moan, then with a roll of the head.

"You're safe, Mrs. Kip," Nora said. "You're in bed now." Turning to Aidyn, she whispered, "She needs to rest."

Aidyn nodded. Strangely, the dismissal brought no relief, despite her eagerness to jet out of there as fast as possible. As she gathered her belongings, Nora continued to talk with her awakening patient.

"I'm going to listen to your heart, Mrs. Kip. You'll feel me poke the stethoscope under your shirt."

Aidyn quickly strapped on her bag and headed for the door, eyes averted. When she was nearly to the hallway, Nora called out to her. "I think Mrs. Kip is trying to tell you something."

Surprised, Aidyn turned. "She is?"

Nora leaned closer to Mrs. Kip's mouth. The old woman's lips moved, but her voice was too quiet to travel far.

The nurse listened carefully, then looked up at Aidyn with her brow knitted in confusion. "I hope you know what she means, Miss Kelley. She said, 'Write those down. They're good.'"

A hot wave passed over Aidyn.

The woman had heard every word.

Jarred.

The word played over and over in Aidyn's mind as she walked down the north hallway of Sacred Promise. *Jarred* was the perfect word to use should anyone ask how she was doing, should Jimmy cross her path or Rosario come out of the office to ask how the interview went.

Aidyn quickened her pace and envisioned herself reaching the freedom beyond the front doors. She prayed no one would get in the way of that goal.

Her mind insisted on replaying snippets of what had transpired in Mrs. Kip's room—the winces the old woman tried to hide, the way her body slumped like a rag doll, the weak moans, the threadlike ankles, the unsettling way the old woman responded to Aidyn's suggestions. All of it out-provoked Mrs. Kip's request for an extraordinary death.

All of it propelled Aidyn out the front doors.

Safely in her car, Aidyn exhaled heavily and took several minutes to regroup.

How did I get into this mess?

Regardless of what had happened—or how bizarre Mrs. Kip's request was—Woods expected a completed, well-written draft. Soon. No excuses. And based on everything

Aidyn had seen and heard and smelled that afternoon, Mrs. Kip was ever closer to her real death.

Time was quickly running short for Aidyn to get what she needed. If she was going to redeem herself, she had to work fast. And she had to work according to rules she had no say in.

Whatever it takes.

She took out her phone and texted Rahmiya.

> Need your help. Come over for dinner? I'll order Thai.

She reached into the outer pocket of her bag for her keys and felt the forgotten cookies inside. Repulsed, she quickly found her keys and started her car.

On her drive back to the office, she attempted to look past all the weird things that had happened and thought about where their next conversation might lead. What more had Mrs. Kip done after her husband died? When and how had that fierce love of hers begun to bloom? What exactly had the "new life" entailed?

On the latter, her mind swirled for several miles.

"Ours is a God of new life," Mrs. Kip had said.

What exactly did she mean by that?

Later that evening, Rahmiya arrived at Aidyn's apartment door, bearing two to-go coffee cups. "Got you a vanilla latte."

"You're a saint." Aidyn took the cup her friend held out. "You have no idea how badly I needed this. And a friend."

Rahmiya frowned. "Why? What happened?"

As they settled in the living room alongside their respective curries and coffees, Aidyn explained everything. From Mr. Slesher's decomposing body, to his startling response, to Mrs. Kip's passing out, she didn't mince a single detail. Horror steadily shaded her friend's face.

"This sounds like the worst assignment in the history of ever," Rahmiya said at the end.

Journalists faced far worse conditions for a story. Still, Aidyn nodded, appreciating the sympathy more than the need for accuracy.

"So, what are you going to do?" Rahmiya asked.

"I have to do what it takes."

"You mean the new-death thing?"

"Yes. It's the only option. Which is why I need your help."

"Me? What can I do?"

"You can help me brainstorm different ways for her to die."

Rahmiya laughed. "You're joking."

"No. I really need your help. If I can only ask three questions for every new death I suggest, I figure I'll need dozens of ideas, depending on what she shares."

Her friend shook her head. "This is way too morbid for me, sister."

"It's not exactly a walk in the park for me either. This is going to take a depravity I don't have."

"I don't have it either, Aidie."

"Please, Rahmi. I can't do this part on my own."

Rahmiya stirred her food thoughtfully for a moment. Suddenly she smiled. "If it's a twisted mind you need, I know someone who fits the bill better than I do."

Aidyn righted. "Who?"

"He's super annoying, but he does know his action movies and video games, which seem to be a treasure trove for what you need."

"Who?" Aidyn asked again.

Her friend took out her phone and waved it.

Minutes later, they watched through FaceTime as Rahmiya's teenage brother, Ahmed, grinned impishly at their request for help. "Dude, this sounds awesome."

CHAPTER 14

July 1, 1975

Clara leaned closer to examine the map sprawled out on Martha's kitchen table. The thick red line drawn by the Red Cross caseworker showed the proposed route for the Khab kids' covert evacuation. It snaked through infested jungle terrain Clara had never seen nor could imagine, and it pinged towns whose names she could not pronounce. If Portuguese had been hard for her tongue to acclimate to, Lao was next to impossible.

Mai's shoulders trembled under Clara's hands. Clara tightened her grip on her friend. Across the table, Mai's husband, Mahasajun, stood behind the caseworker's chair, arms crossed, brow creased. Like the military leader he was.

Martha and her husband, Erik, sat together at the head of the table, watching and listening carefully.

"The idea is to get the kids here." The caseworker pointed his pen at a spot in the northeast quadrant of Thailand, just south of the Mekong River that separated the country from

Laos. "Right here, in the Ban Vinai refugee camp, in the Pak Chom District of Loei."

Mahasajun nodded grimly, as if knowing exactly where that was and not liking it.

"The camp is about sixteen kilometers south of the Mekong. Once they cross the river, their trek will get much easier. But it's this part here, between Vang Vieng and the river, that will be the hardest." The caseworker drew an imaginary circle around the stretch of red line between a city and the thin blue squiggle representing the river, several centimeters apart.

Though Clara couldn't calculate how many miles that constituted, without question it was many more than young children deserved to dare for freedom.

"The State Department has operatives who will get them to the Mekong and across, if your family can get the kids to the outskirts of Vang Vieng."

Heavy silence hung around them. That word—*if*—weighed the most. *If* confirmed the worst of fears. *If* meant danger could ravage the children at any point, even within the walls of their grandparents' home, where they were at that moment.

"What about my in-laws?" Mahasajun asked. His command of English outpaced his wife's, but his accent was still strong.

"We will do our best to keep our eyes out as they travel," the man replied.

"They're not evacuating too?" Clara asked with surprise.

"The US government has heart for only so many Lao," Mahasajun spit.

"Mahasajun!" Mai reprimanded with a fierce, quiet voice. "They save our kids!"

Her husband clenched his jaw and looked off to the side.

The caseworker kept an even countenance. He likely had heard much worse from the other Laotian officers trapped in the US, caged warriors unable to protect their own families, let alone their country, from the blood-seeking Communists.

These were the very same men who bravely risked everything to help the US fight in exchange for the promise of protection and reward. A gentlemen's agreement had brought Mahasajun and Mai to specialized training in the first place. But with President Ford's sudden order to withdraw from Laos, the US effectively reneged and abandoned the people to face the consequences of their allegiance. Alone and unarmed.

The news reports had not been pretty.

Clara was angry for them, but Mai was right. The kids needed all their attention in that moment, regardless of international politics.

"How long will this journey take?" Clara asked, hoping to move the conversation forward.

"We estimate they will arrive in the camp by the end of the month," the caseworker said. "It will take several more weeks at that point to process all the paperwork, visas, etc."

"How will they cross the river?" Mahasajun asked.

"On a fishing boat."

"Belongs to government?" he prodded.

"A local villager," the caseworker replied. By the look in his eye, Clara could tell he knew the answer would not please the officer.

Mahasajun stepped to the side of the caseworker's chair, prompting the seated man to look up at him. "That's too risky."

"They have been vetted," the caseworker said. "They're friends."

Mahasajun huffed. "I don't trust the US definition of friend."

"Regardless, Lieutenant, it's the only option you have. It's the only option your children have."

Mahasajun stared at him for a long, bated moment. Then, in a swift, sudden movement, he turned his back and stepped away. The brave man who had seen war from all sides now saw it from the side of helplessness. He could not maneuver men through this part. His specialized training was worthless. He was relegated to the sidelines, asked to trust people who had already let him down, and trust them with the lives of his two children.

Mai quietly rose to her feet, forcing Clara's hands to fall away from her shoulders. She went to her husband's side and slid her arm through his.

The others at the table watched in silence.

Clara imagined the two young faces she had seen only in pictures. The precious ones, ages five and twelve, likely already terrified, crying night and day for their mom and dad. Now they were being asked to go on a trip that might result in their death or that of their grandparents, or both.

Clara hoped, for their little hearts' sakes, they did not know the dangers in their path.

When the caseworker left, the five adults knelt in the middle of the living room. Erik led them in fervent prayer.

Clara stayed the night at Martha's, sleeping on the couch so Mai and Mahasajun could have the privacy of the guest bedroom.

She stayed the next night too, when the children's treacherous journey began. The friends' prayer vigil lasted until well past midnight.

Over the course of months, Clara came back and stayed each night the Khab children were moved to the next place on their journey to reunion. First to the refugee camp. Then to Bangkok. Then to Washington Dulles International Airport. Finally, in September, the children boarded their last flight, to Kansas City International Airport.

Martha and Erik offered to pick them up in their conversion van. Clara rode in the back with Mai and Mahasajun. None of them spoke the entire drive. They waited at the gate, the parents huddled together in a pair of chairs. Clara and Martha paced the lounge. Erik stared out the window at the tarmac.

Finally, at nearly 11:00 p.m., the plane eased up to the jetway.

Mai and Mahasajun rose from their seats. Clara barely breathed, afraid of waking everyone from this impossible dream.

The moment the children appeared in the doorway, Mai wailed. Mahasajun fell to his knees. Two small, thin humans raced across the lounge, shedding their meager bags along the way, and thrust themselves into the open arms of their parents. The family's tears spilled together. Their cries blended into a symphony of relief.

Answered prayer despite insurmountable odds, joy birthed from pain, life brought out of death.

Clara's tears flowed as freely as the family's.

She was there to help them settle into bed that night, safe and together at last. She was there to help them explore their new city. She was there to help Mai learn American cooking—to boil hot dogs and bake chocolate chip cookies. She was there to walk her friend through the school enrollment process for her kids.

And she was the first one to whom Mai dared to whisper her heart's desire.

"My family. They must come too."

Thursday, June 9, 2016

Clara roused to the brilliant morning colors painted across her picture window, a lingering ache in her bones and a sure knowledge in her heart that Charles Slesher would die that day.

She needed to get to him. Whatever business he had outstanding with the Lord, it could not wait.

She wrestled off the bedsheet the night nurse had cloaked her in and unclipped the call button. Once free, she sat up and pulled the tray table closer. Linearly arranged on top were her glasses, her Bible, and the cup of water the nurse had left for her. Clara ignored the water, put on her glasses, and gathered her Bible.

Her house slippers were stationed next to the bed. She guided her feet into them, paused to pray for strength, then pushed herself up onto her legs. The shaky limbs protested at first but soon steadied. She headed to the bathroom for her dentures. The rest of her, the bunny-adorned yellow sleepwear and mussed hair, would just have to stay as it was.

Time was short, the work imperative.

At the door to her room, she poked her head out and peered down the hall. Finding it empty, she ambled forward. The closer she got to Charles's room, the more intense the draw on her heart became.

Lord, be near, she prayed and pushed open his door.

He lay with his face pointed to the ceiling. The head of the bed was angled upward at twenty degrees. The staff had stuffed pillows under his calves and feet, making his legs bend at the knees like a plateau.

Clutching her Bible, she shuffled to his bedside.

His skin had taken a distinctly ashen tone. The edges of his mouth were bluish-gray. The conviction proved true. He had a matter of hours.

"Good morning, Charles. It's me, Clara." She lowered into the armchair. "Did you have a good night?"

Silence hovered where raspy inhales once were. She counted, listening for an inhale. *One, two, three, four . . .*

When she reached ten, he finally took a breath, a rumbly, throaty inhale that drew his lower jaw slightly downward.

A laboring mother counted the shortening breaks between contractions to estimate the time to the first breath of her baby. Loved ones of the dying counted the elongating pauses between inhales to estimate the time to final breath. Of the many ironic reversals of life events, that one was perhaps the most bitter.

She opened her Bible. "Shall we pick up where we left off

yesterday, friend? We were working through the Psalms, if you recall. How about I find a morning Psalm? Seems fitting considering the beautiful sunrise outside. What do you say?"

She paused and listened, partly believing if she held still long enough, she could hear his response deep inside the chamber of his being. She studied her friend's face, imagined seeing it as the Father would. She traced its contours and the angle of the brow, the shape of the nose, the wisps of hair on his spotted scalp, the oblong ears with lobes that hung like fat teardrops. A unique human, created with his own mold. Created with adoring attentiveness, the Father falling deeper in love with his masterpiece with every brushstroke he made.

"I sure wish I had been able to see pictures of your life, Charles," Clara said softly. "To know more about you as a young man. What a treat that would have been."

She slipped her fingers around his limp hand. Brokenness joining to brokenness. Warmth covering cold. Love and pulsating hope reaching into the dark.

As she held on to him, she whispered the same words she had so many times over countless babies and hurting hearts she'd encountered since coming to know what her Savior had done for her.

"You are precious. Do you hear me? You are seen. You are known. You are longed for. Do you believe that?" She squeezed his hand. "So long as we have breath, the Lord calls to our hearts. And he is calling to you now, Charles. You can hear him, can't you? It's a wondrous sound. A wondrous invitation. A miracle! And it was written for you. Given for you. Freedom is there, Charles. Run to him, friend." She leaned closer and whispered with all the pleading stored up for him in her heart. "Run to him."

She cupped his hand in both of hers. *Lord, have mercy.*

She knew her Lord unfailingly heard those who stood in the gap. She knew he would move according to his will.

And she knew she wouldn't find out what would become of Charles Slesher until she stepped over heaven's threshold and called his name.

Still, she offered up all her strength for his sake.

Aidyn sat at her desk with her notebook opened to the dog-eared page. Of all the things she thought would end up on the pale blue lines, a list of possible ways for a seventy-nine-year-old woman to knock off never entered her mind. Yet, there they were. Forty-five possible demises.

Whatever Rahmiya thought of her younger brother's mind, it proved highly useful.

Pen in hand, she went down the list and starred the ones that seemed most appropriate based on what Mrs. Kip said she wanted. In the first fifteen lines, several suggestions earned a star.

Attacked by native tribesmen while attempting to rescue the kidnapped daughter of an emissary.

Rappelling off a skyscraper to save her family from a madman intent on blowing up the building.

Deep-sea diving to find a rare, endangered fish; attacked by ridiculously large shark.

Caught in a brutal typhoon while trying to kayak between the islands of Hawaii.

Carried off the bow of a crab boat by a massive swell in the Bering Strait.

Swallowed while trying to surf a thirty-foot wave.

Aidyn paused, noticing a pattern in the last few suggestions she'd starred. "Hope you like water deaths," she mumbled.

"You hope I like what?"

Aidyn looked up with a start.

"What are you babbling about?" Shayna set her off-brand bag on her desk.

"Nothing." Aidyn closed the notebook. "Thinking out loud."

"How about think in your head?"

Despite her instincts, Aidyn shot back, "You do realize 'think in your head' is redundant?"

Shayna halted unpacking her bag and narrowed her eyes. "Big talk for someone who takes three days to write an obituary."

Aidyn drew her lips into a hard line.

Shayna smirked. "Exactly." She finished unpacking and plopped into her chair.

Aidyn started to set her obnoxious neighbor straight that it had, in fact, been *two* days—but one simple question halted her tongue. How would Mrs. Kip handle someone like Shayna? Probably nothing like what Aidyn had in mind. She kept her mouth closed and let Shayna's slight float off to the corner of the room like the puff of air it was. Besides, more important things needed tending to, like checking her email for the latest tasks from Woods.

Her inbox indeed contained several requests, but it was a

message from Phyllis in Archives that drew her. The subject line read, "Follow-up on John Kip request."

She clicked it open and read,

Give me a call when you have a chance.

Curious, Aidyn picked up her desk phone and dialed the archivist's extension.

Phyllis answered on the second ring and got to the point. "I wanted to follow up on my email yesterday. I mentioned the search engine pinged on several other articles with the name Kip."

"Yes, I remember. They weren't for John, though, right?"

"Correct. But curiosity got the better of me and I read them. They appear to be about his wife."

Aidyn sat bolt upright. "You mean Clara?"

"You're familiar with her already, then?"

"In a manner of speaking." She turned to a blank page in her notebook and grabbed her pen. "What did these articles say about her?"

"It appears she had a rather interesting role in the history of Kansas City."

"You're kidding." Aidyn's pulse quickened.

"She and a woman named Mai Khab did a lot together. Have you heard of her?"

Aidyn jotted down the name. "Doesn't sound familiar."

"I have a feeling you'd remember if you had heard of her."

Aidyn put a big star next to Mai's name, along with a question mark.

"There are some pictures too," Phyllis continued. "I have

everything gathered in a folder if you want to come take a look."

Aidyn vowed to hug Phyllis as soon as she saw her. The break could not have come at a better time. With any luck, the articles would tell her all she needed, and the game of "Rewrite My Death" would end—giving her the open path to redemption and better, *actual* reporting work.

"I would love to take a look," she said as she tucked her pen inside her notebook. "I'll be right there. Thank you." She hung up the phone and leapt from her chair, drawing a scowl from Shayna.

"What's got you on fire?"

"Nothing." Notebook in hand, Aidyn turned to leave.

The ring of her desk phone stopped her. The screen showed the receptionist's extension, a signal someone had called the switchboard for her.

Though she itched to get to the archives, the rarity of a switchboard call was too intriguing. She peeked at her computer's clock. A little after 9:00 a.m. The department meeting was at 9:30. If she had even ten minutes in the archives, it should be enough. She snagged the receiver off its cradle. "Aidyn Kelley."

The receptionist announced, "I have Rosario Dia on the line for you."

Aidyn frowned. "Thank you. Put her through." She waited for the click of the transfer, then said, "Rosario?"

"Sorry to bother you at work."

"No worries. What can I do for you?" Aidyn considered sitting back down but held out hope that the conversation would be quick.

"I wanted to talk to you about Mrs. Kip. I heard what happened yesterday during your visit. That must have been scary."

Jarred. Still the most appropriate word to use. "I'm just glad I was able to catch her," Aidyn said, echoing the nurse's sentiments from the day before.

"Yes, me too, and that you weren't hurt in the process."

Risk to herself hadn't even been a consideration. She had simply reacted.

"Were you planning to come today?" Rosario asked.

"Yes, about three."

"Would you by chance be able to come earlier?"

"I'd have to check with my boss. Why?"

Rosario paused.

Something was about to drop.

"Mrs. Kip had another fall this morning. Unfortunately, no one was around to catch her."

A pinch of sympathy. She sat down. "Is she okay?"

"She has a black eye. By some miracle, it wasn't worse. So, in terms of the physical, she's doing fine. Emotionally, though, she's not doing well."

"She's embarrassed?"

"No, angry. At us."

"Why is that?"

"As you can imagine, we're deeply concerned about her safety and have strongly encouraged her to use a wheelchair to help avoid future falls."

"I'm sure she's completely on board with that." She glanced at the clock again. So much for a short conversation.

"Sometimes we don't see our own limitations," Rosario

said. "She is such a feisty woman, the staff is fearful of leaving her alone. Jimmy is with her now, attempting to keep her occupied, but she is a sharp woman and sees right through it. As a result, she's become rather agitated and sullen. Jimmy is doing his best to cheer her up, but it isn't working. Plus he really needs to be available for other patients. I was hoping you'd be willing to come now and be with her."

"Me?"

"Yes. I think you would be able to settle her down better than we can."

Aidyn guffawed. "I'm flattered you think I have some kind of magical influence over her, but honestly, I barely know her. I don't think I would make any difference. She doesn't exactly listen to what I say either."

After a brief silence, Rosario said, "Miss Kelley, let me be clearer. It's not whether you can get her to obey the rules, it's about you being there to represent what we can't."

"I don't understand."

"You remind her of good things," Rosario said tenderly. "Of things that are *possible*. And she needs that right now."

The words smacked into Aidyn. Something in her chest clicked open, like a tiny door unlatching. "But I barely know her," she insisted.

"The point is, she knows you. Will you come?"

The folder waited for her in the archives, the meeting was about to start, the to-do list in her inbox grew by the minute. And most of all, there was the jarring sight of a slack old woman. All valid excuses to say no, to insist she would come in later as originally planned. Yet caught in the middle of the swirl of reasons was the distant song of Mrs. Kip's giggle.

The old woman's bemused face, so delighted with herself and the life she had. Thin lips pulled back to oblivion, small eyes twinkling.

It hooked into Aidyn, sucked her toward that tiny door.

Her body clenched even as she said, "I'll see what I can do."

CHAPTER 15

Aidyn stood inside her editor's doorway, messenger bag already strung on her shoulder, and explained how "circumstances for Mrs. Kip" necessitated that she go to Sacred Promise immediately instead of that afternoon, which meant she'd have to miss the department meeting. She gave no details and certainly avoided any mention of her supposed persuasive powers over the deceasing woman. Such a detail would indicate the two of them had an emotional attachment, which first of all wasn't true (despite Rosario Dia's assertions) and second of all directly violated a cardinal rule of engagement with interviewees.

No emotional attachments. Ever.

Woods mulled over her request. "You can miss the meeting. But"—she held up a stubby finger—"I need you back here ASAP. You still have other jobs to do. Everything I sent you needs to be done today."

"Will do. I should be back by lunchtime." She took a step backward.

"How's it going with this woman, anyway?" Woods asked.

"Slowly. But getting there."

"What do you mean, 'slowly'?"

"Let's just say she has a way of drawing things out."

Woods puckered her brow. "And you're letting her do that why? You're in charge of the interview, Kelley. Find a way to make her talk. This is an obit, for crying out loud. It shouldn't take this long."

"I know, and like I said, I'm getting there. I have some good notes." Desperate to get the scowl off her editor's face, she added, "There are articles about her in the archives as well."

"Is that right?" Woods tilted her head a bit to the side. "What do they say?"

"I'm not sure. I haven't read them yet." She realized, much too late, her folly in the admission.

Woods blinked once, deliberately. "You haven't read them?"

Heat filled Aidyn's cheeks.

"You do know how to be a reporter, right, Kelley?"

Why was it she always made a fool of herself in front of Woods?

"I mean—I just found out about the articles. I was on my way to the archives when I got—"

Woods held up her hand, putting an end to the ineffective monologue. "You're really testing me."

Aidyn shifted on her feet.

"I'm going to give you three more days on this. That's it. Three days to turn in a Sifford-worthy obit."

Aidyn opened her mouth to defend herself further, then quickly decided against it. She gave a single, submissive nod. "Understood."

With a flick of her hand, Woods sent her on her way.

Nora leaned in, her face so close Clara could see the grayish-blue tint of her irises. With a gentle tap of her index finger, the nurse felt the swollen area around Clara's right eye. "Does that hurt?"

"Stop fussing over me. I'm perfectly fine."

"Should I take that as a yes?"

"You can take it however you please, I suppose."

"Scale of one to ten, what's your pain level?"

"Negative three."

Nora pursed her lips.

"I told you, I'm fine," Clara insisted. "Please go deal with other patients more in need of your skills."

Nora stood upright and crossed her arms. "You going to be mad at me all day?"

Clara shrugged. "I'll find out at the end of the day."

Shaking her head, Nora left Clara sitting in her armchair and skirted around the bed. "Jimmy, she's all yours."

The young man sat in one of the dining chairs with an amused look on his face.

"I don't need a babysitter either, thank you very much!" Clara called after her.

If the nurse heard her, she kept walking as if she didn't.

"Mrs. Kip, I'm just here to keep you company," Jimmy said.

"You're here to keep me guarded, honey. And I'll say it for the thousandth time: I need to get back to Charles. There was a reason I was in his room."

"And there's a reason you're in *your* room now." Jimmy pointed at her eye. "That was a nasty fall, Mrs. Kip."

Clara didn't remember if it was or not. She recalled praying, then waking up in her bed. Whatever happened in between she pieced together from what the staff told her. Chief among the details was the fact she was no longer trusted to navigate the whole thirty yards between her chair and Charles's chair by way of her own legs.

At least they had the good sense to let her get out of the godforsaken bed.

"I'm more hardy than I look, you know," Clara told the young man.

He grinned. "I do. Why do you think they have me on guard?"

Clara huffed, in no mood for wit, and turned toward the window.

"We could go anywhere you want to in the wheelchair," he said. "The chair's not so bad, is it? It looks comfortable. I bet it feels like riding on a cloud."

She glanced at the obnoxious thing on the other end of the loveseat. It sat there, waiting—mocking.

She looked square at Jimmy. "The only cloud I want to ride is the one Jesus gives me."

Her final say on the subject. She returned her gaze to the outside world.

The sky wore several wispy clouds on its chest that day. They possessed such simple elegance, such gentle promises of free flight. She longed to be among them, longed for the view from the other side. Where hospital beds and wheelchairs and death rattles didn't exist.

175

Questions circled Aidyn's mind as she drove. Newer, more pressing questions.

Who was Mai Khab? At what point did Mrs. Kip know her? Was she still around? What could the pair have possibly done to influence the history of a city?

Regardless of what the archives had waiting for her when she got back to the office, hopefully Mrs. Kip herself would help her begin to piece the story together.

When she arrived at Sacred Promise, she signed the guest book as usual, leaving her name on the second line under June 9. After two days of visiting the facility, hers was one of only a few names in the registry. Not entirely unexpected considering how the place still gave her the willies. The atmosphere sagged around her, as if even the structure of the air succumbed to the weight of depression.

Clutching her bag's strap, she started for the activity room with light steps, careful not to disturb the eerie quiet.

"Miss Kelley, wait up!" Rosario came down the hall after her. "You made good time."

"It's 9:45. Not much traffic."

"We so appreciate you doing this. Mind if I walk with you? I was headed that way anyway."

"Sure."

They fell into a slow stride.

"Has Mrs. Kip settled down any?" Aidyn asked.

"She's started referring to Jimmy as her parole officer, if that answers your question."

"She's taking it that hard?"

"We've had worse."

Heaven only knew what that meant.

After a few paces, Rosario continued, "It's really no surprise she's having such a hard time with the loss of independence, after the life she's had."

Aidyn perked up. How much of Mrs. Kip's story did Rosario know? Until that moment, she hadn't seemed like a source. With measured coolness, Aidyn began to fish. "She's had quite the life, hasn't she?"

"Oh my goodness, yes. Isn't it just amazing what she and Mrs. Khab did?"

Aidyn tingled. Clearly Rosario knew the story.

"Absolutely," she replied, then tried out the archivist's opinion. "They changed the history of the city."

"Have you had a chance to read her journals, then?"

Aidyn held fast to her even expression, refusing to give herself away. "Not all of them."

"I'm so curious what they say. What details they give."

"Me too," Aidyn replied calmly. *Me too!* she screamed internally.

Journals. There were journals! They had to be somewhere in Mrs. Kip's room. She traced the room in her mind, attempting to locate them via memory.

They rounded the corner into the north hallway, and Rosario suddenly came to a stop. Aidyn did too.

Rosario turned to her, a pleading look on her face. "Knowing what you know about who she is and what she's been through, I'm sure you can appreciate how important it is to feed her spirit. Can't you?"

Not sure what to say, Aidyn nodded. "Of course."

Rosario looked down for a moment, as if gathering her thoughts. "The loss of independence is hard to overcome for spirited folks like her. I've seen too many of them go downhill fast once they reach this point, and it's never easy to watch. The bitter irony of it is awful."

Sadness gathered at the edges of Rosario's eyes.

"I know you're here because you have a job to do. But, Miss Kelley, I ask you to remember what you represent to her. As staff members, we represent the need for her to accept her situation as it is. But you? You represent something far more meaningful to her. Something far more craved by her soul. You represent a world beyond her limitations. A world where stories have life."

Aidyn listened and tried to discern what she was supposed to take from it all.

"Keep reminding her of what's possible," Rosario continued. "Help her find ways to cling to that indelible vibrancy of hers. Quite selfishly, I'm not ready to see her spark fade."

Every ounce of Rosario's plea pressed in on Aidyn—a plea she was wildly unsuited to fill.

You severely overestimate my role, she wanted to say. *You've got the wrong idea. This whole assignment is just a reprimand.*

Response after response marched forward in her mind, ready to be counted legitimate, true, undeniable. She had come only to get her interview for the day—hopefully her last—and then go back to the office to finally put together a winning draft that appeased her editor and proved she was not incompetent.

How had she ended up in the middle of someone else's mess?

But once more, Mrs. Kip's laugh called across the chasm.

The innate desire for connection that Aidyn had been trained to keep locked up awoke, and it rattled the bars of its cage.

February 17, 1976

Clara vowed not to take "no" for an answer. A "maybe" was equally unacceptable. Only a "yes" would do.

She stood patiently on the other side of housekeeping manager Gary Henderson's desk as he glanced through the handful of applications she had given him.

He looked up from the papers with a frown. "This is not how we normally do things."

"I'm aware of that, Henderson. But they don't speak English. *Yet*, that is. I'm working to resolve that minor detail."

"That's hardly a minor detail, Clara. They don't understand the language we speak. How would I give them instructions if I can't talk to them?"

"No offense to you, but sweeping floors and cleaning up spills is a pretty universal skill. It doesn't exactly require special talents."

"Some offense taken, actually, but I'll excuse it because you're clearly passionate about these men."

"I am. I will vouch for every single one of them. And their sons, their daughters, their dogs, their gerbils—whoever. These men are hard workers. You have never seen harder workers, and they are hungry to work. They have been through hell, Henderson. All they want is a new life, a chance at—"

He threw up his hand. "Thank you, Clara. I get it."

"I doubt it," she muttered.

His brow narrowed, but he let the comment slide. "Look, it's nice what you're trying to do." He let the papers fall from his hand onto the desk. "It truly is a noble thing. But I can't see how this could possibly work."

Clara clamped her hand to her hip. "Why not? Tell me what the problem is."

"You mean, besides the fact they can't speak English?"

"*Yet*," she said. "Can't speak English *yet*."

"Yet or never—for my purposes, it's the same difference."

"There is nothing in the job description that says an applicant must speak English."

"The job description is written in English. It's implied." A vein began to bulge in Henderson's forehead.

Clara dug in. "You want people who can do the work, and they are motivated to do the work. Let's find a way to make this a go."

"No, Clara. The roadblocks are too numerous."

"What are they?" she asked. "Tell me. The top five."

Henderson stared at her in disbelief or irritation. Likely both.

She arched an eyebrow in challenge.

Finally, he sighed. "This conversation is going nowhere. The dangers of having non-English-speaking custodians are too great to patient safety. Period."

Clara crossed her arms and glowered at him. "You know something, Henderson? I have never seen the vast smallness of American minds until I've attempted to get them to wrap around the concept of hospitality toward outsiders."

"You're being a little overdramatic. Not to mention increasingly insulting."

"Good! You need a little knock against the pedestal."

He started to say something, but Clara cut him off.

"Have you had to sneak through your own country in the dead of night because both the indoctrinated citizens and the crazy men who took over the government want to murder you? Have you ever had to risk the lives of your children in order to find a safe place to sleep or to forage for food?"

The manager sat back against his chair, the joints of his jaw bulging.

"Have you ever had to put your life into the hands of a complete stranger in the hopes of escape, praying to God they would not sell you out for a few dollars?"

Henderson didn't say a word.

"These men will do whatever you tell them to do. They are more than qualified, and they are insanely thankful to be here. The language barrier will dissipate soon enough."

After a brief pause, Henderson cleared his throat. His voice was quieter. "That may be, but the reality remains that patient safety is at stake here. The hospital has sanitation standards—state-issued standards—that we must follow. I can't teach them those things, plus how to properly handle biohazards, not to mention how to navigate secure areas, if we don't speak the same language."

She lifted her chin. "Of course you can. All you have to do is show them."

Though he moved his mouth, no words came out, a sure sign he found himself in a corner.

"Let them shadow your people for a month, Henderson.

They will learn fast. I guarantee it. These are smart men. Clearly. They outwitted the Communists, for crying out loud."

Henderson reached up and rubbed the stubble on his chin.

It was clear he could still go either way. Clara took a step forward, planted her hands on the edge of his desk, and leaned toward him. "I can appreciate your hesitation, Henderson. You care about standards, and that is also noble. But let me point out to you that one of these men was a dentist in his home country and another was a construction manager. They *get* standards, and they will respect every one you show them. The first time, every time. Believe me, you will not regret hiring these men."

Henderson stared at her for a long, silent moment. Then he looked at the pile of applications.

All four Laotian refugees received night-shift job offers the next day.

Within three years, fourteen refugee men had supported their newly resettled families with similar facilities-related jobs on the campus of KU Med.

CHAPTER 16

June 9, 2016

They whispered about her with hands over their mouths, as if such measures magically hid it all. Clara attempted to ignore the three of them—Rosario, Jimmy, and Aidyn—and gazed at the clouds. How lovely it would be to sail among them, floating serenely above the fray, above the earthbound reality she was stuck in.

But the hushed chatter on the other end of the room proved too irritating. She tore her eyes away from the sky and scowled at the group. Rosario saw her first, followed quickly by Aidyn. Their twittering stopped. The girl startled at seeing Clara's full face for the first time that morning. Hopefully someone had warned her about the bruised eye.

Jimmy, bless him, tried to break the ice. "Look who's here, Mrs. Kip!" He held out both arms like a game show host to indicate Aidyn.

"My afternoon schedule changed, so I decided to come this morning," the girl offered.

"Mm-hmm," Clara replied. It was pretty clear what had caused the so-called schedule change.

"I hope I'm not interrupting anything," Aidyn added.

"Only my imprisonment."

"Mrs. Kip," Rosario reproached gently.

Without replying, Clara resumed her study of the outside world. Truth be told, Aidyn's arrival earlier than expected was delightful. Things felt better with her around. If Clara could extricate the girl from the influence of the big worrywarts currently taking up unnecessary residence in her room, then she could have Aidyn take her to see Charles without the nuisance of a wheelchair.

She had convinced far more stubborn people of far more difficult things.

As the quiet conferencing continued, Clara turned toward the pergola alone on the lawn. She ached to sit once more in the shade of its vines, the breeze whispering over her cheek, the warmth of the sunbaked earth rising up to embrace her. She closed her eyes, snuggling further into the daydream.

The soft thud of a door closing brought her back to awareness.

Only Aidyn remained in the room, looking even more uncomfortable than the day before, which seemed impossible. What had Aidyn been told to make her don an expression like that?

Slowly the girl came over and settled herself and her bag on the loveseat.

They stared at each other, both ready to get on with other plans.

Finally, Aidyn cleared her throat. "So. How's it going?"

"Splendid," Clara replied flatly.

The girl tapped her fingertips together, clearly searching for something to say. She peeked to her right and noticed the wheelchair parked insultingly close by, then turned to Clara. "Have the hummingbirds been by today?"

"I don't really know, honey. I've been a little preoccupied this morning."

"Right." She dropped her gaze to her lap.

Clara winced at the resigned reaction. She was being a heel, a superb heel. The girl was trying, and besides, she had nothing to do with why Clara was in a tizzy. Quickly Clara thought of something friendlier to say.

"I suppose you noticed my shiner." She pointed to her eye.

"I did. How'd that happen?"

"Got into a scuffle over the last cookie."

The girl grinned, obviously knowing the truth. "Sounds like an eventful day."

"That's one word for it." Clara sighed, then gestured at the wheelchair. "You also noticed my new luxury ride."

"I did."

"Straight off the showroom floor, apparently. What do you think?"

"I can tell you don't like it."

Clara curled her top lip in disgust. "What's to like? It's the color of a headstone."

"A headstone?" The girl examined the wheelchair. "Why do you say that? Because it's black and gray?"

"Exactly. It's like a precursor."

"But it's also shiny. See?" Aidyn pointed at the bars connecting the different parts. "Headstones aren't shiny."

"It's still a repulsive piece of machinery, and I have no use for it."

The girl looked at the wheelchair thoughtfully, then back at her. "It's not the most attractive, but it does look comfortable. Maybe it's a really smooth ride."

Clara eyed her. "They told you to say that, didn't they?"

By the look on Aidyn's face, Clara had guessed correctly.

"Of course they did," she muttered. "Squares."

"They care about you, Mrs. Kip. They don't want to see you get hurt."

"Bless all their hearts. If only they would care a little less obnoxiously."

Aidyn's quiet laugh came as a surprise. Their gazes locked. A hint of empathy showed in Aidyn's expression that hadn't been there the day before.

"You know, Mrs. Kip, I was thinking." Aidyn clasped her hands. "It's a nice day. What if we took our visit out to the courtyard again? You love being out there, don't you?"

Clara glanced at the window, at that pergola and the promise of a warm embrace from creation. The ache flared. "You want to bust me out of here?"

"Sure. If you want to go."

"You going to make me ride in that thing?" She gestured at the wheelchair.

The girl lifted her eyebrows expectantly.

"No thank you, then."

"You're going to be sitting outside anyway."

"I said no thank you." She turned away. The refusal felt as childish as it sounded. But she simply couldn't bring herself to entertain the notion of using a wheelchair. She still had strength in her legs. Surely she did. If only everyone else would listen.

Silence lingered.

At last, Aidyn suggested, "What if we put a new life to it, Mrs. Kip?"

Curious, she faced the girl.

Aidyn scooted forward on the loveseat, leaning onto her knees. "What if we rewrote it to be something . . . extraordinary?"

Clara's heart lifted like a balloon, but she stayed cautious. "Continue."

"I can think of something else that is black, gray, and shiny."

"What?"

The girl grinned. "A motorcycle."

The floating sensation spread throughout Clara's body. Her imagination begged to come alive, to run free, right alongside the girl's.

"The Harley kind," Aidyn continued. "With rumbly mufflers."

Clara tried fruitlessly to keep a smile in check. It ticked up the corners of her mouth. "The kind that disturbs dogs and scares young children?"

"And rattles windowpanes."

Clara's smile broke loose. "That's a thrill, isn't it?"

Aidyn chuckled. Then she swept her arm toward the wheelchair. "Ever ridden a Harley?"

When Clara's eyes fell on the repugnant contraption again, it seemed to have taken on the colors Aidyn painted. The colors of extraordinary—and compassionate—strokes.

She peeked at Aidyn. "You really want me to get in that thing, don't you?"

"You said you wanted to bust out of here."

They both turned and studied the one thing that stood in the way of the courtyard.

Into the quiet, Aidyn's soft voice floated. "Clara Kip was a renowned test driver for Harley-Davidson's innovative Atomic Force line, which pushed the limits on speed and agility." She spoke with inflection, like a narrator on a documentary. "During a test run of the latest AF-40 prototype, Kip was thrown from the bike after swerving to avoid a fox kit that had wandered onto the track. Her final words were, 'Did you see me fly?'"

Little by little, the tale soaked into Clara, the way the girl's nervously whispered suggestions had the afternoon before, when she didn't know Clara could hear her. The imaginative new life Aidyn gave the thing that Clara despised dethroned her pride and tickled every inch of her body.

"Where have you been hiding that creativity, Miss Kelley?"

The girl laughed. So did Clara.

She nodded. "All right, honey. Let's ride."

———

Aidyn crouched and unfolded the footrests. "Right foot first, Mrs. Kip."

The old woman obeyed, lifting her foot and easing it onto the rest.

"Now the left."

Aidyn smiled internally. Rosario had been correct. She did possess some kind of influence over Mrs. Kip. An influence she needed to appreciate. That sway could work to her advantage, but how remained to be seen.

With the old woman settled safely in the chair, Aidyn stood and adjusted her messenger bag on her shoulder. "How do you feel?" she asked.

"Like an outlaw biker."

"In this case, that's wonderful news." She stepped around to the back of the chair and unlocked the brakes. The chair glided forward easily at her command.

For the first time since she'd arrived, she had the chance to scan the room. Rosario had said Mrs. Kip had journals, but where?

Two nondescript white boxes sat on the dining table. No labels, no explanations, no hints. Only a basic 1 and 2 numbering system. That had to be them, surely.

"Still have some unpacking to do, Mrs. Kip?" she asked.

"That stuff isn't staying here," the woman said simply, then gestured toward the door. "Come on, honey, let's get out of here while I'm still conscious."

Aidyn slowed as they neared the boxes, wanting to press the issue. Reluctantly, she steered away from the table.

When they got to the hallway, she turned the chair to the right, toward the exit for the courtyard. Thankfully, Mrs. Kip did not ask to see the man next door. From what Aidyn could tell when they passed by, he was still alive. That was enough information for her.

She hit the automatic door assistance button and rolled Mrs. Kip outside.

The midmorning sun had warmed the earth to a pleasant seventy-two degrees. Overhead, birds swooped from treetop to treetop, singing all the way with glee. The massive blue sky stretched wide, coaxing all it dominated to look up at its brilliance.

Aidyn squinted and silently lamented the fact that she'd left her sunglasses in her car. Mrs. Kip, meanwhile, tilted her head back and let the whole of her face be kissed by the rays, the same reaction she'd had the last time they visited the courtyard. As if she breathed in the open with her entire being. Inspired, Aidyn, too, lifted her face to the sky and filled her lungs with the smell and feel of the created world.

Admittedly, heaven did seem closer.

She guided the wheelchair along the path. "I'm glad you wanted to come out here, Mrs. Kip."

"I'm glad you convinced me."

Aidyn grinned. "I came up with a pretty good suggestion, didn't I?"

The woman laughed. "Indeed, that was quite the extraordinary death."

"Thank you." Even Aidyn was surprised by her creativity. Maybe Mrs. Kip also had an underappreciated influence. "So, if I'm not mistaken," she continued, "that means I get three questions."

"That's our agreement, Miss Kelley. And I am champing at the bit to hear what you've got."

Where should she even begin? She needed questions that would give her the most words in return, the most clues, and hopefully she could back into the story of Mai Khab and the tale of history being changed. Finally a great kick-off question formed.

"You obviously like extraordinary stories. What was something you did in your life that others would consider extraordinary?"

"You're assuming a lot with that question," Mrs. Kip said as they reached the edge of the pergola. "I told you my life is exceedingly unimpressive."

"I seriously doubt that. You're too impressive to have lived unimpressively."

"My, you sound like a writer."

Aidyn parked the wheelchair by the same bench as last time and came around to face Mrs. Kip. "And you sound like you're stalling."

The old woman pursed her lips, clearly knowing Aidyn had seen through her. Finally, she relented. "I suppose there was this one thing."

Aidyn sat and retrieved her notebook and pen from her bag.

Mrs. Kip looked off in the distance as she recounted the memory. "I once knew this boy named Joshua. He was from a very poor family that had immigrated to America. They had nothing. Not even beds for a long time. Joshua was the sweetest soul, and he had such a hard time adjusting to living in this country. He came as a twelve-year-old, so he didn't know the language, and he didn't understand baseball, and he didn't know any of the comic book characters. So, as you can imagine, school was torture for him. His mother worried constantly. His younger sister did okay, but Joshua was such a shy guy, and the odds were stacked against him from the beginning. One day, I asked him if he wanted to learn to play baseball. Well, of course, he lit up and said he did. I decided I would teach him myself. Just the basics, mind you, I'm no Joe McCarthy."

Aidyn put a plus sign by the name, her shorthand for "look up that guy later."

"To help, I gathered other boys who could model for him the fundamentals of playing. We met twice a week after school on the playground's baseball field. Over time, Joshua learned to hit a ball, how to throw and catch, how to run the bases, and how to steal a base—which was his favorite part. But the beautiful thing was, along the way, he started to pick up English, especially the way the other boys spoke it. He also made a couple of friends who helped him out in school. They would pack extra food in their lunches for him to have when he needed it. Eventually he joined a summer league team with those boys, and they remained close until Joshua and his family moved away." Mrs. Kip looked at Aidyn. "That may not sound extraordinary to some people, Miss Kelley, but we should never underestimate the life-changing gift of friendship."

The last sentence caught Aidyn and drew her attention away from her notes. She stared at Mrs. Kip, attempting to process the wisdom, as it deserved.

Mrs. Kip jiggled a finger at the notebook. "Write that down, honey. That was gold I just gave you there."

Aidyn smiled. "It was. Thank you." She jotted notes as several follow-up questions to the Joshua story swirled in her mind. So many possible directions to go, details to mine about how Mrs. Kip met Joshua's family and where they had emigrated from. But she couldn't waste her remaining two questions on rather narrowly focused inquiries. She needed to lead Mrs. Kip to Mai Khab.

Perhaps the concept of friendship was the key.

"How has friendship made a difference for you?" she asked.

The woman took a deep breath, as if pulling in air would help her line up her thoughts better. "Friendship has saved me more times than I can count, Miss Kelley. Like having Martha after Johnny died. She was a godsend. Those first years were brutal. Life had been flipped on end. All my plans and dreams changed the instant that knock fell on my door. Unless you've been through something like that, it's hard to understand what it's like. Every minute detail of your existence is ripped away and replaced with something foreign. You begin to wonder if you're even the same person."

Aidyn watched Mrs. Kip speak as much as she could between taking notes. The details of a person's expressions are where a quarter of any story is told.

"When things like that happen, you need friends, Miss Kelley. You need the Lord more than anything, but in his benevolence, he often shows up in the form of friends. Like Jonathan for David in the Bible. People like Martha were the Jonathan for me in those years. Did I tell you she was the one who got me to go to counseling?"

Aidyn shook her head.

"I still love her for that. She knew I needed it, and she had been a friend enough to say so. I was grieving something awful and couldn't see how it was limiting me. One of the things I had a particularly hard time with was letting go of the dream John and I had of caring for the orphans in São Paulo. After he died, I tried so hard to honor our dream and go to Brazil, even for a short-term trip. Several times I had plans in place, but each time, the Lord said no. It wasn't my story to live."

The hurt of it rang through Aidyn. A lifelong dream never being realized after so much work and prayer seemed too painful a fate. And unfair. What if that happened to her? "I can't imagine how hard that must have been."

"Hard is a good word for it, honey. But God was good to provide a better story. His stories usually are better than anything we can come up with. He gave me lots of friends and love and adventure, right where I was. I was short on family, but I was never low on blessings."

Aidyn took her time to write down those words. They lit her mind and stirred her heart.

Mrs. Kip had revealed so much in that one answer. So many things Aidyn could dig into. But only one question remained before she had to break momentum and suggest a new death. The old woman was on such a roll, the worst thing would be to interrupt it.

The time had come to stop pretending she didn't know an important detail of Mrs. Kip's life. It was time, at long last, to get to the core of things and to find out if the "better story" Mrs. Kip referenced was indeed what she suspected it to be.

"Mrs. Kip?" She waited until the woman met her gaze, because she especially needed to see the expression that would come. "Who was Mai Khab?"

CHAPTER 17

Hearing Mai's name unexpectedly on Aidyn's lips was one of the most startling—and most beautiful—moments Clara had experienced in a long time.

Her heart leapt at the thought of what this would mean for Aidyn. God was connecting the chapters he was authoring in the girl's days. Threads weaving seamlessly as only the Master can do. The breeze from his busy hand tickled Clara's soul.

"Oh, Miss Kelley," she breathed. "The Lord is up to something. Even now."

Aidyn frowned. "What?"

Eventually she would understand. Someday.

"Never mind my babble, honey. Tell me how you found out about Mai."

"Actually, I sort of just happened upon her name in connection with yours. I don't know much about her, other than she was a friend of yours and you two did some big things together."

"Big things, huh?" Clara chuckled. "Anything we happened to achieve was God, not us. Of that I can assure you. We were bumbling fools half the time. More than half the time, really."

Aidyn readied her pen. "Sounds like a story I'd love to hear."

Her eyebrows were pointed up in anticipation, her eyes open to see, her ears open to receive. No doubt she would indeed treat the story with love, as Bella Woods had predicted.

It was the story Aidyn had been meant to find.

Clara settled into the wheelchair and began. "I met Mai in the hallway of KU Med in May 1975."

Over the course of the next several minutes, she laid out the events in the first months after meeting Mai with as much accuracy as she could muster, thanks to the journals. She explained the sordid Vietnam-era politics between America and Laos, and how two parents found themselves completely at the mercy of a foreign government they didn't understand or necessarily trust. She spoke of the long nights holding Mai's hand, kneeling in prayer. The waiting. The crying. The sore knees. She told of the agencies involved and the daring escape plan. She shared what she knew of the horrors in the refugee camp, where the two terrified children stayed for weeks with only a single change of clothes and lonely dreams of their parents' voices.

Then, in joyful crescendo, she told of the miraculous day the children finally stepped off the plane, safe and relieved, and leapt into their parents' aching arms.

Recounting it welled up all the old emotions, as if the events were as fresh and real as when they first happened.

More than ever, Clara longed to reunite with Mai, wherever she was.

When Clara finished, she turned to Aidyn, who sat stock-still, jaw hanging loose, taking it all in.

"Wow," Aidyn said softly.

Her reaction made Clara giggle. "You bet, wow. That's a big-God wow right there."

The girl shook her head, clearly still in amazement. "I had no idea anything like that happened back then."

"Many times over, honey."

"What happened after the kids arrived in Kansas City?"

Though she kind of hated to do it, considering the massive headway they had just made, they did have an agreement, one Clara was bound to keep. She cleared her throat. "Well, I very much want to answer that question, but I do believe that is number four."

Aidyn's expression melted. "Seriously?"

"Annoying, isn't it?"

"A little bit." Aidyn sighed from the unjust burden, then quickly perked up. "You died fighting against Communist insurgents in the name of liberty and justice for all."

Clara laughed. "You are one clever girl, Miss Kelley!"

"Or maybe I'm just getting to know you better," she replied with a grin.

"That could be too. But really there's only one thing you need to know about me. It's the only thing I want anyone who ever has the misfortune of hearing my name to know about me."

"What's that?"

She jiggled a finger at Aidyn's notebook. "Write this down

and put a star next to it. I want it to be known that I did my utmost to leave in my wake the love Jesus first gave me. I came to trust him later in life than most, when I was thirty-six, after many years of being angry at him for all he had taken away from me. But he is a God of new life, Miss Kelley. A God of rescue and redemption. Always has been, always will be. After I surrendered my life to him, he gave me plenty of opportunities to share the love he first gave me, starting with the babies in the KU Med nursery. I did what I could for those babies and then for everyone else who was put in my life, regardless of how long or short my time was with them. Even when it cost me something dear, I loved. No effort in Jesus's name is ever wasted. Am I making sense?"

The girl nodded, writing.

"That's the heart attitude I carried forward into everything that happened next, which I promise I'm going to tell you once this ramble ends."

Aidyn laughed softly and continued to write.

"I did nothing amazing, Miss Kelley," she insisted. "Despite what you've been told. I simply tried to love people as best I could for as long as I was privileged to be with them. We don't stay long in each other's lives—that's the crux of our humanness. You have to be the friend people need while they are there with you, because it's the only chance you'll get."

Clara watched Aidyn take down the quotes. Maybe some of them were headed for print, maybe not. Either way, she prayed the words would find root in the girl's soul.

"More than you asked to hear," Clara said.

"It's okay," Aidyn said. "I appreciate all you shared."

"But really you wanted to know the answer to your question . . . which was what again?"

The girl chuckled. "I asked, after the Khab kids arrived in Kansas City, what happened next?"

"Next?" Clara thought for a moment. "Next we got the others."

September 28, 1978

Clara rubbed her friend's hands between her own. "It's going to be okay, Mai. I'm right here with you."

"I don't speak English well," Mai protested. Her unaccustomed tongue still bent English sounds in ways they weren't supposed to go. She had raised the same protest repeatedly since the phone call from the *Star* reporter.

"Whatever you have trouble saying, you tell me," Clara said. "I'll explain it to him, okay?"

Mai nodded, though she clearly harbored reservations.

They waited for the reporter outside the main doors of Clara's church, as he'd requested. Students for the evening classes continued to arrive. They smiled, nodded, and sometimes hugged the pair of women, greeting Mai in Lao and Clara in their beginning English.

"Well done," she told each one who dared the adopted tongue.

Considering how difficult Lao was to her, she always graciously told them "well done" even if they butchered the pronunciation or placed emphasis on the wrong syllable, which happened often. Her attempts at Lao didn't sound much more lyrical.

By 5:37 p.m., the last of the stragglers had arrived for the sessions that had started seven minutes prior. Clara and Mai found themselves alone on the front stoop of the church, watching for an unfamiliar car to turn into the parking lot.

The time and location for the interview were by design. The reporter "definitely" wanted pictures of the classes.

"This will help, yes?" Mai asked. "You sure?"

"Stop worrying, friend. Your story is worth telling, and you are going to do a fantastic job at it. It will certainly help the mission, as well as other refugees."

Mai did not look convinced. "Maybe Mahasajun need talk to him." She took a step for the door.

Clara caught her and pulled her back. "He's already started the Bible class."

"He better speaker."

"Your husband sent you for a reason." She reached over and lifted Mai's chin with her index finger. Doubt gathered in those big brown saucers as they stared up at Clara. "Do you trust him?"

Mai nodded.

"Do you trust God?"

Mai nodded again.

"Then lean into that. The Lord will give you all the words you need. It's not about whether they sound pretty. It's about what he will do with them. Hear me?"

Mai looked at her for a moment, then nodded once more.

"Good."

Movement at the edge of the parking lot caught their attention. A leather-brown Cutlass pulled in.

"That's them," Clara said.

Once the car had parked, two men stepped out, one shorter with a camera bag draped across his torso and the other taller and carrying a small notepad.

"I'm here with you," Clara assured her friend.

The reporter smiled at them as he came up the front sidewalk with his colleague. "Clara Kip and Mai Khab, I presume?"

"You presume correctly." Clara stepped forward with her hand extended. The man's strong grip matched her own.

"Sam White," he said.

"Glad you could come, Sam." Clara released her grasp. "Welcome to the New Life Christian Mission evening classes. This is my friend Mai Khab."

He offered his hand to Mai. "Pleasure to meet you, Mrs. Khab."

Still unused to Western manners between the genders, Mai hesitantly reached out and gave a quick, weak shake.

"I hear you all are doing great things through the mission," the reporter told her.

Mai nodded, looking him in the eye only briefly.

Clara wrapped her arm around Mai. "We can't wait for you boys to see for yourselves what goes on here and how far these amazing people have come in such a short time. They will surprise the socks right off of you. Right, Mai?" She jiggled her friend's arm to entice her to speak.

"Yes," Mai replied softly. "Good things."

Clara smiled. She motioned for the men to follow them.

"Let's get to it." As she turned herself and Mai toward the door, she whispered to her friend, "Well done."

Mai lifted one end of her mouth in a half grin.

For the next hour, Clara and Mai escorted the *Star* men from room to room of the host church. They started with an adult classroom, where two members of the church, with the help of translators, taught the recently arrived refugees basic skills for living in America. The troop tucked into the back of the room and watched the lesson unfold.

"As you can see," Clara whispered to the reporter, "tonight's lesson is on how to shop at an American grocery store."

"No barter," Mai added hesitantly. "Big change."

The photographer moved about as deftly as possible to get several angles of students listening with intent.

The next stop was the children's rooms, where more church members helped kids from toddler through high school age practice reciting the English alphabet and identifying sight words.

"Many of the children will be the main teachers for their parents," Clara passed on to the reporter, who wrote similar words in his notebook. "We do offer conversational English classes for the adults too, but sometimes it's easier for their kids to help them on a daily basis."

The final stop was the chapel, where Mahasajun stood in front of the roomful of men and women with an open Bible. He spoke in Lao.

"What is he teaching?" the reporter whispered.

"The book of John, specifically," Clara told him. "He's teaching them the basics of Christianity."

"Are the people Christian?"

Clara turned to Mai, but her friend motioned for her to speak.

"Most of them are lifelong Buddhists," she said. "They heard about Christianity in the refugee camps. Several became Christians there and were hungry to learn more about the faith when they came to America. They are like sponges! As you can imagine, though, Lao-language Bibles are a bit hard to come by in Kansas, so he has to teach this way."

The reporter made notes as the photographer snapped more shots. "Seems like a big change. What made them become interested in Christianity?"

Clara looked expectantly at Mai, who rolled her lips inward in nervousness. Clara nodded toward the reporter, a gentle command for Mai to speak her story. To speak the people's story.

Slowly Mai leaned toward the waiting reporter and whispered with poignancy, "It give hope."

The reporter regarded her, processing her answer. When he looked down at his notepad to record her response, Clara took her friend's hand in her own and smiled proudly at her.

In that moment, standing there in the back of the chapel, as the Word was spoken over a room filled with people who looked nothing like her in a language she did not understand, Clara caught a glimpse of something breathtaking. A brief vision of Mai, bold and strong, helping hundreds upon hundreds of weary souls find hope.

A shiver trembled through her. She knew the Lord had even bigger plans for her friend.

Before the *Star* men left, the photographer insisted on a

picture of Clara and Mai together outside the host church's front doors.

Smiles. Arms around each other.

It was the picture that later graced the article.

The picture Clara treasured for the next four decades.

<hr>

June 9, 2016

<hr>

Aidyn stared in amazement at the words lining her notebook. An insider's look at the mission and the friendship behind it. Five pages' worth. Dozens of stars. Almost as many plus signs. *That* was a story Woods would be stoked she found. She shook her head, bewildered, and looked up at the woman who had lived the words.

That woman, now spindly and vulnerable to falls, had once helped reshape the city's cultural dynamic. A woman who hadn't fought a war or influenced the law of the land or won a major game, but rather, with quiet courage and immeasurable compassion, had helped ensure that refugees were not left to their own devices. The everyday woman who befriended and loved complete strangers, who stood in the gap between two clashing cultures not ready to wholly trust each other.

It all began because Mrs. Kip, intimately familiar with pain, once stopped amid her daily rush to comfort a grieving mother and unwittingly found herself in the center of world history.

Aidyn regarded the wilted woman before her and breathed

in wonder at all she had heard. "Mrs. Kip . . . that is stunning."

"The Lord deserves all the credit," she said.

"I think you deserve some of it too, though."

Mrs. Kip laughed off the suggestion. "Honey, I told you I was a bumbling fool the majority of the time. I had maybe five minutes of brilliance. And those Laotian friends of mine were largely self-sufficient. They just needed a good welcome and a little boost. Nothing Mai or I or anyone else did was out of line with common decency."

Aidyn raised her eyebrows. "I think you vastly overestimate common decency."

The woman reverently shook her head. "No, Miss Kelley. You vastly *under*estimate it. People are more compassionate than the media leads you to believe." Apparently remembering to whom she spoke, she quickly added, "No offense, of course."

"None taken," Aidyn replied with a shrug.

"You know better than I do, love, that negativity sells. But the truth is, sometimes people just need a little coaxing into—" Pain caught her, forcing her to shut her eyes momentarily and finish through clenched teeth. "Compassion."

Aidyn immediately tensed. The harbingers she had witnessed the day before were seared into her mind. She lowered her pen in caution.

Quickly the woman recovered and flashed a smile. "I'm totally fine."

Not convincing. Aidyn glanced at her watch. They had been at it for more than thirty minutes. No wonder the woman ran low on steam, especially considering the morning she had endured. With all Mrs. Kip had shared, certainly

Aidyn could find out the rest in those archive files, or in those journals, if she could get her hands on them.

"Would you like to go in?" she asked.

"But I'm having so much fun mesmerizing you," Mrs. Kip replied. "Surely you have other questions."

"I have a ton of questions, but I don't want you to wear out."

"Don't worry about me. Please continue."

Aidyn bit her lip. The phantom weight of the old woman's limp body pressed into her shoulder. "Are you positive?"

"One hundred and fifteen percent positive. What else would you like to know?"

Mrs. Kip appeared to be her normal, gregarious self again. Still, only a few more questions seemed wise, then Aidyn would insist they go inside, where at least the call button would be close by.

"You were saying people sometimes need a little coaxing toward compassion," she said. "What did you mean by that?"

"I mean that sometimes you have to find the tender spot in someone's heart. What would motivate them into action? What commonality do they have with the person in need of help? I searched for those tender spots, then used them to coax the people to compassion."

Aidyn mulled that over and aligned it with what Mrs. Kip had shown of her personality. The implication was clear. "You got in people's faces, didn't you?"

"A few times, yes."

Aidyn chuckled.

"Personal persuasion, Miss Kelley. That's what we'll call it."

Aidyn shook her head and jotted down a few notes. "You are something, Mrs. Kip."

"I have no regrets, except that I didn't start earlier. I would've helped a lot more people if I had."

"Did you 'personally persuade' people to do things besides help out at the New Life Christian Mission?"

The old woman looked off to the side in thought. She stayed quiet so long Aidyn began to worry. Finally, she responded, "You know, Miss Kelley, now that I think about it, this probably is a good time to go inside."

"Are you not feeling well?"

The woman sighed in exaggerated irritation. "Honey, I promise I will tell you if I'm not okay. Either that, or I'll pass out and there'll be no question in your mind."

"That's comforting, Mrs. Kip. Thank you."

She winked at Aidyn.

"Why is it you want to go inside, then?"

"There's something I want to show you. Actually, it's something I want to *give* you. I think they will answer your questions well."

Aidyn perked up. The journals. Immediately, she agreed, packed up her notebook, and stood with her bag draped over her shoulder. As she grabbed the handles of the wheelchair, Mrs. Kip made another of her signature odd requests.

"Listen, I'm not sure when I'll get out here again. They want to keep me caged like a dog, you know. So do me a favor, would you?"

Aidyn hesitantly asked, "What's that?"

"Let's ride like the wind on the way back. One last grasp at open freedom."

"You mean you want to go faster?"

"This is a Harley, isn't it?" She gestured at the chair. "Let's throw open the clutch. I want to feel my hair move."

Aidyn grinned. "Indelible vibrancy," indeed. Rosario had been spot-on about that too.

"As you wish, Mrs. Kip." She pushed forward across the pergola's decorative patio at a trot.

"Faster!" Mrs. Kip demanded.

Aidyn sped up to a light jog, her bag thumping against her backside. "Fast enough?"

"No! Shift it out of third, Miss Kelley!"

Aidyn started to run.

"Now we're talking!" the old woman shouted.

The cheer spurred Aidyn on. She ran faster down the sidewalk.

The woman howled with laughter.

Aidyn ran as fast as the wheelchair would allow, and Mrs. Kip spread out her arms, as far as a seventy-nine-year-old hospice patient can, to feel the air glide under her palms.

The same rush of air breezed over Aidyn's cheeks and tickled the edges of her hair. Such a simple act brought a thrill to the woman in the chair, a woman who seemed to possess more life in her final days than some people possessed in their whole existence.

Including Aidyn.

If only she could run forever, to keep the smiles on both of their faces, and allow the moribund woman's childlike laughter to continue echoing into the vast blue above.

She wanted to keep being the friend the old woman needed.

In far too short of a time, however, they reached the door.

CHAPTER 18

Undeniably, a spark flashed in Aidyn's expression when Clara mentioned having something to give her. Did she somehow know about the journals already?

Either way, the reporter was about to get even more of her story. From there, redemption—and whatever new doors were about to open.

How great God was to let Clara be a piece of Aidyn's unfolding story, and to give her the chance to glimpse him at work as he quietly connected the dots for his treasured young daughter. The Author of Life truly was a masterful yarn spinner.

How great are your works, O Lord, and how profound your thoughts!

"That was a fun ride," Aidyn said as the wheelchair bumped over the slight threshold of the door.

"It was, wasn't it?" But Clara's share of the delight quickly diminished when a new sense prickled her heart.

When they neared Charles Slesher's door, the prickle intensified.

"Hold up, Miss Kelley."

The wheelchair came to a stop. "What is it, Mrs. Kip?"

"Let's go check on my neighbor first. Do you mind?"

"If you'd like," the girl replied, a hint of apprehension in her tone. She directed the chair to the partially ajar door of room 309. When they were close enough, she leaned forward and pushed it open, giving them space to go through.

Heavy silence hung in the room.

Two paces in, Clara held up her hand for Aidyn to stop.

"I can take you closer," Aidyn whispered.

Clara shook her head and whispered back, "We won't be staying long. No sense disturbing him."

The white sheet covered Charles from neck to feet, his body barely pushing the cloth above the mattress. His jaw hung loose. The shadows around his eyes had darkened, off-setting his increasingly pallid complexion. When he took a breath, she counted as before. *One, two, three . . .*

At twenty-five, he inhaled.

Grief gathered in her chest.

She kept her voice low so Charles wouldn't hear. "He's going to die tonight."

"Are you sure?"

She nodded.

Aidyn came to the side of the wheelchair and knelt. "How do you know?"

"Because I'm seventy-nine, honey."

They turned and watched the man in the bed.

"I bet that will be hard on you, Mrs. Kip. You seem to care about him very much."

"Loss is hard no matter how many times you've been

through it." Clara studied the contour of Charles's profile, the slope of his forehead, the angle of his nose, the gentle drop of his lips. She etched them into her memory.

As if sensing Clara needed a few minutes in the room with him, Aidyn stayed still next to the wheelchair. After a moment, she leaned close and whispered, "What was it about Mr. Slesher that made you connect with him?"

"The fact he's a human."

"I mean specifically."

She turned to the girl. "That's as specific as it gets."

Aidyn didn't seem to understand. "It wasn't because you both have no family here with you?"

"We may have that in common, but I connected to him because he was here, and quite frankly, I had nothing better to do."

Aidyn grinned at the levity, then dropped off into thought. "May I ask you a personal question?"

"You may ask me anything."

"Do you ever wish you had children?"

Not a surprising question. Many people had asked her over the years.

"I wouldn't be honest if I said I never did have that longing or that it didn't hurt. But I learned a long time ago that women have the lion's share of God's tenderness attribute because it's one of our greatest opportunities toward others." She gestured at Charles. "Case in point."

Aidyn glanced at the man.

"I was still a mother, Miss Kelley, just not by the world's definition. I mothered people whether they liked it or not. And I was endlessly blessed by it."

The girl held her gaze. "I can say with confidence they were blessed too."

Clara held out her hands, and the girl slid one of hers into them. The youthful warmth invigorated Clara's weary bones. "Regardless of what's ahead for you, darling girl, I hope that you will use your love wisely. Give it away for its intended purpose, and don't be afraid to risk loss. Promise?"

Aidyn nodded.

"Authentic love is the greatest joy there is, Miss Kelley, but it requires a thousand little deaths to self."

Aidyn regarded her for a long moment, searching her expression. "That's beautiful, Mrs. Kip."

"Thank you. I'm sure I lifted it from someone much smarter."

"I'll give you credit anyway."

"Fair enough."

They turned once more to Charles. The words about love echoed through Clara's mind as she watched the fire fade within yet another friend, another person in whom she had invested. The thousand deaths part may have been an understatement. Surrender was an agonizing struggle.

"Mrs. Kip," Aidyn said, drawing Clara's attention, "what about your church family? Are you still a member of that church that hosted the mission?"

"I am, but I've been a shut-in for several years now. Those who are my age have their own health issues, so even if they wanted to, they couldn't get out to see me. It's too far."

"But surely the pastor will come."

"He will, at some point. He visited me in the hospital. But he's newer, younger, and he doesn't know me very well.

Plus pastors today have a lot more on their plates than they used to."

Aidyn looked uneasy. "So, you're basically alone?"

"Honey, I'm not alone. I never was. I may have been in between friends, but I was never alone. Somehow I always found myself with companionship right when I needed it the most."

Though the girl nodded, skepticism coated her expression.

After a moment, Aidyn asked, "Whatever happened to Martha and Mai?"

Clara grinned. "I do believe you've well exceeded your three-question maximum."

The girl rolled her eyes playfully, making Clara giggle.

"Come on, honey. Let's leave Charles to his beauty rest and go get those journals."

Aidyn agreed and rose to her feet, never asking what journals Clara meant.

April 28, 1979

"Which street is it?" Clara asked.

Mai looked at the directions Martha had hastily scrawled onto a piece of notepad paper. She scrunched her face and brought the paper closer to her eyes. "Oh-ttwa-ah?"

Clara attempted to look at the paper while still keeping her eyes on the road ahead. "Tell me how it's spelled."

"O-t-t-a-w-a."

"Ott-ah-wah," she pronounced slowly. "Ottawa. Okay, let's find it."

Together they searched for the street sign with the correct name.

"There!" Mai pointed at the street to the right only a dozen yards ahead.

Clara touched the brakes of her truck, but they approached the street too fast to slow down completely. "Hold on to your hot cross buns, Mai. We're going to do this!"

The force of the turn shoved both of them sharply to the left. Clara pressed against the door while Mai yelped and attempted to brace herself against the dashboard. The cargo in the back thumped against the bed.

Clara completed the turn and straightened out the truck. "Whoa, Bessie! Now that was fun!"

Mai, eyes wide and hands planted firmly on the dashboard, shook her head.

"Be a sport, Mai. I bet Pastor Otis got a kick out of it." She peeked in her side-view mirror at the pastor's white truck, which had noticeably slowed to make the turn in a more responsible manner. In the reflection, Clara could see the pastor laughing along with his passenger, Mai's oldest, Joshua.

"He think you crazy and so do I," Mai said, letting her hands come back to her lap.

"It helps to be a little crazy, friend. Makes life more fun."

Mai huffed playfully and directed her to more pertinent matters. "White house on right."

The destination was halfway down the block. The front door stood open, and stacks of boxes waited on the front porch. Despite a shutter missing from its picture window and the yard in dire need of mowing, the little house had charm. It was about the size of Clara and John's old place.

"I knew the Hollises would come through with something nice," Clara said as she parked along the curb. "Looks like they're already here."

The familiar Lincoln sat in the driveway, next to Martha and Erik's van.

"Nice couple," Mai said.

"They are. They just needed a little coaxing, right?" Clara giggled, and her friend smiled. "How many families does this make now?"

"Twenty-one."

Clara shook her head in wonder and repeated, "Twenty-one."

The federal government's laxation of private sponsorship of refugees "just so happened" to coincide with Mai's plea for help to get her loved ones out of the camps. Confident it was providential, Clara convinced Mai they needed to take full advantage of it. Together, the two women approached everyone they knew, particularly the church members, to step up to be sponsors for fleeing Laotian families. Mai had been especially gifted at turning hearts through no other mechanism than recounting her own story. The *Star* article extended her reach, just as Clara had predicted it would.

Clara looked again at her friend in admiration. "God is good, Mai."

"All the time," her friend finished.

They climbed out of the truck and met Pastor Otis and Joshua on the lawn.

"That was some trick move you had back there," Pastor Otis said.

"It was like a Steve McQueen stunt," Joshua said.

"I ride back with you, Pastor," Mai said.

They marched into the house to find it alive with activity. Clara paused to take in the scene.

The newly arrived couple stood in the living room of their new rental house talking in Lao with the Saysomphengs, who now boarded with Martha and Erik. The couple looked happy, relieved, and utterly exhausted. Their three children zipped in and out of the room with the two Saysompheng kids.

Keith and Evelyn Hollis were already busy unpacking boxes of household supplies and groceries donated by many church and community members. Martha and Erik helped ferry the items to the intended rooms.

A beautiful sight. It never grew old.

The Hollises had been among the hardest to convince to be sponsors, though they had both the resources and the heart. Fear was a powerful enemy, and Clara and Mai had to diligently address each of the couple's concerns. Then Mai had the brilliant idea to have Evelyn shadow Martha in her sponsorship duties with the Saysomphengs.

The Hollises submitted their application days later.

With a satisfied heart, Clara called out over the happy fray, "Furniture is here!"

The adults stopped what they were doing and looked toward the door.

The Lao women threw their hands and voices high at the sight of Mai, who scooted over to embrace each one.

The men, American and Laotian, shook hands with Pastor Otis, then followed him and Joshua out to the loaded trucks.

Martha approached Clara. "Did we get everything they need?"

"Almost. No one had a couch to donate, and we could only get one double bed."

"I'm sure we'll be able to get bunk beds for the kids at some point. And couches always have a way of appearing."

"I asked several people in our Sunday school class to keep their eyes out," Clara said. "And to help find more clothes for the kids."

Martha smiled and hugged her. "Can you believe we get to witness new lives beginning? It's like the nursery, but bigger."

"I think that's the most apt way to describe it, friend."

For the rest of the morning, the dual-culture crew worked to set up the little white house in the middle of the block in the middle of the city in the middle of the country. Save for that one goal and their shared humanness, they had virtually nothing in common.

Somehow it didn't matter.

It never did.

At lunchtime, Martha and Evelyn prepared a simple meal of turkey sandwiches, apples, and chips for the adults and Joshua. Meanwhile, Clara and Mai collected all the younger children into Martha's van and continued the welcoming tradition Clara had started with Joshua and his younger sister.

Their first taste of McDonald's golden fries.

CHAPTER 19

June 9, 2016

By the time Aidyn reached her desk again, it was nearly lunchtime. The white storage box landed with a soft thud on her desk as she set it down. Though Mrs. Kip had given her both boxes, one was all she managed to lug into the newsroom from her car in a single trip. Before she could remove the lid, her phone pinged.

Rahmiya
Can't wait to see what you got. Be there in a few.

Aidyn slid her phone next to her keyboard and prepared for Rahmiya's arrival. She hadn't left the Sacred Promise parking lot before texting her friend to implore her to meet up at her desk. Four exclamation points capped the message, in case Rahmiya had any doubts about the necessity of the meeting.

"These boxes hold a stretch of my lifetime," Mrs. Kip had

told Aidyn when she presented them to her. "The first one has journals from '71 to '74, and the other has journals from '75 to '80 or thereabouts. I wrote a lot about the people and the mission. If you read closely enough, you should find a lot of the answers to your questions in them."

Aidyn had eagerly reached to open the boxes right then, but the old woman stopped her.

"Please, honey, don't read them here. Go ahead and take them with you. You let me know tomorrow if you still have any questions. I need a little beauty rest myself."

Aidyn had agreed, then asked Jimmy to help transport both boxes to her car. Now here she was, the box labeled 2 waiting on her desk, fully hers. She shook her head in bemusement. The story had been right under her nose the whole time.

She glanced over at Shayna's desk. Conveniently, the senior reporter was out again, giving Aidyn the freedom to explore the box without prying eyes. Especially for a story as tender—and as headline worthy—as Mrs. Kip's, Shayna didn't deserve to be anywhere near it.

She pulled the box lid off. An undiscovered world—a hidden lifetime—opened wide its arms to receive her.

A dozen hardcover journals of various sizes and thicknesses lined up in a row at the bottom of the box. On top lay a single newspaper clipping, browned by age and air, along with a stack of pictures.

Aidyn gingerly picked up the clipping and unfurled it, careful of its fragile folds. In the faded photo accompanying the text, two young women smiled at her. One a younger, healthier version of Mrs. Kip, and the other a small Asian woman.

That first glimpse of Mai Khab pierced her heart. It was no wonder Mrs. Kip had been drawn to her.

Mrs. Khab had the smile and presence of someone who represented safe harbor. Instantly welcoming and interesting. An intangible quality that can only be possessed, not taught. She had long, dark hair tucked behind her shoulders and dark eyes set deep in their sockets yet twinkling boldly with her smile. She stood under the embracing arm of her friend, who was slightly larger in physical stature and clearly larger in personality. Mrs. Kip's smile had remained mostly the same since her younger days—hospitable and ornery. The last part claimed a bigger share.

What a joy it must have been to be in the same room as those two.

Aidyn grinned and took in the rest of the article, starting with the headline: "All in a Day's Work: Two Women Use Creativity, Connections to Help Resettled Refugees."

The article began with a rather dry but decent recap of the Khab children's journey to a Thai refugee camp. The reporter—a man named Sam White—could have done a better job of drawing out the heartrending nature of the event. He'd respectably explained how New Life Christian Mission came to be, as well as its services, but he clearly had approached the story in much the same way Shayna would have—strictly factual, more in honor of the inches allotted by the editor than to honor the lives the words represented and would potentially affect.

Aidyn shook her head. The story had been told, but not well. Not from the perspective of what it *meant*.

She laid the article on her desk faceup. Bypassing the stack of photos, she took out the first journal in the row, since it was most likely to be the first chronologically. On the inside of the cover, in neat, black-ink scrawl, a young Mrs. Kip had written "March 1, 1975." She would have been just shy of thirty-eight years old. Thirty-eight and about to stumble into a life-changing adventure.

"What's all this?"

Aidyn looked up from the journal. Rahmiya glided around her desk.

"Come look at this, Rahmi." She handed her the article. "Read it."

Within seconds, Rahmiya's lips parted. "Wow."

"I know, right? Amazing."

"It's incredible. This is her?" Rahmiya pointed at the picture of Mrs. Kip.

"Yep. Looks different now, obviously."

"She's cute. They're both adorable."

"I know."

Rahmiya lowered the clipping and looked inside the box. "What else did she give you?"

"Her journals. Some of them, anyway. She documented everything that was going on back then."

Her friend's eyes widened. "You're kidding."

"This is huge, Rahmi. Gold! If I weren't in the doghouse, I'd be pitching this to Woods, like, *now*. This is definitely a feature sitting here."

Rahmiya frowned. "Then why would you not take it to her?"

"I need to focus on getting through the obit first. Redeem

myself. Then, when things settle down, I'll pitch her. I've got plenty of time. It's not like this is on anyone else's radar."

Rahmiya shrugged. "I'd pitch her, but that's just me."

"You'd also email Maper, so . . ."

"Are you saying I give bad advice?"

"No. I'm saying I'm not going to listen to your advice."

"Yes, that's much less insulting."

Aidyn laughed and playfully elbowed her friend's arm.

Rahmiya winked in return, then pulled the photos from the box. She flipped through them, showing flashes of Mrs. Kip and her friend in various settings and poses, often with other, unfamiliar faces.

When she reached the end of the stack, Rahmiya set the pictures aside and surveyed the other contents of the box. "You going to read all these journals?"

"Eventually. If I do have a chance to write about this, I definitely will, and I'll dig deeper with research. I want to keep the story from Mrs. Kip's perspective, and her journals are great, but I need historical facts to complement them. I'll find out what our archives has, maybe hit up the library and the historical societies."

Rahmiya nodded and picked up the second journal in the row.

"Wouldn't it be something if the families were still around?" Aidyn asked her. "And what if they still remembered Mrs. Kip?"

"That would be something. Maybe you could . . ." Rahmiya trailed off, eyes fixed in the distance.

Curious, Aidyn followed her gaze.

Shayna.

The senior reporter moved slowly across the newsroom,

staring at the open file folder in her hands. Whatever was inside made her lips twist in concentration.

Quickly Aidyn put everything back in the box and closed the lid. She managed to hide the box in the shadows by her feet before Shayna sidled up to her own desk.

"Did you know," Shayna asked, reading from the folder, "that between 1975 and 1977, an estimated two thousand Laotian refugees resettled in Kansas City during one of the world's worst humanitarian crises in history?"

The blood rushed from Aidyn's face.

"That seems like an unexplored history highly relevant to today's world—a headline in the making—doesn't it?" Shayna looked knowingly, threateningly, at Aidyn.

All at once, Aidyn remembered the conversation with Phyllis and the folder she had been promised. She tensed. "What is that?"

"Something for you," Shayna said. "I ran into Phyllis in the cafeteria when we were both getting coffee, and she asked me to give it to you since apparently you skipped out on her earlier."

"That was kind of her." Aidyn held out her hand for the folder.

"It was, wasn't it?" Shayna flipped to a new item in the folder. "Makes me curious why you're researching the little-known history of refugee resettlement in the city. This certainly has nothing to do with anything I'm writing . . . *yet*, that is."

Aidyn dropped her hand and clenched her teeth. Shayna's greedy hands on an integral piece of Mrs. Kip's life story boiled her blood.

"Why are you researching this?" Shayna inquired.

"I asked her to help my brother on a term paper he's doing," said Rahmiya, always a quick thinker.

Shayna shut the folder with a huff and looked at Aidyn. "Why are you really?"

Aidyn remained silent.

"You honestly think Woods would give you something like this?"

Aidyn thrust out her hand. "Just give me the folder, Reese."

Shayna smirked. "Sure thing. I saw what I needed to see anyway." Holding out the folder, she added, "Thanks for the lead. You're a fantastic assistant. Good luck with the term paper."

Her phone rang, drawing her attention, and her leer, away from Aidyn.

As Shayna tended to the call, Rahmiya leaned toward Aidyn and whispered, "You might want to rethink that timeline for pitching Woods. The vulture is swirling."

Just a little bit of shut-eye, Clara had told herself after Aidyn left. Just a bit, then back to Charles. There was work still to be done, words to be spoken, because a friend loves at all times, to the very last possible second.

That was her plan. But then it seemed the very next moment, a voice called her name. A familiar voice she couldn't quite place, drifting from somewhere in the distance.

"Mrs. Kip?"

No, not in the distance. Close by. As close as a touch.

She pulled herself closer to it, navigating the swirls and

fuzziness all around her until they slowly calmed and her mind came into focus.

She was in her armchair. Nora knelt before her. Those facts told her she had fallen asleep. For how long was anyone's guess.

She needed to get to Charles.

"Hello," Nora greeted her.

Clara tried to reply, but the dryness in her throat stymied her voice.

Sensing her need, Nora handed her the water cup from the tray table. "Take a drink and try again."

Clara sipped through the straw and swallowed. Her voice loosened. "Better."

"Good. How are you feeling?"

Clara pulled in another sip only to wet her motors, not because she thirsted for it. "I'd be doing better if you'd roll me over to Charles's room."

"I can in a minute. First, I need to do your vitals."

"It's not enough to see I'm still kicking, huh?"

"Unfortunately, no."

Clara glanced at the door. The draw to Charles strengthened. "Can we do this over in his room then?"

The nurse paused. Then, as if understanding completely, she cupped Clara's forearm. "Mrs. Kip, I assure you he's okay. He will wait for you."

Nora's expression told Clara that she, perhaps even better than Clara, knew the encroachment of death.

Relenting, Clara relaxed in the chair and allowed herself to be examined.

Within minutes, the exam was complete. Nora wrapped

her stethoscope around her neck. "Did you want anything to eat? You missed lunch."

"No."

"What about the restroom? Do you want to try?"

"No. I'm fine."

"We should at least check your—"

"My britches are fine, honey. And even if they aren't, what's another couple of hours?"

Nora clearly had a different opinion. Bless her, she nodded anyway. "Let's get you in the wheelchair, then."

As they advanced to Charles's room, the intense presence of death was like another body in the room, big enough to take up space and air. When they arrived, she could see it had already thrown its shadow across Charles's face and put its rattle in his throat.

She gripped the armrests of the wheelchair.

Lord, make a way.

Nora moved furniture to make room for Clara in her wheelchair, then guided it into position next to the bed. Clara had an easy view of Charles's face and access to his hand. Exactly where she wanted to be.

"We didn't bring your Bible, Mrs. Kip," Nora said. "Would you like me to get it for you?"

For a moment, Clara considered it. Then she shook her head. "I've got all I need." At that point, all she needed was the Spirit to lead.

The nurse nodded and headed for the door. "I'll let staff know you're here, and I'll check in with you periodically."

When Nora was gone, Clara looked at her friend. He was frail to the point of snapping.

"Alone at last," she said and forced herself to giggle for his benefit. He should hear only joy at that point. But inside, grief strained her soul, that familiar sensation of sinking.

The shadow was so gray, so ominous.

"I just hate this part, don't you?"

She slipped her hand under his. The coldness startled her. The things and the people of the world were fleeting, never meant to be held on to forever. That she knew, but the truth never did make it easier to let go.

"It's okay to be afraid, you know," she told him. "Fear is an invitation to remember who God is." She looked down at his hand, thin but still hinting at the power it once possessed. "You don't need to be strong anymore, Charles. He will be your strength, if you let him." She lifted her eyes to his face. "Will you let him? Please, Charles, tell him you'll let him. Doesn't that sound like the freedom you've been searching for? There is so much freedom in his embrace."

How many times had people she loved walked away from that offer, stubbornly still carrying their load on their shoulders as if it were a twisted treasure? Like she once had. How many times had her heart cried out in sorrow for them, understanding what it was like to be burdened and what it was like to be boundless?

As long as she had a heartbeat, she would love them toward that release she had found.

"I won't give up on you, Charles." She clenched his hand. "You are too precious to me."

That was the core of the life she had chosen. The sower's job was to sow, trusting her success would be measured by how few seeds remained in her hand.

"I won't give up on you," she whispered.

From that moment on, as Charles's life peeled away bit by bit, she clung to his hand, prayed for his soul, and spoke Scripture over him from the storehouse in her heart.

For three hours, she held on to him, ignoring the tiredness growing in her muscles and the pins in her stomach. She stroked his hair and counted his breaths. And prayed.

Above all, through all, because of all at stake, she prayed.

A few times, he sucked in a rattled breath. Once, he moaned softly.

Then, at 5:17 p.m., his jaw suddenly opened wide. He inhaled sharply once, then twice.

And he was gone.

A piece of her own heart broke away with him. Another small death to self in the name of love. She leaned forward and kissed his hand, letting her lips linger.

Her eyes burned. Her body ached.

The price of loving never got easier to bear.

May 20, 1983

The church had begun to fill. The refurbished little sanctuary still smelled like new carpet and fresh paint.

Clara and Mai stopped in the back just inside the door and drank it in. Clara sighed, satisfied. Seeing this fruit of their labor brought a smile to her lips, despite the rising heartache over what the evening would entail.

Pastor Otis had been the one to tell Mahasajun about the

dissolution of the small church on the outskirts of Olathe. After seeing the *Star* article, the outgoing pastor had approached Otis with an offer to sign over the deed, free and clear, to the burgeoning congregation of refugees. They quickly accepted and set about the work of fixing it up.

They named their new home Hope Church.

Clara hooked her arm through Mai's. "I think we did pretty good with this place."

Her friend nodded, trying to smile. But her chin began to tremble.

"Come on, now." She nudged Mai's arm. "No sense crying until we absolutely have to. We're both wearing mascara."

Mai smiled under watery eyes.

Clara, too, welled with emotion. It grabbed hold of her vocal cords. This evening would be the last time for who knew how long the two friends would worship side by side. But she couldn't think about that. Not yet.

Live in the moment. It matters most.

She tightened her grip on her friend's arm. "I love you, Mai."

"I love you too." Her friend leaned against her shoulder, and together they walked down the main aisle.

They slipped into the reserved row of chairs in front. The kids and Mahasajun soon joined them. The youngest Khab, sweet baby girl Ruby, then thirteen, settled next to "Auntie C." Behind them sat Martha and Erik. The Hollises were there, along with several other sponsor families, sitting among the Hope congregation. Brothers and sisters from two sides of the world together for one bittersweet evening.

At 6:00, the newly installed Hope pastor came to the pulpit, and a hush fell over the room. Every word he spoke was in Lao, but Clara didn't have to understand the language to understand what was happening.

After speaking for several minutes, the pastor gestured to Mahasajun and Mai, who rose and joined him on the short platform. The couple stood shoulder to shoulder, looking out over the fellow countrymen they had loved and coached, nurtured and trained. Husband and wife smiled at them, and at the sponsors who had helped provide a space and an opportunity for them to work and to follow the Lord's hand on their lives.

Then, at the pastor's invitation, the body of believers rose, came forward as one family, and laid hands on the two people who would return to Southeast Asia, taking with them their children, their faith, and their God-given dream to minister in the refugee camps. Daily, desperate men, women, and children flowed into the Thai camps, seeking hope. Mahasajun and Mai understood which hope was worth clinging to.

First out of her seat at the pastor's invitation was, of course, Clara. With one hand, she held on to baby girl Ruby. With the other, she reached forward and placed a hand on Mai—a grip filled with hope, with fear, with unshakable love.

Her heart cried.

God, be her way. Jesus, be her words. Spirit, be her protection.

Three promises Scripture gives every believer to call upon in times of need.

Within two years of Mai's departure, Clara had lost all contact with her.

For the rest of her life, Clara could only trust that God kept every promise.

CHAPTER 20

June 9, 2016

For the remainder of the day, the smug look stayed on Shayna's face, and box 2 of the journals stayed well hidden under Aidyn's desk.

In her heart and mind, a fierce debate waged over what to do about her (yet another) error, one that had allowed Shayna to find the lead for the resettlement story. Such a basic rookie mistake.

To Aidyn, the story was more than just a collection of telling facts. It was breathing life. Life that she had seen, heard, and held. Life that was meant to spill over into others and illustrate the effects of love crossing boundaries in a boundary-laden world.

But all of that would be gutted, thrown away, and lost to the wind under the cold command of Shayna. For her, the story was a prize to be won, a badge to wear proudly and loudly in the face of the cub reporter, another hash mark in the tally of bylines attained.

As Aidyn attempted to work through her tasks for the day, she thought of the old woman's giggle, her flippant humor that somehow always worked, and her gentle way with people unable to return the favor. Her stomach knotted at the thought of having to surrender the boxes and interview notes into the possession of Shayna for her to pick through like a buzzard. But what could she do?

If she did nothing, Shayna would pitch Woods and get the story. Or Woods would get angry at Aidyn for not bringing the lead first, raging at her for her incompetence, and Shayna would get the story.

Or, if Aidyn did pitch, Woods could get angry at her for not listening to instructions—again—by pitching an article when she had been expressly told not to even think about writing one, and Shayna would get the story.

Or Woods would love the pitch but hold fast to the no-byline-for-you mandate, and Shayna would get the story.

By the end of the day, Aidyn's head throbbed, and her heart hung so low the pull hunched her shoulders.

She waited until Shayna left for the day, well after 5:30, then snuck the box out to her car via a back stairwell. She would do whatever she had to do to protect the full story for as long as she could.

As she slid the box into her trunk next to the other one, she sighed heavily. The effects of doubt flinging against hope had left her drained. She tried to turn off the inner noise for one second at least. But it refused.

Lord, what do I do with all this?

Not that she expected otherwise, but the question went unanswered.

On the drive home, the mental wrestling was flared by the external battles of rush-hour traffic.

By the time she exited the interstate to merge onto the thoroughfare leading to her apartment, the urge for silence had intensified. She detoured to the neighborhood park a few blocks from her building. The oval-shaped park, tucked away from the busy street, comprised a couple of acres of lush grass horseshoed by centuries-old Kansas oaks, cottonwoods, and maples. A paved walking trail circled the campus. Except for a small playground and pavilion at one end, the park was an open field, a sanctuary of stillness amid the barrage of human noise.

Aidyn parked her car by the pavilion and stepped out into the warm evening sun. Pausing, she closed her eyes and breathed in, the way Mrs. Kip would have. The sun had lowered enough behind the trees on the far side of the park that their shadows stretched thick and plentiful over the belly of the horseshoe.

She passed a few patrons enjoying the playground and followed the trail to that far end, where a bench waited. Settling in, she lifted her gaze to the sky partially covered by the outstretched tree limbs. It was as crisply blue as it had been that morning, calling those below to look up, beckoning them to swim in its tranquility.

That same sky had witnessed the day Mrs. Kip met her husband. The day he died. The day she lost her dream for São Paulo. The day she met Mai Khab. The day she saw the children run to their parents. The day she posed for the *Star* photographer.

Every day Mrs. Kip had lived.

Every day she had loved.

Every time she had won, and every time she had lost.

Oh, the stories the sky could tell.

Aidyn tilted her head back farther and studied the tree branches reaching their fingers to the sky. A light breeze slow-danced with the leaves. She imagined their silent hum to a melody only they could hear.

Out of the corner of her eye, she caught sight of it—a falling leaf. It glided back and forth in long zigzags to the ground. The thin, fragile leaf touched down with little fanfare and no one to notice its excellent journey except for Aidyn, who happened to be in the right place at the right time to see and to remember.

Suddenly, all doubt melted. In its place settled a steady, peaceful call.

Somehow she had to write Mrs. Kip's story. Somehow *she* had to be the one to bring it—and the history it entailed—to the world. And she had to do it now. Despite the odds stacked against her.

She hurried back to her car and to the boxes and the notes.

To the beauty she had found in the death.

Nora lifted the washcloth from the basin next to Charles's leg. Water streamed over her fingers, gentle as cleansing rain. Carefully she wrung the excess, leaving just enough wet in the material to effectively clean his skin. She held the cloth out to Clara. "Let's start with his face."

In all the times Clara had sent loved ones off to the life beyond, she had never experienced the moments just after the soul departs, the thick stillness and intimate care involved.

John had died an hour before anyone knew. Baby Elijah had been whisked away. Martha had been tended by family in the hours afterward. But in the death of Charles Slesher, Clara became privy to a facet of compassion so few had the ability to experience.

As she gathered the warm cloth in her hand, she thought of the women at Jesus's tomb. How tender would their touch have been? How broken their hearts? How much did they consider it an honor to pour back onto Jesus a tiny ounce of the love they had first received? Such was the heritage of compassion in which she participated.

A lump formed in her throat.

She leaned forward in her wheelchair and touched the cloth to Charles's forehead. Jimmy, on the other side of the bed, steadied the man's head and jaw, keeping Charles's face pointed to Clara to make her work easier.

Gently she swiped the delicate skin along his left temple as fondly as a mother. His expression was relaxed in his final rest. No more deep folds of pain and worry along his brow. No hint of fear on his lips.

The cloth left a glistening trail across his skin as she moved it down the sides of his jaw, over his cheeks, and across the bridge of his nose. On the broad stroke across his chin, her hand began to shake from the strain.

"Let's rinse the cloth now," Nora said, likely seeing the tremble.

Clara sat back, fighting the pinch in her abdomen, and handed Nora the cloth.

Jimmy reverently rotated Charles's head to a neutral position and began to remove the hospital gown.

"We'll do his shoulders and arms next," Nora explained as water splashed into the basin once more. "We'll go one at a time."

Clara took the cloth from Nora as Jimmy leaned across Charles's torso and pulled the man's left arm free from the gown. He laid the arm bare at the man's side, ready for Clara's attention.

She stroked downward, over the thin space where his bicep once was. She imagined it bulging as a young Charles carried bags of mulch to the back corner of his yard or moved the dresser so his wife could find a lost necklace.

Emma.

Was he with her now? Did he have that strong body again? Or a new, beautiful one? An undefeatable one?

Had the seeds turned into fruit? Was he laughing with his Emma? Was he joyful and glorious and free, like Clara had prayed?

Would she see him again?

How she longed to see him. And Martha, and Elijah.

And John.

The lump grew larger.

Johnny.

What would it be like to see him? Would he rush to her and pick her up off her feet and twirl her around? Would he tell her he had missed her and loved her and never wanted her to leave?

She glided the cloth down Charles's arm, remembering the feel of Johnny's arms around her as they embraced, the heat from his chest blanketing hers.

Would she have that same pleasure again? If so, when

SARA BRUNSVOLD

would the Lord allow her to find out? She wanted to find out. She was ready to find out. So ready.

Her hand trembled harder. Her fingers lost control of the cloth, and it fell to the bed. She bowed her head.

"Mrs. Kip?" Nora touched her arm.

But Clara couldn't answer. What would she say even if she could?

Gingerly, Nora took Clara's hand. "Let's let Jimmy finish. I'll take you to your room."

For the first time, Clara did not argue against the insinuation of rest. She nodded and kept her eyes closed until they arrived at her bedside.

Without a word, Nora took Clara's slippers off and placed them on the floor next to the bed. Then she helped Clara rise from the wheelchair and swivel to the mattress.

Clara leaned back against the pillow and allowed the nurse to help unstiffen her legs and pull the sheet over them. Every little movement told Clara her power—whatever she'd had to begin with—drained at a pace she was not allowed to influence.

"You did a wonderful thing for Mr. Slesher," Nora said softly, and Clara knew she meant more than the final bath.

The tightness of her throat barely allowed her whisper to escape. "I won't forget him."

"I won't either, Mrs. Kip."

As sudden and forceful as a clap of thunder, Clara began to sob. Tearless cries filled the room. Cries that pleaded with heaven for grace and endurance.

Nora sat on the bed and wrapped her arms around Clara. She didn't speak. She didn't try to stop the cries. She only held her.

"I'm so tired, honey."

Nora snuggled her tighter. "I know, Mrs. Kip. I know."

Aidyn brewed a cup of green tea in her favorite mug—a soft-yellow enamel with a silhouette of a white bunny emblazoned on the side. She brought it to the couch with her, along with her notebook. The open storage boxes sat side by side in front of her on the floor, eagerly offering up their contents. The story, the true depths of which only Aidyn had been personally invited to explore, waited to speak. Waited to be drawn out into the light, page by page.

She set her cup on the side table and looked down at the journal spines lined up along the bottoms of the boxes. What more could they add to the story that she didn't already know? What did they contain that made Mrs. Kip want to give them all to her? What pieces of the story was she still missing?

She leaned forward and pulled out the first journal of box 1.

August 25, 1971.

She traced Mrs. Kip's neat penmanship with her finger. The young widow had kept her cursive tidy, like it was a small grasp at control in an existence so out of control. The entire first page was filled with similar script.

The words contained the soul of their writer. Words Mrs. Kip wrote in faith that they had value, if only to herself. After all, how could that young widow foresee a twentysomething cub reporter, still decades away from being born, one day opening that journal, tracing her pen strokes, and poring through her words in search of meaning?

For four hours straight, well after her tea was gone, Aidyn read through five years' worth of Mrs. Kip's life. The entries were not the dry "Dear Diary" variety, but prayers. Fervent, honest, often heartbreaking prayers.

> Take this anger from me. Take this pain. It is too much to bear.

> I do not see the point in this life, God.

> I don't want to go on this way, Lord. Help me to see your path. I give my life to you.

> HALLELUJAH! Thank you, God, for saving me!

> Lord, give Mai the courage to live and the renewed hope she will see her children again.

> Protect your hurting people still trapped in the camp, Lord. Provide for them in miraculous ways, especially sustaining food and clean water.

> Raise up your people, Lord, to be who we are called to be. May we together surround these families and bring them into safety and the saving knowledge of your Son.

> Break every hint of pride to accomplish your will in my life and in those of my brothers and sisters.

> Lord, you are so good, and your love holds everything together.

That last prayer was repeated the most frequently.

Through the humble entries on the pages, Aidyn watched the progress Mrs. Kip made from lost young widow trying to survive the day to godly warrior who could see wider, go bigger, and believe bolder, and who left a long, wide wake of hearts in better shape than how she found them.

Tears spilled.

By the time Aidyn reached the last journal in box 2, the urge to write had nearly overwhelmed her. She retrieved her laptop from her bag and began to pour out the words she believed would have value, if only to herself.

She captured the story of Mrs. Kip and Mai Khab not only from the facts she had noted but also from the way it *felt*. The way it affected the minds and hearts of those who had lived it. She pulled herself into the being of Clara Kip, often speaking the very words Mrs. Kip herself had written.

She wrote and cried, wrote and thought of the old woman alone in her room. A woman she had seen only as a means to an end. An assignment to survive. How very foolish of her.

Suddenly she stopped, her fingertips hovering over her keyboard. She looked to the ceiling and felt a familiar prayer rise to her lips.

"Lord, break every hint of my pride to accomplish your will." A new wave of tears cascaded down her cheeks. "I don't know why you led me to Mrs. Kip, but, Lord, I am listening."

CHAPTER 21

Friday, June 10, 2016

Pain swept over her about midnight. The enemy's schemes find their strength at that hour. Clara barely had the presence of mind to press the call button.

For what seemed like years, Michelle, the night nurse, sat with her, held her hand, and sang to her softly. With each surge of pain, Michelle offered her the morphine. "The doctor said you could have it."

"Not yet," Clara said each time. She remembered what the pain meds had done to her in the hospital, the way they fogged her mind and strangled her voice. "Not yet," she would tell Michelle, because there was Aidyn. "Not now."

But then a big wave came that sucked the wind out of her.

Michelle stroked her hand as she moaned. "Just enough to get you through the night?" the nurse whispered.

Clara relented.

Whatever amount constituted "just enough," it rescued Clara from the sharp, angry clutches and let her drift into the smooth, cool night.

When she woke with the first light of morning, Michelle was gone, but a dull pain lingered in her gut. Her limbs drooped heavy on the bed. Her mind felt like it had unshakable cobwebs in the corners. She knew that before long, the just-enough dose would wear off completely and the cycle would repeat. The pain would be worse, longer, harder. And the dose would be higher, longer, stronger.

The doctors had told her this point would likely come, but it had arrived far too soon. Honestly, she had hoped the Lord would knock her out before it did.

The new day that broke outside her window undoubtedly would be the last she would enjoy the freedom of mobility, however limited it may have been.

She turned to the picture window. The first touches of orange seeped into the inky blue. She longed to bathe in the sunrise as it bloomed overhead, to savor each stroke as if it were made with her in mind, her name hidden within.

Her eyes drifted to the pergola. There was no better place to be at that moment.

Willing her muscles to rouse, she sat up. She retrieved a small notepad and pen tucked into the nightstand drawer and brought them to the tray table. It took a minute to come up with what to write. She wrote in a jagged scrawl that looked nothing like her youthful penmanship.

Honey—

Don't panic, I'm using the wheelchair. Be back soon. Do not disturb, and if applicable, DNR. You'll ruin the party.

She drew a little heart underneath, then signed her name. She left the note on the very edge of the tray table where hopefully it could be spotted easily.

With considerable grunting, she heaved herself onto her feet, unclipped her call button, and shuffled to the wheelchair parked by the dining table. "We enable each other, yes?" she said to the contraption.

It didn't have the courtesy to answer back, but it did have the decency to catch her when she flopped into the seat.

To her pleasure, she found she could turn the wheels with fair ease, as long as her arms had the gas to do so. She breached her doorway less than a minute later—messy hair, pajamas, denture-less smile and all.

Briefly she paused outside Charles's room and peeked in. The blankness had returned, the room ready to receive the next voyager, stripped and sterilized of anything that was of him, as if he was never there.

But he had been. The empty place in Clara's being proved it.

The heart is designed to give far more love than the brain can calculate and to endure far more loss than the body anticipates. Clara had lived that truth many times, yet the fact still amazed her as she sat outside her friend's door.

"Godspeed, Charles," she whispered into the open room.

Turning away, she focused all the energy she could into her arms and wheeled through the outside door.

Once over the threshold, she stopped. As in every other instance, she closed her eyes and breathed in as deeply as she could. Crisp, fresh, and scented by the nearby flowers. The last first breath of outside.

She began a slow, steady roll toward the pergola. After

a short distance, her arms began to complain. She willed them to keep moving. Each push forward, though, seemed harder than the last. Each movement a little more arduous. The uproar spread from her arms to her lungs.

Stopping momentarily, she looked toward the pergola again. She had made it only a third of the way. The rest of the distance might as well have been miles.

Determined, she gave another push on the wheels and moved another foot. Five more times she pushed, each time advancing no more than a stride. Her arms shook with the exertion. Her breathing sounded like she had just emerged from an aerobics class.

She pulled her exhausted arms into her lap and tilted her face to heaven, ready to cry out for one last jolt of strength.

But then she saw the sky.

There on that open sidewalk, Clara had an unobstructed view of the canvas above, at the perfect time and perfect place to see a sunrise unlike any she had ever beheld. The brilliance of purple and indigo, pink and yellow, streaming from corner to corner, as bold as if they themselves were the power of the Creator. The colors streamed through her, their magnificence saturating to her innermost parts, taking her breath away.

Beauty that had no end. Wonder that extended for eternity.

If that was the splendor she could see on earth, how much more was there to behold in glory itself? How small the glimpse!

What a speck I am compared to you, Lord.

Yet she was a speck he loved. The same mastery that had spun the colors before her also wrote her small collection of days with the same attentive care, as if she were something.

To her Abba Father, she was everything.

Every reason he needed to send his Son.

A yearning gathered within her. If she could produce tears, they would have traced down her cheeks.

How she wanted to go home. How badly she longed for it. To finally see the face she had sought for years. To hear the voice she could only imagine and see with her eyes that for which she hoped. To be free at last. Free of the pain. Free of the grief. Free to walk. Run! Fly! Soar!

At last.

She wanted to find the place where lightning bolts were stored, to discover where the wind began, and to watch as love poured down in generous waterfalls into hearts that moved in its current. What a joy to be among the chorus when one more of those hearts turned to the Son. How loud the sound must be.

I can be loud, God. I will find a way to be the loudest.

She closed her eyes, felt the brilliance still coursing through her, like her body had already joined back with the elements of creation.

With all that she was, she presented what would be her final request.

Please, Father, let me come home.

At 6:45 a.m., quiet blanketed the newsroom, the sliver of rest between when the presses ran and when the news cycle churned anew. The small sea of desks sat empty, phones silent, few lights burning. One of those lights belonged to Woods.

The section editor's early-bird habits were familiar to all

staff. It was the only time of day Aidyn could catch Woods in her office without interruption. Aidyn needed the pitch to be perfect. The right timing, the right angle, the right research, the right words.

The right everything.

She walked softly toward her own desk, messenger bag flapping gently against her hip, and rehearsed what she planned to say.

She would start with the obit. That part was straightforward. Then, somehow, she'd segue into the pitch for the longer profile piece, deftly handing Woods the completed outline. Somehow.

The flimsy master plan was the best she could do on little sleep. The two pieces had kept her up until 1:00 a.m. writing, then for another hour fretting over them as she tossed and turned in bed.

She laid her bag down on her desk, looked furtively at Woods's office door, then pulled the printouts of the two pieces from her bag. Her pulse raced. Her head felt light. She took a deep breath and prayed, *Lord, I don't know how you're going to do this, but . . . I guess, just make a way.*

Her prayer life had some progressing to do to catch up to the likes of Mrs. Kip's. Still, hopefully it would be enough.

Without giving herself another minute to delay, Aidyn strode to the office door and peeked in.

Woods sat bowed over a book laid open on her desk. Her eyes were closed.

Tentatively, Aidyn knocked on the doorjamb.

Woods looked up, first with surprise, then with her signature bulldog frown. "You're here early, Kelley."

"I was hoping to talk to you before things got too busy." She stepped into the office, hanging by the door until or unless directed to move closer. "I have the obit to show you."

"Is that right?" Woods shut the book and slid it off to the side. In the movement, a word that looked an awful lot like *Faith* appeared in the book's title. "Let's see it."

Dutifully, Aidyn stepped forward and handed her the top page of her printouts.

Woods adjusted her glasses, then propped her chin in one hand, elbow on her desk.

As Woods read, Aidyn clasped the other two pages with both hands and waited. One sentence in particular, if it did its job well, was bound to snag Woods.

Sure enough, after a moment, Woods's frown released some. "Is this true about the mission?"

"It is," she replied. "I found historical records to support it."

Woods glanced up, an unspoken instruction for more detail.

Aidyn obliged. "Mrs. Kip gave me boxes of her old journals, which document everything. It appears she helped shape the cultural landscape of Kansas City."

That caught Woods's attention as well. "Interesting."

Aidyn nodded, ready to share more and set up a perfect segue to the outline, but Woods asked, "Has she seen this obit yet?"

"Taking it to her this morning."

"If she's happy with it, then it's a go." Woods nodded toward the other two pages in Aidyn's hands. "What's that?"

Though she should have been prepared for such a reaction from her eagle-eyed editor, a wave of panic swept through

Aidyn. She sent up a plea for help. What had she practiced so brilliantly in the car on the drive in? It had sounded so profound.

She looked down at the draft of the outline, mustering the words. "I . . . know I still have a long way to go with proving myself . . . and I appreciate the opportunity to even try . . . As I was writing Mrs. Kip's obit, it became apparent her story is much bigger than a simple memorial can contain. I already have—"

"Kelley, are you pitching me?"

Aidyn sucked in her breath. "Yes," she said with as much boldness as she could manage. "A human-interest story—low risk."

Woods closed her mouth into a hard line.

"It's rich with themes that resonate with today's audience," Aidyn continued. "The content could also serve to bring attention to nonprofits currently doing similar kinds of work in the city. Like Don Bosco or Mission Adelante."

Her editor's face was impossible to read. It remained set, unmoved.

"Low risk," Aidyn repeated, softer.

Woods's scrutiny bore into her. Finally, she asked, "That's the outline in your hand, I assume?"

Aidyn nodded.

Her editor jutted out her hand, and Aidyn slid the two pages into it. All she could do then was wait as her editor scoured her words. That, and remember to breathe.

Woods flipped to the second page. Read. At last, she looked up at Aidyn. "Tell me why you want to write this."

She thought for a moment. "Because . . . it's a good story."

Woods looked at her over the rims of her glasses, clearly wanting more.

"Because . . . the world needs more Mrs. Kips. It needs to be inspired by people like her." The words of the old woman rushed to her mind. "People are more compassionate than the media makes them out to be. Sometimes they just need a little coaxing."

Woods raised an eyebrow. "Learn that from her?"

"I did, actually."

Woods stared at her another moment. Then she leaned back in her chair and exhaled. "Give me a thousand words of a sketch draft by Monday. Proposal purposes only."

Aidyn's mouth dropped open.

"If it's good, I'll take it to Maper. He'll need to okay an assignment like this."

No way was that real. Aidyn stood there slightly dazed.

"And I need a working title, for crying out loud," Woods said. "You forgot that part. Titles are part of the selling point."

Finding her voice, Aidyn replied, "Yes, of course. Thank you."

"Don't thank me yet. I haven't said yes."

"Right." She took back all three pages from Woods's outstretched hand and corrected her phrasing. "Thanks for the consideration."

With the typical flick of her wrist, Woods dismissed her.

Aidyn turned to the door and exited in stunned silence.

Mrs. Kip had been right—the Lord's hand was moving.

The brilliant oranges and pinks slowly burned off, revealing the magnificent blue underneath. The sun inched higher, expanding its reach over the courtyard and sending signals of the full summer heat to come. Birds raised their sweet symphony of praises over top the dull thrum of traffic drifting over the trees.

The day was fully awake, and Clara was nourished on the foretaste of glory. With palms opened to heaven, she finished her time before the throne.

Lord, you are so good, and your love holds everything together. Give me joy in every minute I have remaining here in this place you have called me to. If I have any work remaining, please give me wisdom and grace to complete it. Amen.

The Lord never failed to answer a prayer for work to do.

Full from the communion, she turned the wheelchair and directed herself toward the door. Push by tired push, she wheeled back to the building. It was hard to judge how long she had been in the courtyard, but certainly the staff had noticed her "noncompliance" and were not thrilled about it.

Putting her head down, she pushed as much as her arms would allow, nudging her closer to the building. When she was still a few yards out, the door opened.

Nora stepped out, arms crossed, a slight purse to her lips.

Clara halted. "Oh boy," she muttered. Pushing a few inches closer, she asked, "Did I cause a kerfuffle?"

"What do you think?"

"You kids never let me have any fun."

Nora grinned and came out to meet her on the sidewalk.

"You going to let me have it?" Clara asked.

"Oh, Mrs. Kip." Nora took hold of the wheelchair handgrips in back, relieving Clara of the burden of movement. "I don't intend to say a word about it."

The implication tugged at Clara's heart. "You are too much."

"No, Mrs. Kip. You are. And I sincerely mean that."

Clara laughed. "I have no doubt."

The nurse pushed her to the door and pressed the automatic door opener. "I'm just glad you had your quiet time safely."

Clara frowned. "Were you watching?"

"Yes."

"How long?"

Nora paused. "A while." She left it at that.

The thought of the nurse standing sentinel even for five minutes, not interrupting or trying to corral, made Clara appreciate her more than words could express.

"You won't give up on me, will you, Nora?"

"No, Mrs. Kip. I won't."

A silent understanding settled over them as they finished their trek to room 310.

When they arrived, Nora parked the wheelchair next to the bed. "Ready to get dressed for the day?"

Clara still wore her pajamas. Her dentures were still on the sink's edge, and her hair probably stood up at various angles in the back. "Sakes alive, I'm a mess, aren't I?"

"You look beautiful."

"You're too kind."

"Would you like me to get your clothes?"

Clara shrugged, torn between two equally strong forces. She'd expended so much energy for the sake of her quiet time that going back to sleep—in bed—didn't sound atrocious. But these were her last hours of mobility. What a dishonor to the blessing to spend them *im*mobile.

As if hearing the debate in Clara's mind, Nora intervened. "I have an idea, Mrs. Kip. How about a bath?"

"A bath?"

"Yes. A real one."

Clara raised her eyebrows. "You mean in the soaker? Not this washcloth-in-the-shower business you've had me on?"

The nurse nodded. "In the actual bathtub. I can even put in lavender oil."

"And bubbles?"

"If that's what you'd like."

Clara grinned. "You're making dreams come true, honey."

One vitals check and a half hour later, Nora wheeled her into the bathroom in the east hallway, where a specially designed whirlpool tub awaited. It featured chest-high walls with a cushioned bench seat and a pocket door that rolled up from the base.

The nurse helped her disrobe and then guided her through the opening in the tub and onto the seat. Once the door was rolled down and latched, Nora turned on the hot water.

Warmth that had for so long eluded Clara seeped first through her feet, then her ankles, then up her calves and higher. She leaned her head back against the cushion, relishing the sensation.

Nora added several drops of lavender-scented bath oil and a scoop of bubble bath, then turned on the jet sprays. The churn kicked up the bubbles and the smell of blooming flowers. A froth formed on top of the water. The pops of tiny bubbles tickled Clara's skin.

The bath thrilled nearly every one of her senses. The lulling sounds of the sprays, the fragrance of lavender, the roiling water gently massaging her muscles and joints.

When the water level reached her shoulders, Nora turned off the faucet and let the whirlpool do its work.

Clara's body hungrily absorbed the feeling of weightlessness, releasing its aches into the roil. She melted into it.

Sweet, rewarding freedom.

"How's that, Mrs. Kip?" Nora asked.

Clara sighed contentedly. "Like heaven."

CHAPTER 22

She expected to see John first, the one she longed to see more than any other. Instead, she saw Mai. Beautiful, amazing Mai! Her heart leapt, and she ran to her friend, arms wide and voice high like those of the overjoyed Khab children that night at the Kansas City airport. But Mai showed no reaction; she stood perfectly still.

Confused, Clara slowed and lowered her hands.

The closer she got to Mai, the more she could discern that her friend looked past her, out somewhere in the distance over her shoulder. Concern puckered Mai's brow.

"What is it, Mai?" Clara turned around and tried to see it too. "What is it? Show me."

Far away, a blur of angry red and throngs of black gathered into two shapes. Bit by bit, they sharpened into focus, crisper and crisper, until Clara had no doubt what she saw.

A child. Alone. Armed with only a small sword and a thin shield, standing in the shadow of a beast five times its size.

The child was not equipped to fight alone, not yet ready

for the battle—but tried anyway. The small one swung the sword at the beast. Unfazed, the creature slithered its tongue at its prey, taunting.

"No!" Clara cried, but the child did not hear her. She turned to Mai.

Her friend pointed to the unfolding battle, a silent instruction for Clara to look again. When she did, the child was suddenly recognizable. Long blond hair, delicate features, and a messenger bag slung over her shoulder.

Clara gasped. She cried out again and again, unable to move, like her feet were cemented to that spot. She screamed without words, cried with no tears, trying to get to the child. Deaf to the noise, the child continued to take fruitless swings. Clara strained and strained, attempting to move toward her.

Something shoved her.

She tumbled away from the scene, falling, falling, until she landed somewhere soft. Her vision morphed to a new place. And when her mind caught up to what her eyes saw, she realized she was in the armchair of her Sacred Promise room.

Nora stood over her. "Mrs. Kip?" she asked with a puzzled look. "Everything okay? I think I startled you."

Clara glanced to the right and left, looking for remnants of the scene she had just witnessed—it seemed so real—but she found none. She tried to shake it away. "I'm okay, honey. Just . . . in my own world, apparently."

"I was asking if you were finished with your breakfast." Nora indicated the untouched plate of food on the tray table.

Clara couldn't remember the food arriving, much less if she had considered eating. "I'm finished, thank you."

Nora paused as if trying to read something in her expression.

Quietly she picked up the tray. "I'll take this to the hall, then. I hear the dining crew out there with their carts. When I get back, let's do a check."

As Nora left with the tray, Clara turned to the picture of John on her nightstand. His strong, confident stance on the São Paulo balcony, that inciting look of "join me" ever on his face. She longed to be where he was. Her handsome Johnny. The embrace waiting for her. But the image of Aidyn swinging helplessly hung heavy around her.

She whispered to John, "Looks like I'll be delayed a bit longer, darling."

Then she closed her eyes and exhaled. The initial rumbles of pain rattled in her gut. She felt weaker than she ever had. More ill-equipped than she ever had. But she knew the Lord's nudging when she felt it. And she knew he had answered her prayer from the courtyard—to give her joy and wisdom if any work remained for her.

Lord, my life is yours. Show me the way.

His instruction arrived before the nurse did. It was simple and vague—and just like the Lord.

Psalm 16.

Aidyn sped through her other tasks for the morning, the singular goal in mind of getting back to Mrs. Kip as quickly as possible. The permission to write a sketch article opened the door wider for her to capture more of the woman's story, above and beyond what an obituary required, and Aidyn itched to talk to her . . . and maybe bring her a legit chocolate chip cookie in celebration.

Finally, a little after 11:00, she slid her notebook into her messenger bag and reached to lock her computer. A second before the screen switched to lock mode, an IM came through. Though she caught Rahmiya's name, she didn't have a chance to read the message her friend had sent.

Eager to get moving, she jumped to her feet and headed for the door. She vowed to follow up with Rahmiya as soon as she returned. The questions had piled up for Mrs. Kip after a night of reading her words, then there were the details of the conversation with Woods. So much to discuss!

The Lord's hand was definitely moving. Wow, was it moving.

She cruised through the doors of Sacred Promise with a lightness in her step. She would leave the facility that day far richer than she came. That promise propelled her through the activity room and down the north hallway. The urge to get her notebook ready began to fill her fingers.

All her zeal came to a halt, however, as she approached Mr. Slesher's door.

It gaped open. Darkness spilled from the room. A telltale sign.

"Oh no." She held her breath and moved to look inside.

The bed lay empty, bare. The shades were drawn. A room in mourning.

Her heart sank. Bare beds were the reality that existed within the walls of Sacred Promise. Her gaze drifted to Mrs. Kip's room.

The woman had told her loss was never easy, no matter how many times she had been through it. How was Mrs. Kip handling the loss of Mr. Slesher?

Slowly, Aidyn walked toward the sunlight streaming through the open door of room 310.

Mrs. Kip slept peacefully in her favorite roost, encased by the sun's rays, holding an open Bible on her lap and wearing a bright red tracksuit.

Aidyn quietly made her way to the loveseat. Without the woman's giant personality and captivating smile to distract, Mrs. Kip's true state was evident. Even asleep, she looked exhausted. She appeared more shrunken than before. The wisps of her white hair looked like strings of cotton candy that would melt upon touch. The blackness around her right eye had deepened, offsetting her pale skin, which seemed to have lost more of its peach tint. Her chest moved slightly with her throaty breathing. Her gnarled fingers wrapped around the edges of her Bible, the smoothness of the pages making the wrinkled, splotchy skin contrast all the more.

It all paralleled Mr. Slesher's appearance. Aidyn's chest hitched.

She leaned forward and gingerly slid the Bible out of Mrs. Kip's grip. Predictably, the woman had been reading the Psalms.

"You're a creature of habit, Mrs. Kip," she whispered, laying the Bible open on the tray table. She sat for a moment and watched the old woman sleep.

How many Psalms played happily in that mind of hers? How many of them had gotten her through the deepest valleys of life? How many of them had been her praises during the highest highs?

How many resounded in the woman's contagious giggle?

Oh, that giggle. It could tell a thousand stories.

In that instant, every goal Aidyn had brought with her gave way to a bigger, glorious mission. Every question she'd intended to ask suddenly didn't seem to matter. Every task she'd set out to do, a shallow achievement.

Aidyn simply wanted to sit under Mrs. Kip's words, whatever they might be. Whether a straight line or a divergent rabbit trail. She wanted to be still and listen. To be the friend Mrs. Kip needed in all her heartache and noticeable pain and indelible vibrancy.

The yearning bloomed within her. She watched the sweet woman and prayed, *Lord, show me how. I'm listening.*

Tenderly, she rubbed the woman's arm. "Mrs. Kip?"

After a couple more tries, the woman finally roused, blinking until she came into full awareness.

"Hey there." Mrs. Kip's voice came out faint and scratchy. She coughed dryly and looked toward the tray table.

Following her gaze, Aidyn saw a cup with a bendy straw and handed it to her.

Mrs. Kip took a sip, her movements slower, more weighted, but she smiled all the same. "What a sight you are to wake up to, honey. I've been looking forward to our visit."

"Me too," Aidyn said with an honesty that warmed her. "How has your morning been so far?"

"Can't complain." She gave the cup to Aidyn. "But I will if you want me to. I have a few things I could get off my chest."

Aidyn grinned and returned the cup to the tray table. "How about we start on a better note? I have a surprise for you."

"A surprise? How thrilling."

Aidyn reached into her bag and retrieved the oversized

chocolate chip cookie in a paper sleeve from Homer's Coffee House. "I thought you might enjoy a special treat, something a little better than those cookies up front."

The woman's eyes widened. She took hold of the cookie with both hands, looking as tickled as if she had been handed a hundred-dollar bill. "It's a monster!"

"You can enjoy it while we chat," Aidyn suggested.

"What a happy thought that is." Mrs. Kip slipped the cookie out of its sleeve and broke off a portion. "Here, honey. It's rude to eat in front of one's guests. Have a morsel with me."

"With pleasure." Aidyn lifted the portion and took a healthy bite. The buttery cookie practically melted in her mouth, the gooey chocolate coating her tongue.

Meanwhile, Mrs. Kip broke off a piece so tiny it was barely visible, a near-literal morsel. She placed it in her mouth and declared, "Delicious."

Aidyn started to comment on the ludicrously small bite, but for reasons she didn't fully understand, she left it alone. Something told her it was the friend thing to do. Instead, she sat and gobbled what was left of her portion. "I started reading your journals last night," she said.

"Any good?"

"They're brilliant."

Mrs. Kip guffawed. "Let's not oversell it, honey." She laid the partially eaten cookie next to the Bible, a move Aidyn also respectfully ignored.

"They were fantastic," Aidyn insisted. "In fact, they inspired me to finish your obituary. Would you like to read it?"

"I'm *dying* to," the woman replied with a wink.

Aidyn rolled her eyes playfully. "Walked into that one."

She pulled the copy of the obituary from her bag and handed it to Mrs. Kip. "We still need to land on an 'extraordinary' ending, of course."

"We can work on that today, I'm sure. Let's take a look at what you've got." The woman adjusted her glasses and read the obituary aloud. When she reached the end, she looked up at Aidyn with amazement. "Oh, honey."

"You like it?"

"Like it? I love it! Absolutely love it. You made a mediocre life sound magnificent."

"It's hardly a mediocre life."

"You're right. It's an exceedingly unimpressive life."

Aidyn chuckled. "You like to think that, but I have some more good news to share that may influence your opinion." Excitement surged as she delivered the news—the words she had waited all morning to share. "Your life story has inspired a potential human-interest feature."

Mrs. Kip righted at the words. "It has?"

Aidyn nodded.

"Are you writing it?"

"If it's approved, I would be."

A smile slowly spread across Mrs. Kip's face. "Miss Kelley, that is indeed wonderful news!"

"I thought you'd get a kick out of it."

"It's a beautiful thing, honey. Very beautiful. That editor of yours is a genius."

Aidyn's smile drew in. "What?"

But Mrs. Kip continued as if not hearing. "She had every confidence you'd locate those journals. You sure did take your time about it, though, I have to say."

Aidyn blinked. "Hold on. I think I'm missing something here. What do you mean she had every confidence I'd find them?"

Mrs. Kip giggled, the mischievous twinkle shining brighter in her eyes. She leaned forward on her elbows. "Your editor knew about the journals. Rosario told her the whole history. She just needed to get you here in a way that the grumpy guy would approve of."

Everything went still.

The connections zipped together. The unorthodox obit assignment; the refusal of the first, standardly written draft; the imploring to "go back and listen"; Woods's stunning agreement to see a sketch draft.

Aidyn felt her mouth drop open. "The obit was . . . a cover?"

Mrs. Kip laughed heartily. "Quite the scheme, isn't it?"

Aidyn's mind refused to bend around the assertion, refused to accept it as truth. "But . . . why would she do that? Woods doesn't even like me."

"Oh, I beg to differ."

"No," Aidyn said. "She really doesn't."

The woman regarded her a moment. "That's interesting, because she told Rosario you were the one with the soul to write about the mission story. If that's not a statement of faith in your abilities, I don't know what is."

The revelation smacked into Aidyn. She looked off to the side, trying to reconcile it all. For the second time that morning, she had been dumbfounded by Woods. "I . . . don't know what to say."

"The Lord hides his warriors in the most surprising places, Miss Kelley."

Though Aidyn balked at the reference to Woods as a warrior for the Lord, she had to admit she knew very little about her editor.

"I bet you feel more confident in getting approval now, yes?" Mrs. Kip asked.

Aidyn wanted to share in the confidence, but Mrs. Kip didn't realize an even bigger challenge lay ahead. "Actually, Woods is only the first layer. The harder layer is the managing editor."

"The grumpy guy?" Mrs. Kip asked.

"Yes, him. He'll be a hundred times harder to convince. He's a beast."

Something sparked in Mrs. Kip's expression. "A beast?"

Thinking the woman didn't understand the expression, Aidyn said, "He's notoriously difficult to please."

The old woman curled her lip like a boxer facing an opponent. "In that case, Miss Kelley, there's only one thing we can do." She jutted a finger at Aidyn's messenger bag. "Get that notebook out and let's write a story he can't refuse."

CHAPTER 23

The stories prattled out of Clara's old mouth one after another in a mostly coherent manner. Who knew if any of them would help Aidyn find whatever she needed, but Clara kept speaking as she was led. And for her part, Aidyn kept asking for more, kept taking notes, kept laughing right along with Clara.

Oh, that laugh.

It reached deep into Clara, warming her from the inside out. Everything about their visit did. Each time the girl smiled, each time she raised her light-brown eyebrows in interest, each time she asked another question. The delight that the exchange brought Clara enabled her to tolerate the growing discomfort that drilled upward into her ribs.

The story that seemed to capture the girl the most was the one about Martha taking a Lao mother, who had never so much as sat behind a steering wheel, to a local high school parking lot to learn the basics of driving. Clara recalled so many details she surprised herself, and each tidbit tickled the girl more and more.

"Sweet Martha came away with whiplash," Clara told her. "A shuttle launch would have been a smoother ride. Martha had the patience of a saint, but when the gal nearly sideswiped the parked school bus, that was the end of that."

Aidyn chuckled, egging Clara on.

"Of course, the worst part about it all was the gal had brought her little dog along for this adventure."

"No!" Aidyn said.

"Oh yes. Little purse-pooch thing, light as a piece of hair. Sailed into the dashboard several times. Poor pup was concussed seven different ways."

Aidyn roared. The sound of her amusement filled the room, electrifying everything it touched. It fueled the broad smile on Clara's lips, trumping the pain.

"Oh, Mrs. Kip," Aidyn said between laughs, "is any of that true?"

"Most of it, but good luck trying to prove what isn't."

Aidyn shook her head. "You are too much."

"So I've been told."

The girl's chuckles slowly subsided, and she looked at her notes in thought. "What ever happened to Martha, anyway?"

"She passed, honey. August 5, 1997."

"You remember the day?"

"You never forget the day you watch your best friend take her last breath."

Aidyn quieted.

"She had cancer too," Clara explained. "I went with them —her and her husband, Erik—to MD Anderson for an experimental treatment. But she didn't make it home."

"I'm so sorry."

"That loss was one of my hardest, for sure. Mai was another."

Aidyn raised her eyebrows. "Did Mai pass away too?"

Though Clara wanted to answer according to her instincts, she instead offered what Aidyn appreciated more: the truth, as far as Clara could prove it.

"Mai and Mahasajun left on May 21, 1983, to be missionaries in Thailand."

Aidyn wrote down the information. "Wow, that brings a whole new dimension to the mission story."

Clara nodded. The girl didn't know the half of it.

"Did you stay in contact with her?"

"Tried to. But that was the eighties. No internet back then. For the first couple of years, we wrote on a regular basis. Then one day, her letters stopped. A short time later, my letter came back marked 'return to sender.' I tried to get someone from Hope Church to tell me what had happened, but none of them had heard either. The Red Cross told me it wasn't something they could help me with, though believe me, I did my best to persuade them. Unfortunately, that was one time I couldn't coax anyone into action."

"So what did you do?"

Clara shrugged. "After a couple of years, I kind of stopped pursuing it. I trusted that eventually I'd find out what happened to my friend. If not this side of heaven, then from behind the pearly gates."

Aidyn shook her head empathetically. "What a hard thing to carry all these years, Mrs. Kip."

Pain jabbed at Clara's insides, hard enough for her to wince.

The girl froze, watching with a worried expression.

"I'm okay, honey," Clara said.

The girl bit her lip, obviously not convinced. Diversion would be required to give that lip the freedom it deserved.

"You know," Clara said, "you owe me about five hundred extraordinary death suggestions at this point." She tried to giggle, but the movement hurt.

Fortunately, Aidyn obliged and took the redirect. "Lucky for you, Mrs. Kip, I have a stockpile to choose from."

The acceptance was an even more generous gesture than kindly ignoring the partially eaten cookie on the tray table.

"Let's hear them, then," Clara said.

The girl flipped to a dog-eared page in her notebook. A list of ideas stretched down the page.

"Goodness, honey. You spent some time thinking about how I might give up the ghost."

"Don't be too impressed. I definitely had help with this."

Clara craned her neck, trying to see. "Any of them top the Harley one?"

Aidyn smiled. "We'll see." One by one, she ticked off suggestions.

Running with the bulls in Madrid.

"Too cliché," Clara said.

BASE jumping off the Grand Canyon.

"Sounds more dumb than extraordinary."

Breaking up illegal dogfights in Mexico.

"Only if it was the people who got me, not the poor dogs."

Covert CIA operative rooting out a terrorist cell leader.

"Definitely."

Attempting to bring clean water to the remotest parts of India.

"I like it."

Oil-rig worker sent on a mission to outer space to break apart a meteor headed straight for earth.

"Now you're just making up nonsense."

When the list of maybes had grown to twenty, Aidyn looked up. "At some point, you'll have to choose one of these."

Clara waved it off, the effort sending a ripple of pain through her torso. "They're all delightful, honey," she said through her wince. "You pick one."

The girl looked too worried to argue that Clara was breaking their agreement. "Should I ask the nurse to come in, Mrs. Kip?"

"I'm totally and completely fine. Besides, I'm having too much fun with you."

Pink tinted the girl's cheeks. "I'm having fun with you too."

No doubt she meant it.

"But I should get back to the office now," she added with a note of reluctance. "My editor is probably looking for me, and you've given me a lot to sort through."

"You think it was enough?"

Aidyn smiled. "It was definitely everything I needed, Mrs. Kip." Her assurance seemed to speak to more than just the story.

"I'm glad, honey."

As Aidyn packed up her notebook, Clara adjusted in the chair, trying to find a position that might starve the stabs inside her body. She looked up in time to see Aidyn rise to her feet.

"May I ask you one last thing?" the girl inquired.

"Ask me anything."

"If you really could die any way you wanted, what would that look like?"

The long-held dream stirred in Clara's imagination once more. So alive, so vivid.

So real.

"I'd be in São Paulo, Miss Kelley. I'd see the city for myself. Even if I only had an hour there, I'd take it. That's all I'd need. Then I would have that one missing piece of Johnny and me."

The girl nodded. "That sounds perfect."

"I thought so too."

Pulling the messenger bag strap onto her shoulder, Aidyn continued, "Tomorrow is Saturday, and I was told to come on weekdays only. But if they allow me, would you mind if I come to see you tomorrow?"

The offer lit Clara's heart. "Honey, I would love to see you every day."

"Then I'll see what they say." Aidyn sighed in the way someone does after being filled and satisfied. "Behave yourself while I'm gone."

"You give terrible advice, Miss Kelley."

The girl winked and started for the door.

Needing something to drink after all the gabbing, Clara reached for the cup of water on the tray table. Her eyes landed on the open Bible—and the Psalm that had been her nudge. "Miss Kelley, wait."

The girl turned around.

"Will you do one thing for me before I see you again?"

"Of course."

"Will you read Psalm 16?"

Aidyn's brow pinched. "Psalm 16?"

"Yes."

The girl nodded, though clearly not understanding why. "Sure thing." With a final wave, she continued on.

Clara watched her leave and then nestled against the chair, basking in the warmth their conversation had created in the room.

Her third soak of the day.

"I think that's a wise decision."

Rosario's reply echoed in Aidyn's mind as she exited the main doors of Sacred Promise. Aidyn did not explain her reasons for wanting to visit Mrs. Kip on the weekend. Nor did Rosario explain why she thought the decision was wise. The frail frame, the sunken eyes, the fact that Mrs. Kip never asked to move from her chair, the fact that the cookie lay ignored on the tray table—no more explanation was needed.

Aidyn walked to her car carrying far more than she'd anticipated leaving with. Among the treasures and tribulations were even more questions. What happened to Mai Khab? Where was her family? What happened to the people of the mission? Most confounding of all, why would the Lord not let Mrs. Kip go to São Paulo, her greatest dream?

All the loose ends of Mrs. Kip's life dangled before Aidyn like invitations. As she settled into the driver's seat of her car, she took her phone from her bag and searched for São Paulo on the maps app. The metropolis sat slightly inland, almost directly west of Brazil's more famous major city, Rio de Janeiro. It was 5,298 miles from her current location.

If Aidyn could bend space and time, she would shrink that distance to nothing and stand with Mrs. Kip on the same balcony her husband had once found, and together they would survey the city that Mrs. Kip had dreamed of for decades. Surely she would laugh in delight.

Aidyn warmed at the thought.

On the drive back to the office, she called ahead to the archives, eager to find more historical facts to round out the incredible personal story that had landed in her lap—largely because of Woods's scheme, a truth she still couldn't comprehend. She asked Phyllis to pull any articles related to the Laotian refugee resettlement in Kansas City and the nation between 1975 and 1980.

"Funny you should mention it," Phyllis said. "I figured you'd be requesting such articles, so I've already started curating, if you want to come see."

Aidyn grinned, certain Phyllis's foresight was the Lord's hand at work. "I'll be there in half an hour."

A small pile of printouts had formed on Phyllis's desk. A few bright-pink sticky notes jutted out from various pages.

"I'm still digging, mind you," Phyllis said, continuing to scroll through documents on her computer screen. "Most of what we ran back then was written by wire services for national or regional publication, like this piece." She pointed at an article on her screen. The headline read, "Refugees Headed for Iowa."

"What's the date on that?" Aidyn asked.

"October 22, 1975. Written by the AP."

"Could be good for context. Go ahead and print it, please."

Phyllis printed the clip and moved on to the next. "I flagged with a sticky note anything I found about Kansas City specifically." She gestured to the pile. "You're welcome to go through the stack while I search."

"This is great, Phyllis. I really appreciate your being proactive." Aidyn set down her bag and began to read the article on top of the pile, a page 1 *Star* feature from a wire service published May 26, 1975, a matter of weeks after the Pathet Lao took over Laos. It was titled "Anti-US Tension Surges in Laos."

According to the article, US Embassy staff in Vientiane "accelerated the burning of documents today, and the embassy's Marine guards moved their pistols and riot gas supplies to safer upstairs storage areas as anti-American feeling mounted."

These same embassy staff and their guards would soon be evacuated to safety, leaving behind Lao contractors who would be targeted as traitors and suffer the consequences.

Aidyn flipped to the next article, from August 13, 1975, also by the AP. "Tragic End for Long March by Meo Tribesmen."

The Meo, Aidyn soon learned, were a Laotian minority ethnic group who had also helped America in the Vietnam War. Hoping for asylum with their allies, they had fled their mountainous villages on foot and walked through the thick jungle for three weeks in an attempt to find safe haven in Thai refugee camps, where they hoped to stay only temporarily until getting the nod to emigrate to America. Instead, they found a less-than-welcoming Thai government and a US government that wouldn't recognize them. "They now have nowhere to turn," the article read.

Though their camp lay well across the border, it was still vulnerable to raiding parties from Pathet Lao. About 80 percent of the people suffered from malnutrition, malaria, and anemia, according to Thai medical authorities, and in the Ban Nam Lam camp, starvation was rampant. Refugees had begun to scavenge the surrounding jungle for wild bamboo shoots and other food.

Three-fourths of the Meo refugees were women and children.

Aidyn thought of the Khab children, the youngest only five years old, caught in similar circumstances. The long nights Mrs. Kip had spent on her knees begging God to show favor on two children she had never met suddenly came into sharp, hard focus.

What those months must have been like to live through, on both ends of the ocean.

She glanced over at Phyllis. "These stories are all depressing."

Without looking away from her screen, Phyllis replied, "Read that first flagged article. It's an uplifting one, about a local family."

Aidyn peeled back several printout pages to find the article Phyllis referred to. The top half of the page was filled with a dark and grainy photo of a young Laotian family sitting at their kitchen table, looking through toys.

A sweet baby girl caught Aidyn's eye. She held a new Barbie doll and smiled in the most heart-melting way, all teeth and dimples.

"Family Reunites after Haunting Ordeal," the headline read. The article was published on October 5, 1975.

Aidyn looked at each of the smiling children, then at the mom.

She stopped cold.

Mai Khab.

The cutline confirmed the mother's identity. And the father's: Mahasajun. And the oldest child: Joshua. The Joshua of baseball fame.

Aidyn felt her mouth drop open. Until then, she had only imagined what Mahasajun and the children looked like. Being able to see them, zero in on their faces, discover what shape their lips made when they pulled into a smile, shook her to her core. These people she had only heard about, now in front of her. Proof of their existence and their irrefutable humanness.

She hungered to know more about them and dove into the article.

The details all lined up perfectly with everything Mrs. Kip had told her—that Mahasajun Khab was an officer in the Laotian army, studying for what was supposed to have been a brief period at the Command and General Staff College in Leavenworth. When the Pathet Lao took over, all communication between parents and children, who were left in the care of their maternal grandparents back home, was severed. It took nearly six months for the children to make their way to their parents.

As she read, Aidyn was carried into the depth that existed between the dry facts presented in the article, into the emotion behind those words—the emotion so perfectly and profoundly captured in the pleading prayers of Mrs. Kip. The two innocent children saved from near-certain persecution, or worse. A rescue mission requiring the selflessness of relatives and strangers on at least two continents. The multitude of people it took, the fact that many of them had never met (and probably never did), the fact that they didn't speak the same language but they all had the same driving mission. The secret meetings, the covert operations. Lives risked. All to move the children from point to point safely, then across the Mekong River.

"The Pathet Lao shoots on sight, regardless of who receives the bullet," Mahasajun had told the reporter.

Aidyn's stomach sank. How terrifying it must have been for those kids. The risk those little ones took just to be with their mom and dad again. Just to live.

Aidyn's eyes filled with tears.

"Kelley?" Phyllis's voice broke in.

She didn't attempt to blink away the water. "I can't help it. It's such an amazing story."

CHAPTER 24

By 2:45, Aidyn had amassed a thick file folder of articles related in some way to the Laotian refugee resettlement in America. Although it would have been amazing to stick around to get more, to continue walking around in the world that had existed so many years ago, she needed to finally get back to her desk and finish her "real" work. Heaven knew Woods had probably filled her inbox with tasks.

"I'll let you know if I find anything else," Phyllis offered.

"You have been a huge help, as usual." Aidyn picked up the folder and tucked it into her bag.

"It's what I'm here for. Tell Shayna good luck with the article."

Aidyn blinked. "Shayna?"

A wrinkle formed between the archivist's eyebrows. "Isn't that who you're researching for? She told me this morning she was doing a feature on the refugee resettlement."

Aidyn's face burned. Through the wild thumping in her

ears, she managed to respond, "Yes, she was needing this research. Thanks again."

Quickly she made her exit so Phyllis would not see her jaw clenched tight. She took the stairs down to the newsroom, hoping the exertion would soothe her racing thoughts. All it did was get her out of breath.

Shayna sat at her desk typing away on her laptop. Back ramrod straight, chest out like a peacock. As usual, she pretended not to notice Aidyn's arrival. But Aidyn would not be ignored.

She slammed her bag down on her desk. "The resettlement story is not yours, Reese."

Shayna continued to blithely type, keeping her eyes on the screen. "That's not your decision to make."

"I found that story, and Woods knows it."

With measured movements, Shayna took her hands off her keyboard and turned to Aidyn. "Let me explain how this works. The editor decides which of her reporters has the most skill, experience, and savvy to research and write a story that helps bring in the readers. It's in the editor's best interest to go with the reporter she can most trust. And unfortunately for you, you've proven you can't be trusted to have the paper's best interests in mind. The only thing you have proven is that you really don't deserve to be here."

Aidyn's insides boiled. She had never been tempted to scream in the newsroom, but at that moment, she was on the verge of unleashing a shout that would make Maper envious.

Shayna returned to her computer.

"You pitched Woods?" Aidyn demanded.

"Emailed her this morning."

Aidyn balled her hands into fists.

"She meets with Maper in a bit. I assume it will get brought up." Shayna peered at her. "I would say good luck, but I think we both know how this is going to go."

Before she said something she would regret, Aidyn tore her eyes away and plunked into her chair.

Shayna was right. If Maper knew both reporters had pitched similar stories, it wasn't a question which one he would go with. Even if Woods was on Aidyn's side, as Mrs. Kip had claimed, how much influence would she really have?

"You brought it on yourself," Shayna added.

Aidyn ignored her and logged on to her computer.

If Mrs. Kip was right about God having hidden warriors everywhere, they were already overdue for their arrival.

Rosario read the numbers off the sticky note and dialed them into the cordless phone from Clara's nightstand.

Patiently Clara waited in the armchair. The clock next to the phone base read 2:55. Clara had slept off the exhilarating visit with Aidyn, and now most of the workday had passed. She couldn't waste any more time. The battle was at hand.

Rosario, bless her, had gotten right on it.

Finished dialing, Rosario put the phone to her ear and listened. "It's their automated answering system," she said. "Don't worry, I'll get you to the right spot. I figured out how when I tried to reach Bella Woods."

Clara nodded. "Thank you, honey. You are a blessing to me."

After several button clicks and two requests for an operator, Rosario smiled and handed the phone to Clara. She put it to her ear in time to hear, "How may I direct your call?"

Clara dusted off her authoritative voice. "Managing editor, please."

"I'm sorry, he's in a meeting right now. I can transfer you to his voicemail."

The old "in a meeting" block. As if that had ever stopped her. "Tell him it's about one of his reporters. He'll want to hear this."

A brief pause. "Just one moment. Let me see if he's available to take your call."

Clara grinned at Rosario, who silently clapped.

Nearly a full minute later, a gruff voice spoke into the line. "Maper."

"Mr. Maper, my name is Clara Kip. You don't know me, but I just had an experience with one of your reporters that I think you should know about. You should be aware, sir, of the kind of people you have working for you."

Over the course of the next five minutes, Clara figured out exactly what his motivators were, and she used them to her advantage—to Aidyn's advantage—in order to take down the beast.

She never did feel more alive than when she fought for the sake of someone else.

Aidyn wavered dramatically between two opposing forces. On the one side, confidence that Woods had essentially given her permission to run with the story and would honor that.

On the other, crippling fear that her own naïve gaffe in approaching Maper in the first place would come back to bite her . . . again. Not to mention the fact that Shayna was the more experienced writer and arguably the more skilled researcher, at least in Maper's eyes. In the *Star* newsroom, his was the view that mattered most, other than the publisher's.

In the moments of confidence, Aidyn continued searching online for various information related to the story. She found the website of Mrs. Kip's church and hankered to give them a call. Certainly they had records that would prove useful.

Invariably, at the precise moment she started to move forward with any piece of research, fear would rage. She would relent and go back to the menial tasks she had to get done before the end of the day.

No wait is longer or more tenuous than waiting for a verdict.

On top of the worries, she had finally seen the IM from Rahmiya. It was about their lunch plans, which Aidyn had completely forgotten. Though she tried to reach out to Rahmiya to apologize, her friend's IM status showed "in a meeting." All afternoon.

Finally, at about 3:45, Woods emerged from Maper's office.

Aidyn watched her approach out of the corner of her eye, pulse racing.

The bulldog editor came around the front of Shayna's desk and stopped. "Show me the councilman story before you file it, Reese."

Shayna nodded, her confidence having never left her. "Will do."

Without a reply or a glance toward Aidyn, Woods headed for her office. Aidyn didn't have the courage to speak up.

But Shayna did. "Any word on the resettlement piece?" she called after their boss.

Aidyn's heart felt like it would slam out of her chest.

Woods looked over her shoulder and replied evenly, "I want you on the councilman beat for the time being."

"But what about—"

"I've answered sufficiently, Reese." Woods turned and marched to her office.

In the wake of her departure, the two reporters looked at each other, Shayna clearly shocked and confused, Aidyn beginning to see the invisible armor Woods wore over her clothes.

"Don't even think it means you'll get it," Shayna snapped. "Maper probably needs time to think about it."

But they both knew better. If Woods was going to give Shayna the assignment, that was the moment she would have done it. The fact that she didn't could mean only one thing: Woods's instruction for Aidyn to turn in a draft for consideration was still a go.

Shayna shoved back her chair and walked off.

Aidyn didn't watch her leave. Instead she lifted her eyes to the ceiling.

Hidden warriors everywhere.

Aidyn wasted no time in gathering more research, and the secretary of Mrs. Kip's church, Julie, proved exceptionally helpful.

"We have attendance records from that time period," she told Aidyn. "With the mission meeting here, we had about thirty families attending. They would hold a Lao service in our chapel on Sundays. So few of them understood English well enough at that point."

"Are the records something you could email to me?"

"They're handwritten records, but I can try to scan them for you."

"That would be great. Is there anyone still attending who was at the church during that time period? I'd love to talk to them."

"Definitely there are," Julie said. "I'd want to check with them first before I refer you."

"Understandable. Did any of the Lao families stay at the church?"

"Almost all of them moved to the new church."

Aidyn frowned. "What new church is that?"

"The one we helped them plant in Olathe."

Olathe . . . the same suburb as Sacred Promise. "What's the name of the church?"

"Hope Church, on Maxwell Street. They moved there in 1983."

The same year that Mai left for Thailand.

"Would you like the church's phone number?" Julie asked.

"Yes," Aidyn said. "I very much would."

———

Once more, someone's touch roused Clara from a slumber she didn't know she had fallen into. Falling asleep without realizing it, that lack of awareness of such a basic bodily function, was unsettling. It was as though she lived half-dead. One of many reasons to loathe the effects of morphine, even at low doses.

She blinked awake at the touch, attempting to pull out of the fuzziness the drug had descended upon her. What was the time, the day, the place she was in again? When her eyes came into focus, Rosario's full, smiling face was before her. The clue she was in Sacred Promise, in her armchair.

"Just wanted to see you before I left," Rosario told her. "I won't be in until Monday, so I thought I'd come by while I had the chance."

"That was nice of you." If Rosario was leaving until Monday, that meant it must be Friday. Details about the day began to wander back.

Rosario perched on the edge of the loveseat. "I never asked you how the visit with Aidyn Kelley went earlier."

The visit! Snatches of their conversation drifted back. The girl's smile. The laughing. Psalm 16.

"We had a ball, honey. She's a good kid."

"I'm so glad. And I told her it was okay if she wanted to come see you tomorrow. I think that will be good for both of you."

"Agreed."

A shadow inched into Rosario's expression. It betrayed every unvoiced thought chewing at her mind, every unspoken worry that had really motivated her to come for a Friday afternoon visit. Unlike Aidyn, Rosario knew too much, had seen too much.

On the outer edges of life, a lot can happen in a weekend. Nothing can be taken for granted.

Rosario spoke gently. "Please continue to give yourself the rest you need."

Understanding the plea for everything it was, Clara opened

her palm, and Rosario slid her hand into it. Clara held it with the firmness, thankfulness, and love a final embrace comprised, because for all either of them knew, it would be the last one.

"I will be fine," Clara said. "I will be better than fine. I'll be my very tip-top best, in fact. You enjoy your time and keep being a blessing. I cannot thank you enough for all you did for me this week. You gave me much more than I ever thought possible."

Rosario looked down at the floor.

If Clara had possessed the strength in that moment, she would have collected the woman into a tender hug. "You're a good kid too, honey."

After a moment, Rosario sniffed, then met Clara's gaze with moist eyes. "I'll see you Monday, Mrs. Kip."

Clara winked. "See you Monday."

Rosario stood and walked to the door. She stopped once to wave goodbye and then disappeared into the hallway.

In the silence, Clara sighed long and slowly. That same scene with Aidyn would be much harder.

She glanced at the tray table and saw her Bible still open to the Psalms, still resting next to the cookie the girl had brought her. She picked up the Bible and tried to read, tried to find the promises and solace, but her mind wafted to dreamy images the words evoked. Sheep on a hillside in full sun and a cool breeze. Morning putting on its glory. But her favorite image was of sitting at a large table, the length of which stretched beyond her view. John sat next to her. Then Martha. Her parents. So many others, some familiar but many not. She fell asleep admiring the pictures.

She awoke only when she was made to.

When dinner was delivered that evening, she said her thanks but let it sit on the tray table and went back to sleep.

When dinner was retrieved, she put the leftover cookie on the untouched plate and told the middle-aged woman with the hairnet, "Go ahead and remove me from the distribution list."

Then she went back to sleep.

When Michelle came by for the first round of her night shift, Clara asked to get into her jaunty yellow bunny pajamas and then into bed.

Never again would she resent how the bed held her body.

Mai's grandson. It had to be.

Daniel Khab, freelance photographer. He worked for several US-based news and publishing companies.

Aidyn read his bio on his photography blog's About page again, keying in on the details both overtly provided and those implied. In the accompanying headshot, Daniel appeared to be in his late twenties. The bio reported he was the grandson of missionaries to Thailand who were among "the displaced military families during the Pathet Lao takeover." He'd studied visual arts at the University of Kansas before relocating back to Thailand to be with his parents. He still lived and worked in Bangkok.

Aidyn clicked over to the Contact page and filled out the form, explaining who she was and what she was looking for.

If you have any information that may help, I would appreciate hearing back from you. Thank you for your time.

At the end, she included her personal cell number.

She said a quick prayer and clicked Send. The message to Daniel was the second potentially major contact she had made that day. The first was to Pastor Khounmy Sarn at Hope Church, for whom she had left a message on the church's voicemail. Either one, she hoped, would break open the story in a new way.

With Shayna gone for the day, Aidyn worked more openly and with more fervor, stretching her work hours past 6:00. The stack of printouts continued to grow on her desk.

Among her finds were several 1970s articles that focused on the personal plights of different refugees around the country. She highlighted her way through them, picking up a lot more contextual details about the time period. Of particularly interesting note, the sponsors and support networks mentioned in the articles were, almost invariably, faith-based. Catholics, Lutherans, Methodists, Baptists—they all routinely collaborated on individual or group levels in an attempt to find the best sponsors, the best homes, the best jobs for the incoming asylum seekers.

Mrs. Kip had been a local example of a national movement— a movement that changed significantly with the Refugee Act of 1980, which created the Federal Refugee Resettlement Program, a more formalized way to resettle refugees in America.

After marking up several more articles, Aidyn decided to finally go home. The newsroom was empty by that point, save for the scraps of food and old coffee cups left behind from the day's work—and one office light still ablaze.

Woods.

That woman never did work reasonable hours.

Aidyn gathered up her printouts and laptop and packed them neatly into her bag. As she prepared to leave, she glanced again at Woods's door. The urge to say something to her swelled too large to ignore. Without a plan of what precisely to speak, she padded over to the office. Hopefully clear, meaningful words would magically form.

Woods stared at her computer screen, hand clamped around her chin in concentration. She didn't acknowledge Aidyn in her doorway.

"I'm headed out for the weekend," Aidyn said.

"Do you need to tell me that?" Woods retorted without shifting her attention.

"No. That was just a segue."

Woods harrumphed. "Can't wait to find out to what."

Taking one step into the office, Aidyn stood as straight and square as she could. "I wanted to thank you, Woods. For the story."

"I didn't give you a story," her editor quickly corrected.

"But you cleared the way for me to have an opportunity." The words felt awkward and probably sounded that way too.

Briefly Woods looked up at her, brow low, mouth tight. Then she returned to her work. "Stop with the feelings, Kelley. Write a good story. Don't make me regret it."

The reply amused Aidyn, but she was careful to hide it. "Will do."

There was so much more to say, though. Like why she thanked Woods, and how the floundering rookie had one key thing in common with the bulldog editor with a strong poker face.

In the end, Aidyn wrapped it all into a simple code most

Christians would understand readily. "Have a blessed weekend, Boss."

Woods looked up again, longer. With a subtle nod, she replied, "You too, Kelley."

When the editor resumed her work, Aidyn took her leave, for once thankful she had been placed with Woods. The Lord's hand had been moving for a while, apparently.

Out in the elevator lobby, Aidyn's cell chimed. She slipped it out of her bag. A local number showed on the screen.

When she answered, a young man greeted her. "My name is Palani Sarn," he said. "You left a message for my dad, Pastor Khounmy Sarn, earlier today."

A thrill coursed through her. "Yes, I did."

"Dad isn't as strong in English as I am, so he asked me to return your call. He said to tell you that we would be happy to help."

Aidyn looked up with a giant smile. "That is great news, Palani. I'm so glad."

"Sure." He paused. "So, what exactly did you have in mind?"

CHAPTER 25

"Did you get it?" Aidyn asked Rahmiya eagerly through Face-Time later that night. She waited on her living room floor with bated breath.

Her friend held up the virtual reality headset. "I literally had to hold my breath the whole time I was in Ahmed's room, and I nearly fainted on top of his rancid boxers, but yes. Mission accomplished."

"You're the best, Rahmi! I'll bring you lunch tomorrow in exchange."

"That makes *two* lunches you owe me."

"Again, very sorry I spaced on our plans."

"It's okay. You apparently had an exciting day." Rahmiya laid the headgear aside. "And I have to say, this is quite the plan you've cooked up for your visit with Mrs. Kip tomorrow."

Aidyn grinned. Hopefully Mrs. Kip would love what she had managed to pull together, thanks in large part to Palani Sarn. "Sure you don't want to come with me? See how it all shakes out?"

Rahmiya pursed her lips. "As tempting as that sounds, I'll just enjoy my free lunches instead. Have you heard back from the guy in Thailand?"

"Not yet. I hope he's Mai's grandson, though. How incredible would that be to find out what happened to her? Maybe I could even reunite the two women over video chat." The idea quickened her pulse. "That would be amazing."

Rahmiya eyed her, brow lowering.

Aidyn's excitement dwindled. "What?" she asked.

"Nothing."

"It's something. What?"

"I don't know . . . It just seems you're putting a lot into this woman. Like, more than is necessary."

The Aidyn a week prior would have chafed at such a suggestion. But the Aidyn who had looked into the prayer life of Clara Kip, who had cried, laughed, and cheered along with the words poured out from a broken and worshipful heart, found zero shame in Rahmiya's observation.

"She's an adventure, Rahmi. One I completely misread."

Her friend's expression did not change.

Aidyn let it go. "Thanks again for the headset. I'll be by about noon tomorrow to pick it up."

"Sounds good," Rahmiya replied.

"Go recover from your trauma over the boxers, and I'll see you tomorrow."

"Good luck with the writing."

When their call ended, Aidyn put her phone on the floor next to the research she had organized in a semicircle. Piles of articles, charts, census records, maps, and more were queued up on the hardwood. The take-out container of chicken-fried rice sat nearby, only half empty.

As exciting as the next day promised to be, a long night stretched before her. It would be filled with highlighting and searching and somehow stringing words together to create meaning out of it all, meaning that would draw others into the years gone by and give due honor to those who had lived them.

She sat amid the pieces, absorbing the energy they exuded, the sense of anticipation they inspired. She could feel the words waiting just beyond her reach, waiting for her to form them into something clear, bright, and good.

She closed her eyes and pulled in a breath.

Help me tell this well, Lord. Help me find the ending Mrs. Kip needs.

A little before midnight, after several hours of typing words that slowly became a draft, a new-message alert popped up on Aidyn's screen. The preview of the message showed the sender's name.

Daniel Khab.

Whatever sleepiness had begun to web around her immediately fell away. She switched over to her inbox and opened the message.

Aidyn—

Yes, Mai Khab was my grandmother. I'm so sorry to hear about her friend Clara Kip. Although I'd be glad to talk to you, I think the best person is my father, Joshua. My grandmother died before I was born. If you want to email me your questions, I'll forward them to him. Hopefully that works with your deadline.

Daniel

Aidyn stuck on the words "died before I was born." Her heart panged. Until that moment, she had not realized how obstinately she had clung to the idea of a miraculous reunion of two long-lost friends. A show-stopping, Hollywood-rivaling crescendo to an amazing story of friendship across borders.

She recoiled at the thought of telling Mrs. Kip.

Pushing it away, she typed a reply to Daniel. She included questions she thought Mrs. Kip would want to know too. When did her friend die? How? Was she sick? Was she happy? Did she accomplish all she had set out to do? Did she ever have regrets? Did she ever talk about Mrs. Kip? Did she feel the void left by her friend? Did she ever try to come back to Kansas?

Perhaps it was more than the young man expected, especially considering he had never met the woman of his family's stories, but Aidyn had to take advantage of the source while she had it. Had to press in where the frail woman with fading strength could not.

She clicked Send and hoped for a speedy answer.

Saturday, June 11, 2016

The morning rays cut through the room. Clara turned her face toward the window, her hair flattening against the pillow. Though her heart leapt for joy at the new day, her body didn't want to move, didn't want to be disturbed. Her hands didn't—couldn't—take up her Bible from the tray table. The dose of morphine in the middle of the night clung to her, confining her in place.

But her eyes could still see, and her mind could still remember.

She looked out into the canopy of colors and called up the Scripture locked away inside her, where nothing, not even pain meds—or the death they tried to alleviate—could reach and steal it away.

"My lips will glorify you, Lord," she offered in a dry whisper that scratched her throat.

She trusted the muted words overflowing from her lips floated across the room, slipped between the grains of the windowpane, and flew upward on the streams of the wind, where they morphed into a great shout and sailed straight to the ears of heaven. Loud, soft, or silent, all praise was heard by the Lord.

"My lips will glorify you because your faithful love is better than life." Psalm 63:3.

That one she loved more than any others. It was the verse Martha had given her the day she was baptized.

"May this always be the theme of your days," Martha had told her, handing her a small, framed card with the verse written in gorgeous calligraphy. The little framed card sat on Clara's kitchen windowsill for years afterward, but the verse had lodged in her heart forever.

"Yes, Lord." Clara exhaled into the colors outside her window. "It is better than life."

In between the subsequent ins and outs of sleep, as her body involuntarily gave up more of its being, Clara prayed repeatedly for strength and gracious lulls from pain to be able to finish the work she had left to do with Aidyn, to pass on the sword the girl would need for battle.

Just one more day of strength, Lord. If it is your will. She is precious to me.

Rosario had asked Aidyn to keep reminding Mrs. Kip of what was possible. The plea that once pressed so heavy on Aidyn's shoulders had become an invitation. The moment she opened herself up to the privilege, ideas began to connect, one to another. Boom, boom, boom. As if they had been waiting to fall into place all that time.

She walked through the front doors of Sacred Promise, carrying a green tote bag with only two items. So far as she could help it, Mrs. Kip would have the adventure of her earthly life that day. The adventure she had been waiting most of her adult life to take.

Her steps were light, as if the world was at her command and everything was right.

She passed through the activity room. The clock on the wall showed the time had inched past 2:00. The guests she'd invited would arrive in half an hour.

She smiled and zeroed in on the singular goal of making the old woman the happiest Aidyn had ever seen her. Happier even than the day before.

The Lord moved even now in mighty ways. And it was thrilling.

Aidyn strode down the corridor toward room 310, toward the moment that seemed as though it had been appointed all along. Chest up, shoulders back, she came up to Mrs. Kip's door—and stopped cold.

The woman was in bed, the one place she had refused to go. A white sheet stretched over her lower half like a flimsy shield. Her hair was smashed against the pillow, and her head listed to the side. Her lower jaw hung askew, the way Mr. Slesher's had.

How could this be the same woman? Mrs. Kip had been tired the day before, but not bedridden tired.

Aidyn hesitated in the doorway. All she had planned teetered on the edge. Maybe she was too late.

A nudge urged her onward and told her she was exactly on time to be the friend Mrs. Kip needed that day, and she could dare to believe it, dare to trust that what she brought was precisely what Mrs. Kip was supposed to receive.

But could Aidyn do it?

Mrs. Kip had so easily sat with Mr. Slesher, desirously centered on his comfort alone. Could Aidyn do the same? Could she give—and serve—in that way as well?

She swallowed the doubt and clung to the tote handles.

Lord, give me courage.

In Clara's fitful sleep, the table dream returned. She discovered the table sat inside a large dining hall inside a grand mansion, grander than anything ever seen by human eyes. A giant feast lay before her and the others at that table. The food inexplicably gleamed, as bright as the gold platters underneath. It made her ravenous with joy, but oddly not with hunger.

A voice resounded over the people. At first it was deep and rolling. Then lighter. Softer. Feminine.

A familiar voice. It didn't come from the dining hall.

"Mrs. Kip?"

The voice belonged to the girl.

"Mrs. Kip?"

A hand on her arm, gentle and warm—and human. Clara realized she, too, had earthly breath. And earthly beings have eyes to see. She forced hers open, willed them to see the person standing at her bedside.

She tried to say the girl's name, but her mouth felt like cotton.

The girl reached for the cup on the tray table and directed the straw to Clara's lips.

The water blotted out the dryness and peeled her tongue from the roof of her mouth. With concentration, Clara coaxed her muscles to remember how to swallow.

"Miss Kelley." Hopefully her lips showed the smile that lit up inside her. "I'm so glad you came." Clara lifted her left hand from under the sheet. It shook from the exertion.

Aidyn quickly put down the cup and gathered Clara's hand in hers. "Hello to you too." She smiled in return, bright and captivating, like a sunrise. "How are you this afternoon?"

"Spunky as ever." Clara giggled dryly. Even to her ears, it sounded weak. Her hand drooped inside Aidyn's.

The girl chuckled all the same, as if she didn't notice anything had changed. But the haunt of concern in her eyes was clear. The fact that Clara couldn't be more vibrant for her visitor hurt worse than the beast of prey that ate away the inside of her body.

"I'm glad to hear you're feeling spry, Mrs. Kip."

Clara attempted to tilt her head back against the pillow to see the girl better.

Apparently understanding her difficulty, Aidyn let go of her hand and moved a dining chair over to the side of the bed. When she sat, she was more eye level with Clara.

"Better?" Aidyn asked.

"Thank you, honey." A green tote bag sat in Aidyn's lap, where her messenger bag should have been. "You didn't bring your notes today?"

"No, not today."

"I bored you, didn't I?"

"Not in the least, Mrs. Kip. Actually, our conversation yesterday inspired me to bring you some more surprises. Would you like to see them?"

"With unimaginable zeal."

"I hope you like them as much as I liked rounding them up for you." She reached into the tote and pulled out a white paper bag. Grease splotched the outside. She moved the tote to the floor and unrolled the paper bag. "I did some research, and I think this might just tickle your fancy."

She took out something wrapped in deli paper and held it out for Clara to have a clear view as she peeled back the corners. Nestled in the center was a teardrop-shaped, golden-fried piece of Clara's long-held dream.

Clara's chest hitched. "Miss Kelley," she breathed.

"I take it you know what it is."

Clara nodded. The beautiful word John had taught her flowed off her tongue like a fresh breeze. "*Coxinha.*"

She had only seen one of the ethnic croquettes in the picture John had brought back. Had only imagined its taste and texture based on his description. To see one offered up for her pleasure was to believe the Lord had heard every hairline—and hare*brained*—prayer she had ever uttered.

Her throat tightened. "Where did you get that?"

"There's a Brazilian street food restaurant in the City Market. Have you ever tried one?"

Clara shook her head.

"Then it's about time we changed that."

Aidyn stood and pulled the tray table on the other side of the bed closer to them, directly over Clara's lap. She placed the baseball-sized croquette on top and retrieved a plastic knife and fork from the paper bag. Using the deli paper as a plate, she carefully carved the croquette. The crust crunched under the force of the knife and broke open to reveal a layer of breading that protected a scoop of cream cheese–doused shredded chicken.

If only Clara could still smell, to take in the aroma the *coxinha* surely had.

Carefully Aidyn continued to cut, finally picking up a small bit of crust, breading, and chicken on the fork. The tiniest of bites. She held it out to Clara. "Ready to taste?"

The blessing of the gift was overwhelming. Never mind that her taste buds were long ruined too, that her throat was too dry for food, that her jaw was too near exhaustion to chew. She nodded at Aidyn, who gently guided the fork into Clara's mouth.

Clara closed her eyes and held the bite on her tongue. Though the tasters were gone, the feelers still lived, and they danced. The moistness of the chicken, the crispy coating, the dense pillow of breading.

Her imagination told her it was every bit as delicious as John had claimed. She savored it, rolling it around her mouth, feeling it from every angle, thanking God for knowing her every little desire and loving her enough to give her the ones that pleased him.

"How is it?" Aidyn asked.

Clara opened her eyes and pushed the food into her cheek. "So worth the wait."

A wide smile stretched the girl's lips. She could not possibly understand what the *coxinha* truly meant to Clara, but her joy was irrepressible nonetheless.

For that very reason, Clara would not reveal her inability to swallow the bite. It was the only way to keep that look on the girl's face.

So she came up with a plan.

"Miss Kelley," she said. "Do you mind filling up my water cup?"

"Of course not." The girl took the cup and stepped into the hallway for the water fountain.

While she was gone, Clara labored to lift her hand to her mouth—her right hand, the one Aidyn likely wouldn't touch—and spit the food into her palm. Clutching it, she let her hand drop to her side, scooted it under the sheet, and wiped it as far under her leg as possible, where Aidyn likely wouldn't see.

A moment later, Aidyn returned and offered the straw

once again to Clara, who took in a drop and forced a swallow. When she was done, the girl set the cup on the tray table and lowered into the chair.

"Would you like more?" Aidyn motioned to the *coxinha*.

"Maybe after a while, if you don't mind, honey. It was such a wonderful surprise. I can't believe you did that for me."

"I'm glad you liked it, Mrs. Kip. But honestly, I hope you like the next surprise even more."

"I'm not sure I could."

"Oh, I think you can." She leaned forward, reaching into the tote on the floor. Out came a contraption the likes of which were usually featured in science fiction movies. It had a black box-looking thing on one end and a circular strap looped through it.

"Good heavens," Clara said. "What do you have there?"

"It's called a virtual reality headset."

Clara frowned. "What do you do with it?"

Aidyn giggled, clearly unable to contain her excitement. "With this, Mrs. Kip, you are going to walk the streets of São Paulo."

CHAPTER 26

Based on the open mouth of childlike awe and the repeated breathy exclamations, it was evident that every second of Aidyn's planning had been well worth it—beyond what she had hoped. Mrs. Kip's story was coming full circle.

Her heart both lifted and broke, the strangest sensation. But the smile did not leave her face as the old woman, whose shrunken head was comically dwarfed by the headset, lived vicariously through technology and "walked" the major sites of her beloved São Paulo.

Aidyn had come across the video on YouTube, filmed by a native Brazilian who'd captured all the major points of interest in the city. She had watched the video several times, touring over and over the places Mrs. Kip had dreamed of. They were easy to commit to memory, easy to see as if through the old woman's doting eyes.

The shops and entertainment of Avenida Paulista.

The bustle of the Mercadão market.

The natural serenity of Ibirapuera Park.

And last of all but most stunning, the sweeping view from the top of the Pico do Jaraguá mountain, a peak that rose 3,700 feet above sea level, seemingly halfway to the massive blue sky. In the video, the peak was skirted by puffy cumulus clouds, which appeared to be so close that Aidyn swore if she built up enough speed, she could leap onto them with little effort. In between the clouds, the city of millions sprawled out into the distance. Grayish-white buildings sat amid bunches of thick green trees, man and nature finding a way to live in harmony.

For as much as the video footage entranced Aidyn, it clearly meant infinitely more to Mrs. Kip. Through the grace of God, Aidyn had found a way to shrink the five thousand miles between Mrs. Kip and her dream.

"Oh my," the woman kept quietly exclaiming as she watched the video. It was more than enough for Aidyn.

The partially eaten *coxinha* lay in almost exactly the same spot as the cookie had the day before. A lack of appetite was predictable for the end of life, but the inability to swallow was not something Aidyn had accounted for. Mrs. Kip didn't say she couldn't swallow, and she probably never would, but it became obvious in the way she struggled to push down the last sip of water, as if channeling all her effort into the ordinarily voluntary movement.

The woman's first experience of *coxinha* had come not a moment too late. In God's perfect timing.

With Mrs. Kip occupied with the seven-minute video, Aidyn packed up the food and put it back in the tote bag.

Her phone pinged. She looked at the message, and her pulse quickened. The guests had arrived.

Quickly she texted where to find room 310 and where to wait until they heard the code word.

She pressed Send and checked the time. The video would end shortly, with that breathtaking view from Pico do Jaraguá. It should be distinct when that final stop on the tour arrived.

Sure enough, a gasp escaped Mrs. Kip's lips. Her chin began to tremble. She shook her head from side to side. Her chest heaved once, twice.

She was sobbing.

Tearless, soundless, overwhelmed sobs. The cries of a completely humbled soul on top of a mountain.

Aidyn's heart pinched. She reached out and took the woman's hand in hers. Mrs. Kip clung with surprising force.

After several moments, Mrs. Kip took in a loud breath through her teeth and blew it out. "That was spectacular," she said in a small voice.

Aidyn let go of her hand and gently lifted the headset off Mrs. Kip, helping her right her glasses afterward. The woman's eyes were red, as Aidyn had anticipated, but they were bone dry. A natural result from the difficulty in drinking. Fewer tears for emotion, less saliva for eating.

The human body has its being, and its demise, in fascinating ways.

"That was quite the adventure, wasn't it, Mrs. Kip?" Aidyn asked.

"Oh, honey, what a gift that was." Her chin started to tremble again. "Thank you."

The sight of such strong emotion—a first for Mrs. Kip—made Aidyn's throat tighten. If she tried to speak at that moment, her words would come out cracked and tearful. She couldn't cry. Not yet.

Because the final surprise would be even more powerful to give.

As if on cue, feet shuffled outside the door. The guests' arrival gave Aidyn something to focus on, and she cleared her throat. "Mrs. Kip, I learned more about São Paulo in the last day than I ever thought I wanted to know."

The old woman smiled.

"But in the last week, I've learned more about you than I ever thought I wanted to know." She paused to collect her next words, none of which she had rehearsed ahead of time. She fingered the headset in her hands. "You wanted to go to São Paulo to help those who were in need, who needed physical help but also help to know Jesus. And I know it disappointed you to not see that play out the way you dreamed it would. But I hope you also see, the way I do now, that although you weren't called to a different continent to serve, a different continent was called to you so that you could serve right here where you were."

Mrs. Kip nodded. "Yes, darling. That's exactly right."

Aidyn's head went light from the words she would say and what would happen next. She looked Mrs. Kip in the eyes, grateful to be there to witness it unfold. "Sometimes we do things in life without knowing what ripples flow from it long afterward. And I think that's true for you too. There's a lot to your story that you don't know, Mrs. Kip."

The woman frowned. "What do you mean, honey?"

"I could explain it, but I think the friends I invited could do a much better job."

At the word "friends," the feet shuffled again. The guests came into the room and fanned out around the bed. Eight of them in all. Led by Pastor Khounmy Sarn and his son Palani.

"Mrs. Kip," Aidyn said, "these are some of the members of Hope Church."

The old woman's mouth fell open. "Oh my."

———

If only Mai could hear what those surprise visitors had to say! The names, the faces, the stories of those who came after them, and who came *because* of them.

If only.

Aidyn had been correct. The ripples continued to that day. They had rolled unseen, unnamed, until the Lord allowed Clara this glimpse. For one breath of time, he had brought into full view how story connected to story, how one life connected to the next, how it all worked together to comprise his "big S" Story.

Clara leaned into the visit with all the energy she could, fighting for her attention to stay away from growing tiredness and the fact that the pain had started to outwrestle the morphine.

The pastor and his son, whose names slipped right out of Clara's grasp, did most of the talking. The others didn't seem to mind one bit. Except for the pastor's son, they all spoke with Lao-influenced English, the nuances of the American language still a hair out of comprehension.

None of the visitors were related to Mai, it seemed, but all of them had similar stories of finding refuge and opportunity in America. They spoke of how much the Hope community meant to them. They spoke of people and events Clara knew little or nothing about, yet she gained so much meaning from what they shared. Her heart opened to them the way it had opened to the Lao refugees in the mission days.

Dear, sweet Aidyn listened intently from her post in the chair beside the bed. She listened not for the purposes of note taking but for the purposes of absorbing. She embodied the same loveliness Mai had, the same compassion in need of coaxing and a halted courage in need of reinforcement.

Her heart longed for Aidyn the way it had for Mai the night they'd said goodbye.

Would Aidyn remain teachable? Would she grow in wisdom and stature and in favor with God and people? Would she stay on the narrow path to heaven? And the biggest question of all: Had Clara loved her enough?

All the same questions she had pondered when she hugged Mai for the last time. The same questions she had prayed through with countless babies before they left the hospital.

The burden of goodbye had never gotten easier.

Precious Aidyn. Gentle soul. Tender reed. Unexpected friend.

Clara yearned to tuck the girl into the crook of her wing and fly to the blue above, to never let her dash her foot against a stone. If she could, she would fight every beast. She would die at their hands if it meant the girl gained victory—if it meant Aidyn would truly live and never lose her smile, her hope, or her awakening sense of adventure.

But it was not Clara's place, nor her call, to be that for Aidyn. The girl had to learn to do battle—to be more than a conqueror—so she could someday teach that to others. And the only way to learn was to first be fitted with the right armor. With whatever dwindling strength still beat inside her, Clara had to ensure the child knew which armor to take up.

"Mrs. Kip?"

Clara blinked into awareness. Nine sets of eyes rested on her.

Aidyn spoke gently. "Pastor Khounmy would like to pray for you before they go. Would you like that?"

"Oh." Clara looked up at the man, who smiled kindly. Though clearly much time had lapsed since her last active involvement in the conversation, hopefully none of her guests had taken offense. "That would be wonderful, Pastor. Thank you."

Quiet settled over the room as all bowed their heads. The pastor spoke first in Lao, then in mostly whole English. He petitioned for comfort and peace. He gave thanks for all Clara had done in and through Jesus's name. He praised God for the opportunity to meet her. And he prayed for God's will to continue to be done.

"Amen," Clara mumbled.

One by one, the guests came to her bedside to give well-wishes. To each she offered her hand and her sincere gratitude. Her arm quickly grew tired.

Pastor Khounmy came last. He took her labor-weary hand tenderly in both of his. "Many crowns for you, Mrs. Kip." He placed her hand on the bed, satisfying its cry for rest, and joined his flock at the door.

In unison, the eight guests waved a final farewell and left.

Clara turned to the girl sitting in the chair. The afternoon sunlight streamed through the picture window and made her fair complexion and blond hair gleam as if touched directly by heaven, like an affirmation from above that Aidyn would receive the last seed tucked inside Clara's palm.

And it was harder to let it go than she'd imagined it would be.

Unaware of any of these realities, Aidyn sighed with contentment, the joy of the afternoon's events still shining in her countenance. "That was a lot of excitement, huh?"

"You absolutely spoiled me," Clara replied, which made the girl smile.

"You're probably tired now. I should get going so you can rest." Aidyn started to stand.

Clara lifted her fingers off the bed—the most movement she could manage—and waved for her to stop.

The girl sat back down. "What is it, Mrs. Kip?"

"It's my turn now."

"Your turn for what?"

"To give a gift."

Aidyn blinked. "You have a gift for me?"

Clara turned toward the tray table and nodded to her Bible. "Look up a passage for me."

"Is it a Psalm?" Aidyn asked as she retrieved the Bible.

"Yes. The one I told you to look up yesterday before you left." Clara eyed her. "Did you?"

The girl looked sheepish.

"Don't worry about it. Let's read it together. Psalm 16."

Within a few page turns, Aidyn found the correct spot. "You want me to read the whole chapter?"

Clara shook her head. "Just what I starred. Verse 8."

Looking down at the page, Aidyn found the star and read

aloud, "'I always let the LORD guide me. Because he is at my right hand, I will not be shaken.'"

Hearing the girl speak the verse the Lord had popped off the page to Clara made her all the more certain it was right for Aidyn. When Aidyn needed to bear up under the heft of trials, she would have this small prayer to wield. Over and over again in her life, she would lift that sword to her enemy.

"Read it again," Clara prompted.

"'I always let the LORD guide me. Because he is at my right hand, I will not be shaken.'"

"Again."

Though appearing perplexed by the instruction, Aidyn followed it once more and read the verse.

"Say it without looking."

Aidyn paused, clearly caught off guard. Though she did her best, her recitation was clumsy.

"Again," Clara said.

With more accuracy and confidence, Aidyn recited the verse without looking.

"Again."

The girl recited it perfectly.

"Again."

For a second time, Aidyn recited the verse perfectly.

"Do you understand?" Clara asked.

"The verse? I think so."

"Do you understand what the verse is telling you to do?"

For a moment, Aidyn was quiet. At last, she answered, using the words she had just learned to have ready. "'I always let the LORD guide me. Because he is at my right hand, I will not be shaken.'"

Clara continued her test, needing to believe without question the girl understood. "When you don't know what to do next, what choice will you make?"

More quickly, Aidyn realized what she needed to say. "'I always let the LORD guide me. Because he is at my right hand, I will not be shaken.'"

"When the world tries to get you to step away from the narrow path, what will you do?"

The girl's chin lifted, and she answered with assurance. "'I always let the LORD guide me. Because he is at my right hand, I will not be shaken.'"

Clara held Aidyn's gaze, willed every drop of love within her to spill into the girl, to lift her up, and to enliven the boldness those powerful words contained. "Honey, this world is going to come at you. The pain is real, and it is sharp. You know what it did to me. But you also know what I gave back to the world. Despite it all, I returned light for darkness. Remember that."

Her throat cried from dryness, but she forged ahead.

"I am nothing but a feeble bag of bones with a decent smile. I did nothing good—not one solitary thing—apart from God. Whatever empowerment I had came from him. It's the same empowerment you have for the taking. It's walking at your right hand, as close as an ask. Whatever comes your way, you don't need to be shaken."

The girl bit her lip. She clearly understood it was not a trite pep talk. The words were not just a catchy saying. They were life. And though she did not yet realize it, they were also a sendoff.

Aidyn reached out and took hold of Clara's hand.

"Seek him with everything you have," Clara told her. "Follow him even if it means you have to do weird things—like talk to a hospice patient."

Aidyn smiled, but her eyes revealed the emotion rising within her. It pooled just above her lower lids.

Clara futilely tried to wet her mouth. "Will you follow?"

The girl nodded.

"Tell me how you will follow."

With an unsteady voice, Aidyn replied, "'I always let the LORD guide me. Because he is at my right hand, I will not be shaken.'"

Clara nodded. "That's your theme verse. Your sword. Promise me you will keep it close."

Aidyn blinked away the tears. "I promise."

Clara mustered her strength and brought the girl's hand to her dry lips. There was so much more she wished she could say, wished she could give. But her strength had depleted, and her voice was nearly gone. She let their joined hands descend to the bed.

"Listen, honey, I don't want you to be upset with me, but I need tomorrow off. You're running me ragged."

Aidyn laughed quietly and wiped her eyes.

"Besides," Clara said, "you have a story to write."

The girl squeezed Clara's hand. "I have an amazing story to write, Mrs. Kip."

Aidyn had expected the visit with Mrs. Kip to bring a measure of completion, but only for Mrs. Kip. That had been her intention, her plan. In true Mrs. Kip style, though, the old woman had pointed her to something bigger. A divine hand that ceaselessly wove story to story.

Aidyn's heart overflowed with gratitude.

As she walked back to her car with the partially eaten *coxinha* and the virtual reality headset that brought São Paulo five thousand miles closer, she understood that she had left Mrs. Kip's room with more than those two minor connections to the old woman's life. She had left in possession of every treasure Mrs. Kip could impart. Her story and her journals. Her friendship and her counsel. Her admiration of a city and her adoration of the Psalms. Her humility—and her desire to follow God wherever he led.

The latter brought her to a stop under the sky. She looked up, chest aching it was so full, and whispered into the blue, hoping Mrs. Kip could somehow hear it too, "I always let you guide me. Because you are at my right hand, I will not be shaken."

The sword felt so right in her hand.

———

Clara spoke only once more that afternoon. To Joselyn, the weekend nurse.

"I'll take that full dose now."

CHAPTER 27

Sunday, June 12, 2016

The new-message notification drew Aidyn's attention away from sludging through revisions. It was just after 1:00 a.m. Kansas City time, which meant it was more than halfway into Sunday for Daniel and Joshua Khab. Eagerly Aidyn opened the email. The duo's answers were generously long and thoughtful. The level of detail contained within painted vivid images of Mai and Mahasajun tending to hurting people displaced by an evil they couldn't seem to escape. The details drew out with crisp lines and perfect edges what life was like for the Khabs in those early years, the hardship they experienced in the dangerous camp, and the unquenchable hope they never failed to profess. Aidyn saw in Mai Khab the compassion and selflessness Mrs. Kip possessed too.

Who had been an influence on whom? She had assumed it was Mrs. Kip on her friend, but perhaps it was the other way around.

By the end of the sprawling email, Aidyn had all the

information she sought, including how and why Mrs. Khab died. The answer weighed heavily.

She looked to her right, at the picture she kept nearby to inspire her words. The picture of Mrs. Kip and Mrs. Khab smiling in front of the church doors. What would those two have done if they knew what was ahead for them? Would they make the same choices? Would Mrs. Khab still willingly go, and Mrs. Kip willingly let her?

What would it be like to say goodbye to a best friend, knowing it would likely be the last time? Knowing that the pain in this world is real and sharp?

The heartache seemed unbearable.

Aidyn shut her computer and contemplated those things on her bed. Contemplated what Mrs. Kip was doing at that moment, if she was okay, if she was resting comfortably.

When morning came, an overwhelming urge prompted her to go to Mrs. Kip's church, to stand in that spot the women had and walk among the memories. It was inexplicable and weird—exactly how Mrs. Kip described the Lord's nudges.

Sunday worship had begun by the time Aidyn arrived. The church's exterior had not changed much, from the looks of it. The greeters had left their posts to go into the sanctuary, leaving the front doors unattended.

Aidyn paused on the sidewalk, standing roughly in the same place the two young friends had, arms around each other. It was a nondescript spot, easily passed over on the way into the church. But a heartbeat resounded there.

A young mother with three littles in tow rushed past her on their way into the building. The mom stopped her brood just outside the doors for one last check of everyone's hair and clothes. "Remember," she told them, "we're quiet inside."

The little heads nodded.

Apparently satisfied with their appearances and promises, the mom opened the door and ushered them inside.

Aidyn watched them disappear beyond the reflective glass doors and imagined a group of other young mothers from a world away bringing their children to this place. The worries they had carried on their shoulders went beyond appearance and voice volume. Realities had haunted them, and a burning hunger to find hope had driven them.

How very different from any life Aidyn had ever known.

She followed the family inside, stepping into the foyer just in time to see the mom swing open the door of the sanctuary. Music spilled into the foyer. The notes were from the popular praise song of the day, "Good, Good Father."

What would that song have meant to those young mothers?

She looked around the foyer, at its contemporary appointments and design elements. When those Lao families came for mission classes, what did they think of this church building? Did they see the aesthetics, or did they only feel the refuge?

She moved into the sanctuary. The congregation was standing, singing in unison to the Chris Tomlin song. Aidyn spotted an aisle seat a couple of rows down and took her place amid the crowd. She sang the words they sang, worshiped the God they worshiped, did all the usual things for a Sunday morning. But did anyone around her know the story they had inherited? Did any of them live as if that inheritance was a treasure meant to be given away?

More importantly, did she?

Aidyn sang alongside the other uplifted voices, sang of a Father who loves, who is perfect in every way, and who provides the only answers ever truly needed. The words called up a certain image of Mrs. Khab, one her son and grandson had left etched in Aidyn's memory.

Did similar praises grace Mai Khab's lips the day her Communist captors took her earthly life?

———

Clara could catch only a glimpse of the sanctuary. It was enormous. Bigger than anything she had ever seen, with windows so tall and wide they practically overpowered the walls. Millions of souls were there, raising a noise that sounded raucous and melodic all at once.

It was bright. So bright. It smelled like blooming flowers.

And she could move. Freely. Skip around if she wanted.

It was a place she felt whole, a place she could easily make her home.

Forever.

This. This was by far her favorite dream.

Monday, June 13, 2016

The frown puckered Woods's brow deeper than usual. She looked up from the copy Aidyn had slid into her hand moments before.

"There's too much emotion in this, Kelley."

The reaction was predictable, because honestly, Woods was right. The draft contained noticeable sentimentality woven over and between the facts. Facts were supposed to speak for themselves. Facts were king.

Facts were the only thing Aidyn was supposed to present. And yet . . .

"It's the only way I can tell it," she said. "It refuses to come out any other way." She had dozens of rewrites to prove it.

Woods arched an eyebrow. "That's the explanation you'd have me take to Maper?"

The same question had presented itself numerous times in the past day of Aidyn's strenuous editing. "That's the story that wants to be told. Emotional or not, it's a unique story about real people and real Kansas City history, and it's poignantly relevant to current readership."

It was the most she had ever said to Woods in one stretch without hesitation or second-guessing, as if the words streamed through her rather than came from her. She held her breath, waited for her editor to respond.

Woods's stern look burrowed into Aidyn. "So, you're standing by this story as is? Regardless of the risk?"

Aidyn paused. Then she looked Woods straight in the eye and replied, "Absolutely."

Woods stared at her for what seemed like eons. Finally, she gave one small nod. "Spoken like a true journalist, Kelley. I'll pitch the story to Maper today."

The words did not seem real. Aidyn dared to appear unfazed, dared to trust the Lord was making the way and would continue to do so.

"In the meantime," Woods continued, taking up her red

pen, "replace this pathetic hed." She slashed through the working title. "The dek isn't much better." The subhead sentence saw the same inky fate.

Their rejection wasn't much of a loss. Aidyn had ended up putting down whatever came to mind because those two key pieces had refused to click, regardless of how hard she tried to find the right combination.

"I'll keep working on them," she said.

"Do you have any leads on people who were refugees and still live in KC?" Woods asked.

Pastor Khounmy and his church was the best place to start. "I do."

"And find out how many refugees actually came to the city through 1980. You have the one figure until '77, but we need a more encompassing one."

Aidyn nodded.

"Have you reached out to anyone from those local organizations that support refugees and immigrants?"

"I will."

"Wait until the green light. I asked for the purpose of back-pocket information. Email me this draft and do your other work until you hear from me." Woods handed her back the copy. "All things considered, Kelley, you have a solid start."

For a moment, Aidyn half-expected Woods to say something else, perhaps something that started with "But" or "However." Instead, her editor turned and resumed hacking away at her keyboard, bringing an end to their conversation in her exceptionally warm way.

Taking the cue, Aidyn saw herself out and returned to

her own desk. As she lowered into her chair, sketch copy in hand, she looked back at Woods's open door. Almost exactly a week prior, Aidyn had left her editor's office with face burning in shame. This morning, she left with heart swimming in hope.

With Shayna out on assignment, Aidyn had total freedom to bask in the glow of Woods's complimentary response, "A solid start." It might as well have been a pat on the back.

Her morning's tasks, all geared toward helping Shayna write another section feature that she would get no credit for, suddenly didn't seem as demeaning. She threw herself into them, being as thorough as she could, to earn a few more of those "solid" comments from Woods. Hopefully she would have the tasks finished by early afternoon, at which point she could take the news to Mrs. Kip. Perhaps by then, she might even have an answer from Maper.

Aidyn slid into such a groove with her work that only time coming to a complete standstill could have broken her out of it.

At 9:57, time basically did.

Rosario Dia called.

"Mrs. Kip fell into a coma last night."

Aidyn hung up the phone in a state of numbness that was new and foreign to her being. A numbness that left her floundering somewhere between speeding to Sacred Promise and pressing forward with her assignments.

What should be the appropriate response? Why couldn't she figure it out? Better yet, why hadn't she been prepared for such a moment? She honestly—naïvely—thought she had more time with Mrs. Kip. Death took a lot longer in movies, anyway. At least a few days. Enough time to verify facts and approve her "extraordinary" death.

Aidyn shook her head.

Naïve.

Though she attempted to plow forward with her tasks, her mind invariably wandered to an image of a withered Mrs. Kip with slack jaw, alone. Trapped without a giggle. In need of a friend.

Aidyn's heart tugged in two different directions at once. If only someone would tell her what to do. Go? Stay?

Officially, she had no further journalistic reason to visit Mrs. Kip, especially during work hours. If she went immediately on the basis of friendship, she would be seen as emotional—the thing Woods had just chastised her for. If she went under the guise of an interview, she ran the risk of Rosario giving her old chum Woods an update on Mrs. Kip and inadvertently revealing the truth.

She needed input, preferably from someone who didn't have a tendency to overthink, so she IM'd Rahmiya.

> Mrs. Kip fell into a coma last night.

A few moments later, Rahmiya replied,

> That's too bad. Did you get everything you needed?

> For the most part. Draft is with Maper now for consideration.

> That's awesome!

It was awesome, and less than two hours before, the awe-someness had been at its zenith. But in that moment, the weight of the phone call pressed in. Though Aidyn sent back a smiley emoji, what she really needed was not a cheer-leader but a sage. She ventured a roundabout way of getting advice.

> Part of me wants to go see her.

Who? Mrs. Kip?

> Yes.

Why?

In that one word, Aidyn had Rahmiya's full opinion. Her heart sank.

> I don't know.

But a nudge urged her to acknowledge the fact that she did know why, and to honor that reason before others.

Still on for lunch? Your pick this time.

The suggestion of food made Aidyn's stomach clench.

> I'm sorry, Rahmi. Do you mind if we do lunch another day this week?

But you owe me a lunch from last week.

> I know. I promise, another day this week. I'm just not in the mood to eat today.

Rahmiya's end was quiet for several moments. Disappoint-ment dripped from the silence.

At last, Rahmiya replied,

Another day then.

Quickly she followed it with,

Gotta go. Later.

And switched her status to "busy."

More than disappointment. Irritation.

Who could blame her? It was the second time in a week Aidyn had flaked. But her stomach was in no state to eat, and neither was her mind. The IM conversation did little to settle either. She returned to trudging through more of her to-do list.

Shortly after 1:00, Woods summoned her.

Aidyn reported to her editor's office with notepad in hand and heart still sagging.

"Maper replied," Woods said without looking up from her typing. "It's a green light, but as online only and in the Faith section."

The response was no reason to throw up her hands in celebration. "Online only" was code for "restricted circulation." "Faith section" was code for "relatively buried."

Maper was sending a message. Loud, clear, and resounding.

Still, something stood out about the answer, something the Aidyn a week prior would have been too insulted to recognize. But the Aidyn standing in Woods's office at that moment, receiving the news in the context of all that had transpired, realized there was another fact Woods hadn't mentioned. Surely Maper's final response had not been his original one. It couldn't have been. It was too generous.

"You talked him up to that, didn't you?" Aidyn asked.

"That's all the information you need, Kelley."

"So, yes?"

Woods paused in her typing, sighed heavily, then carried on. "Flesh out the research. Write a better hed. Don't make me regret anything."

Her editor's heart had never been on fuller display.

In the wake of that small glimpse of compassion, the nudge returned, urging Aidyn to seek her editor's input about whether to go to Mrs. Kip. Before she could overthink, she blurted out, "Mrs. Kip fell into a coma last night."

Woods's fingers halted again. She looked up at Aidyn. "I'm sorry to hear that." Her stoic expression—that masterful poker face—gave no hints as to her true sentiments.

Feeling immensely awkward and possessing no follow-up statement, Aidyn nodded, as either a thank-you or a that's-all. Then she started to leave.

"Kelley." Woods stopped her in the door. "I'm sure you're eager to get on this piece right away." She paused, ensuring Aidyn held her gaze. "Perhaps some of your research is off-site."

Chills covered Aidyn's body. She had been mistaken. *That* was the moment her editor's compassion shone brightest.

"Thank you, Woods."

Her editor nodded and abruptly returned to her work.

CHAPTER 28

For the first time, Aidyn arrived at Sacred Promise empty-handed. No notebook. No messenger bag. No gifts. She arrived with no other objective than to be where she was nudged to be and to give back some of what she had received.

As she walked through the main doors of the facility, she stepped farther away from her own perspective and closer to Mrs. Kip's. What must it have been like for Mrs. Kip to come there the first time? What had been going through her mind?

How odd it must have been to walk through those sliding glass doors knowing she would never come back out.

How hard it must have been to leave behind her old life—her home, her lifestyle, her relationships—and come to this strange place with only some personal items and two white storage boxes, as if she herself was a kind of refugee.

How difficult it must have been to know that the people she came to live among were not long for the world, and neither was she.

How heart-wrenching.

And yet . . .

Mrs. Kip lived as if death were merely a phase, not an end. She poured out as if she would never go empty. She giggled as if there was no pain.

Aidyn steeped herself in those thoughts as she signed the guestbook for the sixth time in the week since she had met Mrs. Kip.

Only one week. It was hard to believe.

The roots of their short time together had plunged deep into Aidyn's existence. Like they surely had for Mr. Slesher. And all those babies. And Mr. Kip. And Mrs. Khab.

Mrs. Kip's words reverberated in Aidyn's soul, where they had lodged themselves: *I simply tried to love people as best I could for as long as I was privileged to be with them.*

If only one thing Mrs. Kip had ever said was true, that was the one.

When Aidyn arrived at room 310, Nora was bent over Mrs. Kip with her back to the door. The nurse turned when she heard Aidyn, revealing the stethoscope in her ears.

"Sorry." Aidyn began to retreat to the hallway. "I can wait till you're done."

"It's okay, Miss Kelley. You can come in if you want."

"That's fine, I'll give you some privacy."

"Really, it's okay." The nurse waved her forward. "Mrs. Kip gave consent for you to be here."

"She did?"

"Last week." A knowing smile came to Nora's lips. "She hoped you'd keep coming."

A tingle spread through Aidyn—the sensation of being known and wanted. "She thought of everything."

"She's good at that," Nora said. "Come on in and have a seat. I'll be finished shortly."

As the nurse resumed her exam, Aidyn made her way to her usual spot on the loveseat. She sat with the afternoon sun warming her back, and her gaze came to rest on Mrs. Kip.

The woman's complexion drifted closer to the hue of the sheet draped over her lower half. Her hair sagged against her scalp, and her face looked almost unrecognizable without the twinkling eyes to make it shine or the eyeglasses, which lay folded on the nightstand. Despite it all, the woman in the bed was the one Aidyn knew, the woman whose stories and spirit had brought her back to Sacred Promise five times.

Those bony arms, stretched out at her sides on top of the sheet, had affectionately wrapped around countless women who needed hope in a new country, cradled precious ones who needed comfort in a new world, and taught a lost little boy how to throw a baseball and find his fit.

How naïve to think that old woman had nothing of value to give.

Aidyn shook her head. *So naïve.*

Nora slid the stethoscope to different spots on her patient's chest, listening to the throaty breath as it flowed through her lungs. "You're starting to sound a little congested, Mrs. Kip." She withdrew the stethoscope from under the bright-yellow pajama shirt and announced, "I'm going to check your feet. Be prepared for the draft."

As the nurse moved to the end of the bed, she motioned for Aidyn to join her.

Curious, Aidyn followed.

"Do you know why we check their feet?" Nora whispered. Aidyn shook her head.

"I'll show you." Nora folded back the sheet to reveal Mrs. Kip's bare, gaunt feet. Near the arch of her right foot was a light purple spot the size of a silver dollar. "It's called mottling," Nora explained. "It'll get darker the closer her time comes."

Aidyn's stomach knotted. Not from fear. Not from disgust. But from grief.

Mrs. Kip suddenly looked even more fragile.

Within a minute, Nora had finished her exam and replaced the sheet. "You did great, Mrs. Kip. Thanks for being a trooper. I'll leave you so you can enjoy your visit with Miss Kelley."

The woman's only response was a throaty inhale, her cracked lips moving slightly with the effort.

"I'll be down the hall if you need me," Nora said to Aidyn.

"Thank you."

The nurse nodded and stepped outside, pulling the door most of the way closed behind her.

Silence descended upon the room, and it felt disorienting. Silence and Mrs. Kip didn't go together.

It was too hard to believe that Mrs. Kip wouldn't wake up any minute and smile that toothy smile and laugh that laugh and call her "honey." How would she get used to a Mrs. Kip who didn't talk?

She returned to the loveseat and waited, as if something would change.

When nothing did, she admitted aloud, "I'm not used to you being so quiet." Part of her wished the sound of her voice would actually cause the woman to open her eyes, like a miraculous healing in a movie.

She sighed into the unshakable hush.

Mrs. Kip's treasured pictures still stood on her night-stand. The one of her husband and the one of their wedding reception. What a raucous event that must have been, so memorable and joyful—so very Clara Kip. Aidyn traced the lines of the young woman's flushed face, in it a reflection of the vigor with which she embraced her new stage of life, her beloved husband next to her, her dream very much alive.

In that picture, Mrs. Kip was the same age as Aidyn. Her whole adult life ahead of her. And what a life it would be.

The story. The article. The next words to speak rushed to Aidyn's lips.

"You'll be excited to know Maper gave approval for me to write the article."

If Mrs. Kip had been awake, surely she would have raised her eyebrows in eagerness to hear more.

"It'll be published online, probably next week sometime. I can read it to you when it comes out."

She kept the hope in her voice—to remind Mrs. Kip of what was possible.

"By the way, you were right about my editor, Woods. She's good people. Doesn't like to show it, but she is."

Twinges of regret gathered in her chest over what she had said and thought about her editor.

"I wish I would've seen it sooner. Hidden warriors can be hard to find sometimes. I'm sure you had to learn that too."

Mrs. Kip's face showed no signs she heard, no signs they

were still conversing. Already Aidyn ached for the sound of the woman's voice. But somehow her own words continued to flow.

"Speaking of good people, I also found Joshua, Mrs. Khab's son. He still lives in Thailand, and he has a son named Daniel, a little older than me." She paused. "Joshua told me what happened to his parents."

Tapping her fingertips together, she weighed what words to use to explain everything that needed to be explained. The last remaining thread in Mrs. Kip's story waited to be tied.

With a tenderness that matched the nurse's touch, Aidyn revealed that last chapter of Mrs. Khab's life.

"Not long after they arrived in the Ban Vinai camp, the Thai government stopped allowing new refugees into it because of overcrowding. But that didn't stop your friends. In 1985, they were caught trying to sneak in a family and were arrested. Mrs. Khab was forcibly repatriated back to Laos shortly after."

Aidyn looked down at her hands. If Mrs. Kip heard, she would know exactly what that meant for someone in her friend's position. Still, she was compelled to speak it.

"She was killed. The children never found out what happened to their dad."

Saying the words aloud made them undeniably real. Surely they reached into Mrs. Kip and filled a gap that had long been open.

"By a miracle, the children were moved to Bangkok, where they were deemed 'true refugees' by the Thais and allowed to stay. That's where they remained."

She sat in the stillness and drank in Mrs. Kip's face. The skin puckered under her cheekbones and the lines were etched across her forehead like stress cracks in weathered concrete. So many years reflected there, so many selfless prayers.

"Mrs. Khab was a courageous woman. She died trying to save others. That's an extraordinary death, don't you think?"

What she wouldn't give to hear one more "Oh my," to see one more expression of wonder the story evoked.

"I think you had something to do with her courage. You probably disagree with that, and quite adamantly. But you know what? I'm right. I know I'm right because the same is true with me, Mrs. Kip. I'm here now doing this weird thing—talking to a comatose hospice patient I've only known for a week—because I know it's something you would have done. It's something you *did* do."

That moment when Mrs. Kip, unsteady and exhausted, clung to Mr. Slesher's hand as if it were a precious jewel and whispered sweet dreams over him still struck her. Despite what the rules were, regardless of what her own body said it wanted, Mrs. Kip had returned to his bedside and stayed, right to the end.

"You said the mark of authentic love is dying a thousand deaths to self. I get now what you meant by that because I watched you live it out."

Aidyn folded her hands tightly in her lap, trying to distract herself from the rising emotion within her. She couldn't cry. Not yet. It wasn't time to cry.

"I don't know why God brought us together in this way or at this stage, but I'm glad he did. I'm privileged by it. And

I'm positive Mr. Slesher felt the same way. And Mrs. Khab, and your friend Martha, and everyone at the mission . . ." She glanced at the handsome husband in the picture. "And most of all your Johnny."

She swallowed against the tightness in her throat. Mrs. Kip should hear only joy in her voice.

"We can all attest to your thousands of extraordinary deaths."

Her chin trembled, and her eyes again wandered to the nightstand, this time falling on the Bible.

She cleared her throat and reached for it. "Okay, enough prattle. What do you say we read some Psalms?"

Mrs. Kip gave no objection.

For well over an hour, Aidyn filled the silence left behind by Mrs. Kip with the words the woman certainly still sang in her heart loud enough to reach the rafters of heaven.

By the time Aidyn left for the day, the hed and dek for her story had clicked faultlessly into place.

Tuesday, June 14, 2016

"I appreciate your time. Thank you." Aidyn nestled the phone receiver on her shoulder, pressed the button on the cradle to disconnect, and immediately dialed the phone number for the next interviewee, her third Hope Church member of the morning.

Every call started the same.

"Hello, my name is Aidyn Kelley. I'm a reporter with the

Star, and I'm doing a piece on the Laotian resettlement in Kansas City in the 1970s. I'm wondering if you have a few minutes to talk."

Every person invariably said, "Yes."

It was a rare occurrence in journalism.

With each interview, she gained insightful details and nuances that would deepen the richness of the article. More so, it became clear how lives of strangers and friends alike wove together to make one breathtaking tapestry.

The unmistakable mark of a masterful Storyteller.

All morning, she barely stopped moving. More calls to subject-matter experts in immigration and one call to Mission Adelante, whose founder "happened" to be available right then. He patiently and articulately answered a long list of questions about what it was like to help foreigners assimilate to modern-day America.

But her favorite interview by far was with a woman named Evelyn Vanders, one of the church congregants referred to her by Julie, the secretary.

"I'll tell you everything you never wanted to know about that ornery old coot," Evelyn said with a chuckle and a noticeable Southern drawl.

"How did you know Mrs. Kip?" Aidyn asked.

"We were in the same Sunday school class until neither of us could drive anymore. Then my kids moved me to this assisted living facility here in St. Louis. I sure do miss that class. And that church."

"What can you tell me about the New Life Christian Mission?"

"I can tell you I'm not the least bit surprised that Clara

was a driving force behind it all. She had a way of convincing people to do things."

Aidyn grinned. "I've discovered that myself."

Within their thirty-minute conversation, Aidyn learned that Mrs. Kip, among other things, delivered food bank groceries to the rougher parts of the city, was known as "Baby Magic" to the church nursery workers, had a penchant for practical jokes on a certain stern-faced usher, loved all things Bingo, and always ensured her friends had their favorite cookie on their birthdays.

How easy it would be to stay in those stories all day long, basking in the thrill as the vision of Mrs. Kip's younger years came into sharper, richer focus. Evelyn Vanders proved to be a kind of stand-in for Mrs. Kip's silenced voice.

With much reluctance, she thanked Evelyn for her time and moved on to the last remaining piece of research Woods had told her to pursue: a statistic capturing how many refugees came to Kansas City between 1975 and 1980.

The task proved much harder than she'd expected. One source reported that between 1975 and 1978, thirty thousand Hmong were resettled in America. But Hmong were not necessarily Laotian. Another said 3.5 million southeast Asian refugees resettled in America from 1975 through the 1990s, but that was too large of a time frame and included non-Laotians.

Finally, she discovered that the Kansas State Historical Society had an entire section dedicated to Hmong refugees and decided to see whether the curator could point her in the right direction. But as she looked up the society's phone number, her own phone rang. To her surprise, it was Julie.

"Is this a bad time?" the secretary asked.

"Not at all. And thank you again for the names you gave me. Evelyn in particular was quite helpful."

"She is a delight, isn't she? I'm glad I could be of help, because I have a favor to ask of you now . . . Technically, Pastor Levi has a favor to ask of you."

"From me? How can I help?"

"Pastor just got back from seeing Mrs. Kip, and they told him she doesn't have much longer."

"I've been told that too."

"Blessed soul," Julie said with empathy. "We are preparing with heavy hearts for that time. Mrs. Kip requested to have the services here at the church, and she was kind enough to give detailed instructions on what she wanted. Usually Pastor works with the family on the eulogy, though. He talks to them to get a feel for who the person really was. But in Mrs. Kip's circumstance, that's not an option. He was hoping you might have something you could share with him."

Aidyn smiled. The morning's freakishly easy round of interviews—and all she had captured in her time with Mrs. Kip—had another purpose.

Truly the Lord was at her right hand.

"Tell him I'd be more than happy to share."

Aidyn looked over the write-up for Pastor Levi one last time. Having used her interview notes and sketch draft as a starting point, she had pulled together as many facts and insights as she could about the woman he was trying to memorialize. Though she excluded anything she thought her editors would consider too proprietary for the *Star*, what she did prepare to send accurately and vividly captured the person of Mrs. Kip.

Satisfied with her collection, she copied it into an email message to Julie. As she started to type a greeting to the secretary, an IM popped up.

Rahmiya
Miss you. Let's do supper tonight.

Aidyn smiled. Her friend's irritation from the day before seemed to have subsided. Unfortunately, the request could not have come at a more inconvenient time. Visiting Mrs. Kip was a priority. That evening and every evening until . . .

Hopefully Rahmiya would understand.

Carefully choosing her words, she typed back,

> Miss you too! And we definitely have a reason to celebrate. Maper approved the story!

What? Aidie, that's awesome! Let's do something nicer then. Gram & Dun?

Aidyn bit her lip.

> Do you mind if we plan it for next week, after I turn in the story? I'm sorry to keep delaying. Deadline!

A brief pause.

What about a quick happy hour then? We HAVE to celebrate your big step toward Katharine Graham status!

For the first time, her hero's name had a hollowness to it. The woman's accomplishments, which had been synonymous in Aidyn's mind with success, suddenly didn't have as much meaning as they once did. Not compared to what success looked like in Mrs. Kip's life.

The nudge to acknowledge her connection to Mrs. Kip before others returned. The nudge to speak it, regardless of what it might cost.

Chewing on her lip, she wrote back,

> I would like to keep visiting Mrs. Kip after work this week.

> Seriously? How much more could you possibly need from her?

That was just it. Aidyn didn't need anything more from Mrs. Kip. She was meant to be the one serving. A concept Rahmiya might not be able to receive, at least not at that point. Still, she shared the truth.

> She's dying, Rahmi, and she's all alone.

Another pause. The tension was palpable.

Finally, Rahmiya shot back,

> Whatever. Enjoy your visit.

Then she cut out of the conversation.

Aidyn sighed. There was little she could do. She closed the IM and returned to the email for Julie.

As she reviewed the words she had typed for Pastor Levi's needs, an idea came to her. She started a new email and attached the sketch draft.

Rahmi—

This is what your patience is helping produce.

Love you,

Aidie

She pressed Send and prayed for God to move in all the ways she couldn't.

Several hours later, when her workday came to an end, Aidyn gathered her laptop and notes so she could continue working at home later that night.

But first she went to Sacred Promise.

She sat with Mrs. Kip, held her hand, and read her the Psalms until the Lord turned on the colors of dusk.

CHAPTER 29

Wednesday, June 15, 2016

Rahmiya was not yet at her desk when Aidyn arrived at the *Star* office the next morning. Aidyn placed the vanilla latte where her friend would easily see it. Taking a sticky note from a nearby pad, she wrote a greeting to go with it.

Until we can have one together.

—A.

She affixed the note to the lid of the coffee cup and headed up to her own desk. Hopefully the gift would help ease things. The rift weighed on her mind, almost as much as the noticeable decline in Mrs. Kip the night before. The mottling on the old woman's foot had progressed to a deeper shade of purple. Other, smaller spots had also appeared.

Despite the concerns, the day ahead held tremendous promise.

As soon as Aidyn got to her desk, she would turn in the

polished draft of the story. All of the hours, the research, the late-night writing sessions, the frustrations and joys, the discoveries and convictions, would culminate in one final action.

She walked to the newsroom with purpose.

Surprisingly, Shayna was in. The senior reporter typed feverishly on her laptop and didn't look up when Aidyn started to unpack.

"You're here early," Aidyn commented.

"Some of us have legit reporting to finish."

The barb cut. But in place of the typical urge to throw back a jeer was a pang of empathy, brought on by the way Shayna's brow folded in concentration, as if enormous stress pushed down on her. And it probably did.

If Aidyn, as a cub reporter with only one feature to get perfect in a short turnaround, found it difficult to both do her job and appease the desires of loved ones, what must Shayna, a seasoned reporter with multiple competing deadlines, face on a daily basis? More so, what must Woods experience as an editor over noncompliant rookies and egotistical veterans?

It was not a coincidence both women had hard exteriors.

Aidyn replied calmly, "Good luck with your stories, Reese." As she sat down and opened her computer, she respectfully pretended not to see the surprise on Shayna's face.

They both tended to their respective work without further comments.

Aidyn brought up the polished story for one more read-through. As she read, tingles danced over her skin. Not because the writing was genius, but because she knew—she could sense it in her very core—that those words were needed by someone else in the world. Perhaps more so than she had needed them.

Mrs. Kip's was a story the world needed more of.

After a few quick proofing tweaks, Aidyn saved the draft and started a new email. It would be the simplest and most profound of her career thus far.

Woods—

For your consideration: "The Extraordinary Deaths of Mrs. Kip."
Archives has a great picture of a young Clara Kip with Mai Khab.
I recommend using it.

She attached the finished draft, thanked God for bringing her this far, and pressed Send.

Whatever came of the story, whether it saw wide circulation or not, she would be content with whatever God chose to do with it from that point forward. The story would reach those it was meant to reach.

For the rest of the morning, she tackled the backlog of tasks from the day before and tried her best not to watch the clock.

By noon, without word from either Rahmiya or Woods, she grew too antsy to stick around her desk. She started to leave for a bite to eat when a new-email alert popped up on her screen.

From Woods.

Fingers trembling, Aidyn quickly opened it. Seven simple words:

Perfect title. No edits. File for Monday.

She clamped her hand over her mouth, stopping the gasp before it came.

Unbelievable. And yet it was entirely believable.

Because the Lord was at her right hand.

She sent an IM to Rahmiya.

Story goes live Monday!

She left the conversation open until it was time to leave for the day to go see Mrs. Kip.

Rahmiya did not reply.

Aidyn constantly had to remind herself that nonverbal was the new normal for Mrs. Kip.

As the old woman steadily declined, more of that new normal came into focus. Aspects that could be expected and aspects that stunned.

Breathing that fluctuated between rapid and apnea. Increasingly longer stretches between inhales. Rigidity of the limbs. Needing to be repositioned every two hours to prevent skin breakdown. A Foley catheter. Doses of morphine applied to the inside of Mrs. Kip's cheek.

All of it, normal.

"Just keep talking to her," Michelle, the night nurse, encouraged Aidyn. "That will always be her normal."

For two hours, Aidyn read Mrs. Kip the Scriptures, starting with the woman's beloved Psalms, then flipping to the New Testament. "For some variety," she told her. "Jesus said even better things than David did, you know."

She read the Sermon on the Mount and the entire book of Philippians and had started James when Michelle knocked on the door.

"Sorry to interrupt, ladies." The nurse pumped sanitizer onto her hands as she walked in. "I just wanted to check the catheter bag and see if she's made any progress filling it up."

"Of course," Aidyn said. "We were just expanding her biblical reading horizons."

"Yes, I heard some James when I came in. That's a great book." Michelle walked to the side of the bed facing the door and bent down to the bag. "Well, Mrs. Kip, looks like we still have a ways to go."

The meaning was clear: Poor output meant the time drew ever closer.

Michelle took the stethoscope from around her neck and listened to Mrs. Kip's chest. Without comment, she pulled back and draped the stethoscope around her neck again, then she moved to the foot of the bed and quickly lifted the sheet to peek at Mrs. Kip's feet. When she brought it down, stoicism masked her face.

"Thanks for letting me interrupt your visit, Mrs. Kip," she said. "I just need to borrow Miss Kelley for a quick second and then she's all yours again, okay?"

That statement didn't promise anything good.

When Michelle gestured for her to follow, Aidyn's stomach knotted. Slowly she rose and placed the Bible on the loveseat. "I'll be right back, Mrs. Kip," she said. Then she followed the nurse into the hallway.

Outside the room, Michelle kept her voice low. "She's getting close. All the signs are there."

Aidyn's pulse lurched into high gear. "How close?"

"My guess is within the next day."

The news was like a punch in the gut. They all had known

they would find themselves in that moment at some point, but still. It was wrenching.

She glanced over her shoulder at the old woman in the bed. Mrs. Kip looked more vulnerable than ever.

"I could stay with her," she said without thinking. She turned back to Michelle. "I could take tomorrow off to be with her so she's not alone."

"You sound like Mrs. Kip," Michelle said with a grin.

Aidyn dipped her head. "I wouldn't mind being like Mrs. Kip in a lot of ways."

"Same here, Miss Kelley. She's a special lady, and she sure did take a shine to you."

Tears pushed toward Aidyn's eyes. "I could stay with her," she repeated.

Michelle put a warm hand on Aidyn's arm. "I can see how much that would mean to you. If you feel led to stay with her, then I encourage you to. Let me share with you one thing that may influence your decision, though. Some people refuse to let go with a loved one in the room."

Aidyn frowned. "Why is that?"

"For the same reason you want to be here, Miss Kelley—compassion." The nurse rubbed her arm. "The moment of passing can be a very difficult thing to witness. She may want to spare you the heartache."

The revelation struck a deep chord. Aidyn looked again at Mrs. Kip. "That would be just like her, wouldn't it?"

"It would."

Aidyn turned back to the nurse. "You think I should go, then?"

She smiled sympathetically. "I think foremost you should

make sure you've said everything you want to say. Then make your choice. And know that either choice you make, whether you stay or you go, will be an honoring one. If you're unable to stay, one of us will sit with her until the time comes. She won't be alone."

The tears pooled in Aidyn's eyes. Her chin trembled. The time to cry had come, and it took her breath.

Apparently seeing her struggle, Michelle squeezed her arm. "She is blessed to have you for a friend, Miss Kelley."

Through the tightness in her throat, Aidyn managed to reply, "I'm more blessed."

The nurse lingered a moment, her hand embracing Aidyn's arm. Then she smiled one last time, a gentle Godspeed in its message, and left Aidyn alone with Mrs. Kip.

The moment pressed in on Aidyn from every angle, narrowing her focus to one extremely weighty call.

How had Mrs. Kip faced such times over and over? How had she stepped into the heavy and not succumbed to the weight?

Like a whisper, the answer was unveiled.

Because he is at my right hand, I will not be shaken.

Mrs. Kip had thought of everything, and she had known Aidyn would need that sword.

With blurred vision and a growing ache in her chest, Aidyn walked through Mrs. Kip's doorway for what certainly would be the final time. She moved slowly, intentionally, savoring every detail of the place that had been the site of a beautiful, unexpected friendship—details she had only partially paid attention to before. The minimalist furnishings. The simple decor. The large picture window overlooking one of Mrs.

Kip's favorite places to escape. How special that window had been to the woman.

Aidyn bathed in the intangibles that still floated around the room like living water: the conversations they'd had, the wisdom spoken, the legacy uncovered. She stopped when she saw the armchair, the woman's preferred roost, where she had done most of her sharing and her praising.

Driven by the desire to be close to Mrs. Kip in every way, Aidyn scooted the armchair closer to the bed and lowered into the spot where the woman had prayed countless silent prayers, some of which, no doubt, had been for Aidyn.

Her gaze rested on Mrs. Kip. The first tears broke free and slid down her cheeks. She didn't try to stop them.

"I wish I had more time with you."

Every goodbye Aidyn had experienced up to that point had contained a subtle comfort in the possibility to stay connected. Goodbye had never required the encompassing sacrifice asked of her in that moment.

Her heart burned. She reached out with both hands and cocooned Mrs. Kip's, cradling the rigid, chilled flesh with her own warmth.

"I wish I had recorded you, or at least taken a picture."

She swallowed against the lump in her throat, trying to move it aside so Mrs. Kip would still hear her voice.

"Of course, if I'm going to be wishing for things, I wish . . . I wish you didn't have to go."

Her voice cracked.

"I wish you could tell me more stories. I wish I had listened better from the beginning. I wish I could always have you to visit."

A tear dripped off the end of her jaw and splashed onto her hand. She barely got her next words out.

"I wish a good farewell didn't feel so brutal."

She hung her head and sobbed quietly. She clung to the woman's hand and allowed herself to lean into the burden of sacrifice.

After a few moments, the sobs calmed, and she lifted her soaked face to Mrs. Kip.

"I know you're ready, though. And I can't blame you. You have fought the good fight, Mrs. Kip. You are a child-saving, Communism-fighting, Jesus-professing warrior."

She smiled and stroked the woman's hand with her thumb.

"I will think of you every time I eat a chocolate chip cookie or see a Harley or step out into the sunshine."

She chuckled through her cries, the small promise of joy arising from the pain. The strange combination Mrs. Kip must have felt countless times. Yet another cord that would forever tie Aidyn with the odd old woman she had met eight days and one lifetime ago.

With every ounce of humility and love Aidyn could offer up, she said her final words to her forever friend.

"Thank you, Mrs. Kip. Thank you for helping me find a life that matters."

CHAPTER 30

Aidyn brewed a cup of tea and sat down on her bed with Mrs. Kip's journals fanned out around her. The last moments with her friend drove her to be in those words again, to wrap herself in their world, especially this night.

She took a sip of tea, her chest tingling from its heat, and immersed herself in Mrs. Kip's handwritten records. Armed with a greater knowledge of what was happening in the world and the city when those prayers were lifted up, Aidyn found a new depth to them. One she soon got lost in. The sadness the prayers evoked was heavier, the laughter fuller.

Several hours in, as she closed one journal and reached for another one, her phone rang from the nightstand.

Rahmiya. Calling via FaceTime.

Immediately, Aidyn accepted. Her friend's face filled the screen. Apprehension showed in her expression.

"Hey, Rahmi."

"Hey." Her voice, too, was uneasy.

"I'm glad you called."

Rahmiya looked down, seeming to struggle with what to say. "I wanted to thank you for the latte."

Was it lingering irritation or something else causing Rahmiya's reservation? "My pleasure." Quickly she added, "I know a coffee doesn't make up for my absence, but I just wanted to thank you for your patience with me. I turned in the story today."

Rahmiya bit her lip and averted her eyes once more. "I know. I saw your IM."

The admission pricked at Aidyn, but clearly her friend had reasons for not replying. She waited patiently to find out.

After an awkward silence, Rahmiya added, "I . . . also wanted to say I read the draft."

Aidyn's heart lifted. "You did?"

"It was really good, Aidie."

"Thank you. I appreciate your reading it."

Another silence. Aidyn let it linger. Rahmiya needed to know she had her full attention and forbearance.

Finally, her friend spoke again. "How's Mrs. Kip?"

"She's close to the end. The nurse said the next day, probably."

Sympathy tinged Rahmiya's eyes. "Sorry to hear that."

"I was too. She's ready, though. I think she's looking forward to the next adventure." Aidyn grinned. "Heaven better look out."

"Sounds like quite a lady."

"That she is. I wish you could've met her. I know she would've loved you."

Rahmiya glanced to the side. "I think I would've enjoyed meeting her too."

Perhaps the most meaningful thing Rahmiya had ever said to her.

Rarely did they talk about their differences in faith. Rarely did Rahmiya see the gold cross on the outside of Aidyn's shirt. As Aidyn held the screen containing her treasured friend's face, she thought about how Mrs. Kip had never shied away from an opportunity. And the fact that Mrs. Kip, who had thought of everything, had given Aidyn the perfect personal story with which to start. One that spoke of the love streaming from a cross.

"You know, Rahmi, I'll likely have more time this weekend to hang out. What if I shared more of Mrs. Kip's story with you over brunch on Saturday?"

The corners of Rahmiya's mouth edged up. "That sounds great."

Aidyn silently thanked God as they discussed the time and place and agreed to meet outside the doors of the restaurant. When plans were settled, she wished her friend a good night.

"Good night to you too. And, Aidie?"

"Yeah?"

"I'm really sorry . . . for being so . . ."

Aidyn waved it off. "Already forgiven."

Thursday, June 16, 2016

The phone call came at 8:38 a.m., not long after Aidyn arrived at the office. All Rosario had to say was, "Miss Kelley?" and the news proclaimed itself.

Mrs. Kip's faith had become her eyes.

Wiping the tears away, Aidyn opened the draft of the obituary and put in the most appropriate extraordinary death she could think of for a woman with Mrs. Kip's legacy.

Before submitting it, Aidyn reread the whole obituary one final time. She smiled when she reached the last line.

Kansas City Star, June 17, 2016

Obituaries, online edition

Clara Lu (Rooker) Kip, 79, of Kansas City, Kansas, passed away on June 16, 2016. Services will be held at Prairie Bible Church on Monday, June 20.

Clara was born an only child on April 6, 1937, to Henry and Mary (Bauer) Rooker of Granada, Colorado, and was the faithful widow of John M. Kip. Her birth came "after the Depression but before the war," because she liked to be in the middle of things. That remained true throughout her life. Never one to sit still, even in the grip of cancer, Clara dreamed of adventure and wore the tracksuits to prove it. Though she never saw a sunset in any country but America, she found adventure hidden in every moment of every day.

She claimed her life was "exceedingly unimpressive," but in her time on earth, she went toe-to-toe with the most vicious killers, thieves, and liars this world has ever known. They go by the names of fear, grief, despair, hopelessness, and pride. She slayed away at their schemes, inch by hard inch winning territory for the kingdom of God. She fought especially for those who could not fight for themselves, most notably in helping establish the New Life Christian Mission for resettled Laotian refugees.

Clara is gone from the world not because she failed or succumbed or lost. She is gone because her God told her to pull up stakes and leave behind her tent of a body for the best adventure yet. Let it be said that she went home a celebrated conqueror. Let it be said that she died in the most extraordinary way possible. Clara Kip died while loving.

Monday, June 20, 2016

Mrs. Kip had clearly designed her own funeral.

For one thing, there were fresh-baked chocolate chip cookies—at 8:50 a.m.—served on festive yellow napkins. For another, the service took place on the church's back lawn under bountiful cottonwood trees whose birds twittered in the morning breeze. A God-designed sanctuary replacing a man-built one.

Under the generous shade, people filled the seven short rows of folding chairs. They chatted easily with one another, offering handshakes and shoulder pats.

Aidyn took it all in from a few paces off. The atmosphere of the event invited her to find rest from the grief, like being tucked into the down of a mother bird's wing.

In that assurance, she stepped forward and collected a cookie. Then she found a seat near the middle of the huddle and looked around at the people gathered. To her surprise, the young mom who had snuck into Sunday service ahead of her sat in the back row with one of her littles nestled in her lap. The child's face was already smeared with chocolate, but the mom didn't seem to mind. Aidyn made a note to herself to ask the mom afterward what connection she had to Mrs. Kip. Because clearly there was one.

A handful of families from Hope Church sat a few rows in front of her. Aidyn exchanged waves with Palani and Pastor Khounmy.

Most of those gathered were older and unfamiliar to Aidyn. Several were in wheelchairs. None of them wore black.

In front of the chairs stood a simple wood lectern cordoned off by a row of vibrant bouquets. Pinks, yellows, peaches, reds, and blues popped up from their containers like confetti frozen in midair. Off to one side of the lectern, a poster easel proudly displayed a large picture of Mrs. Kip obviously from several years prior. The woman smiled like someone free, her eyes straight on the camera. Appropriately, she wore a tracksuit. Royal purple, with crisp white stripes around the shoulder seams.

Aidyn grinned into that affectionate countenance she had come to admire and took a bite of her cookie, savoring the flavor.

At 9:00, Pastor Levi stepped to the lectern and commenced what he said Mrs. Kip insisted be called a birthday party. "A birthday into heaven," he explained.

Soft chuckles rolled through the crowd, Aidyn's among them. A birthday-themed funeral was the only fitting choice for Mrs. Kip.

When Pastor Levi led them in prayer based on Psalms, Aidyn smiled with her heart. The Scripture was another fitting choice.

When the worship pastor came up with his acoustic guitar and led them in singing, "This is my story, this is my song,"

Aidyn smiled with her soul. No question Mrs. Kip was at that moment belting out praise in the throne room.

And when Pastor Levi began the eulogy, speaking out of the same collection of statements that she had been inspired to write, Aidyn smiled with her everything. Gratitude filled her heart once more for the woman behind the statements and the divinely appointed chance she'd had to meet her. She imagined the words fanning into flame the faith of those who heard them, the way Mrs. Kip would have wanted.

"Clara believed something greater existed than what this life offers," Pastor Levi told the small crowd. "And that something—more spectacular than her vivid imagination could dream up—propelled her into a fully devoted pursuit of it. It was impossible to be around Clara and not be influenced by this devotion and the sense of abandon it encouraged.

"She was the kind of woman who stood up and defended what was right and noble, even when it cost her. She was the kind of person who embraced the freedom found in giving up her own desires for the sake of God's work. But don't ever call her a hero. She didn't like that label any more than she liked wheelchairs."

The crowd again laughed softly.

"If you asked her, she would tell you her life was 'exceedingly unimpressive.' But the truth is, she went toe-to-toe with the most vicious enemies this world sends our way. So many of us find ourselves at their mercy too. But Clara was one who chose to fight back with armor and a sword no enemy can steal away. She fought not only for herself but also largely for others. Especially those who could not fight for themselves.

"This kind of love comes only from a heart given in devotion to God's will. This kind of love, which crosses boundaries and boldly lays down self, is the love she gave freely and generously, because Jesus first gave it to her. She died in body only once, but she died a thousand tiny deaths to self before that.

"So let it be said of Clara Lu Rooker Kip that she arrived home a decorated conqueror. And may the mission she lived by continue to influence our own lives and stories for years to come. May we, too, grow up into a full pursuit of heaven and a life given over to a thousand tiny deaths.

"What a story to tell."

As the "amens" arose, Aidyn tilted her face to the blue peeking through the leaves overhead. Somewhere in the airy ocean beyond, a glorious, ornery grin gleamed back.

Yes, Lord, she prayed. *What a story!*

And I will also make every effort
so that you are able to recall these things
at any time after my departure.

2 Peter 1:15

AUTHOR NOTE

The Laotian refugee resettlement effort represented in this book is based on real Kansas City and world history. The Vietnam War, which began in the 1950s and lasted through the mid-1970s, ravaged Vietnam and spilled into the neighboring countries of Laos and Cambodia. In the spring of 1975, America and its allies withdrew their forces from Vietnam. What followed was one of the world's worst humanitarian crises. Millions of people displaced from their homes or fearful of the new Communist regimes fled their native countries. Many people fled because their lives and those of their families were under imminent mortal threat from the new regimes, due to their alliance with the Americans during the war. People like the Khab family.

Much of the storyline of Mai and Mahasajun Khab is a work of fiction, an amalgam of facts, eyewitness accounts, and reporting. One piece, however, remains closer to the original inspiration.

Mai and Mahasajun's separation from their children in

357

May 1975 was inspired by the experience of real-life couple Penn Mnirajd and her husband, Marith, who was a lieutenant colonel in the Laotian army. He and Penn were in Leavenworth, Kansas, for officer training when the Pathet Lao overthrew their government, leaving the couple stranded in America and unable to contact their five now-endangered children in Laos. Their months-long ordeal to be reunited with their children was featured in the *Kansas City Star* on September 26, 1975. Out of all the personal stories I encountered during research, theirs stood out to me the most.

While the premise of Mai and Mahasajun's situation is based on this real-life couple's circumstances, most of the details and plot points of the Khabs' version are works of my imagination. My aim was to pay homage to what happened to the Mnirajds and others like them in 1975, while also respecting the privacy of this inspiring family. I pray I struck the balance well.

Though the resettlement effort is long over, many organizations today carry on the legacy of caring for the physical, spiritual, and educational needs of refugees and immigrants in Kansas City. Mission Adelante and the Don Bosco Centers, which are mentioned in the story, are two examples of amazing organizations doing this needed work.

ACKNOWLEDGMENTS

English does not contain enough ways to express gratitude.

Many people played a role in the creation, formation, and completion of this novel, and I sincerely hope I have expressed my thanks to each of them personally even if they are not mentioned here.

First, my enduring thanks to you, the person reading these words. Your love of stories calls to my love of creating them. Thank you for wanting to get to know Mrs. Kip and Aidyn.

My agent, Cynthia Ruchti. She saw potential in me and poured so much time and energy into helping this newbie receive the long-sought "yes." Thank you for your counsel, wisdom, prayers, and advocacy.

The Revell team has my full respect and gratitude for believing in and investing in this story. A special thanks to Rachel for championing it and shepherding it through the process. To everyone who patiently led me through the marketing and production process: Brianne, Sarah, Laura, Karen, Jessica, and Julie. And to all of those whom I did not work with directly but who helped make this book a reality. I appreciate you!

Judy Miller for your counsel and the blessing of your friendship. Homer's this Friday?

Sarah Pope for your detailed description of the former *Kansas City Star* headquarters building. It expanded my imagination.

Kevin Wright for answering a million and three questions about how newsrooms function, for your pontification on journalism in general, and for your readiness to talk writing anytime.

Lucas Houk for graciously answering questions about hospice from an administration standpoint.

Brandon Waterman, who not only answered many inquiries about hospice from a nursing standpoint but also ensured that my father-in-law's final days were the most comfortable and dignified possible. God bless you, sir.

Karen Kessler, who first encouraged me to explore the Laotian resettlement story and whose work in that realm inspired more than a few details in this book. You are a blessing to many, Karen.

Julie Italiano for being a sounding board and encourager in many ways as this story first took shape. I hope this book pleases your reader's heart.

Ruthie Burrell for a rich critique and heart for well-crafted stories that stir souls. Thank God for you!

My mom for your unswerving opinion that writing was the way forward, and for your willingness to read anything I sputter onto paper. You gave me birth, and you continually give me life.

E-Belle, sweet girl, whose unshakable belief that this story needed to be told inspired me countless times to keep going, especially when it got hard. You will make a fine editor someday.

K-Tastic, whose creativity is a beast to be reckoned with. God is going to use that in mighty ways! Your cheerleading and sweet notes left on my computer are a boon to my heart.

Robert, for your endless patience and the many sacrifices it took on your part to see this story come into the world. I pray the fruit of our labor extends beyond what we can see this side of heaven. I love you.

Above all, most of all, because of all, our God. Every word was a gift from you. You taught me more than I ever imagined through this process, especially the complete freedom to be found in surrender. You are worthy of all my worship.

Sara Brunsvold creates stories that speak hope, truth, and life. Influenced by humble women of God who find his fingerprints in the everyday, she does the same in her life and her storytelling. Sara's recognitions include the 2020 ACFW Genesis Award for Contemporary Fiction. She lives with her family in Kansas City, where she can often be spotted writing at a park or library.

CONNECT WITH
SARA

SARABRUNSVOLD.COM

SHARE STORIES THAT SPEAK

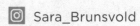 SaraBrunsvoldAuthor   Sara_Brunsvold